# *The* WIDE *Circumference of* LOVE

Center Point
Large Print

**This Large Print Book carries the
Seal of Approval of N.A.V.H.**

# *The*
# WIDE
# *Circumference*
# *of* LOVE

# Marita Golden

CENTER POINT LARGE PRINT
THORNDIKE, MAINE

This Center Point Large Print edition
is published in the year 2017 by arrangement with
Skyhorse Publishing.

Copyright © 2017 by Marita Golden.

The text of this Large Print edition is unabridged.
In other aspects, this book may vary
from the original edition.
Printed in the United States of America
on permanent paper.
Set in 16-point Times New Roman type.

ISBN: 978-1-68324-366-3

Library of Congress Cataloging-in-Publication Data

Names: Golden, Marita, author.
Title: The wide circumference of love / Marita Golden.
Description: Center Point Large Print edition. | Thorndike, Maine : Center Point Large Print, 2017.
Identifiers: LCCN 2017004021 | ISBN 9781683243663 (hardcover : alk. paper)
Subjects: LCSH: African American families—Fiction. | Alzheimer's disease—Fiction. | Large type books.
Classification: LCC PS3557.O3593 W53 2017 | DDC 813/.54—dc23
LC record available at https://lccn.loc.gov/2017004021

# The
# WIDE
# *Circumference*
# *of* LOVE

The words hurl through his lips with a familiar bad taste. His fingers clutch the cool, round object filling his palm. He twists it and pulls. Releasing the orb that he no longer understands is a doorknob, he kicks the stubborn thing looming before him, kicks it hard over and over, then turns from its unmoving gaze. He paces in circles, in straight lines, frenetic and relentless movement. This feeling, dizzying now, pumps into his blood, unearths a fury of words he cannot marshal. Words that are slimy, slippery, burn inside him like a house on fire.

The tattered calendar in his mind reads March 2, 1978. That day. A story that he sees in a million little pieces. There is no beginning, middle, or end to that day; there is only what he would say if he remembered.

He is late for the meeting.

He imagines Mercer cursing in that slow-cured Virginia drawl, "Where the hell you at, Slim? If I can get my black ass here on time, then I know *you* ain't making *me* wait."

Their proposal to design an office building in the U Street corridor—still boarded up, on its knees, and destroyed in the days after Martin Luther King Jr.'s assassination—is finally being considered. Today. Caldwell & Tate needs a break. A big one. He has to make this meeting. He has practiced what he will say. This is the project. He is ready to go.

A pain tightens his temples. To soothe the invasion, he rubs his hands over and over as though washing them and paces the wooden floor in slippered feet. The words now a mumble. Fatigue paralyzes each attempt to move and he slumps on the floor as the words dissolve into a creaky whisper. There is wetness on his cheeks. His mind is the devil. Tears. He no longer knows what they are.

# Chapter One

The footsteps echoed all night long. Her husband, wandering through the terrain of the house they had shared for thirty-five years. A house that for him no longer held memories. A house that he no longer recognized as home.

Locked in the bedroom they once shared, Diane Tate lay in the dark listening to the stuttering dance of footsteps that revealed the path of her husband's halting circumnavigation.

Even at sixty-two, she still possessed a young mother's ears. Once able to hear three rooms away, a quarter mile in the distance, or among the voices of a dozen others for the singular cry of her children, Lauren and Sean, now with the same instinctive precision, she heard Gregory anywhere in the house. Silence was the fear now, for if Gregory was not beside her or near her, then he might be *gone*.

Midnight: his feet hit the hardwood mahogany floor in the den where he now slept. Twelve forty-five: a muffled stomping shook the carpeted floorboards of the living room, its side tables and mantel crowded with photos of the children Diane had borne and they had raised, faces imprinted with Gregory's high forehead and strong jaw. One

9

o'clock: she heard the lighthearted jingle of the small bell attached to the front door as Gregory tried to leave the house.

Punching in the four-digit security code to impose a preventive lockdown was Diane's final nightly ritual, begun months earlier when her slumber was severed by a flood of premonition. A throbbing, cataclysmic knowledge had roused her and she'd run downstairs, opened the front door, and raced barefoot in her nightgown beneath a still dark, early morning April sky to find Gregory, his pajama-clad frame rounding a nearby corner.

Now, Diane tossed aside the lightweight thermal blanket and prepared to get out of bed when she heard the bell stop its tinny vibrations. The silence that followed was interminable until finally there was the sound of Gregory's defeated footsteps heading away from the door.

Diane granted herself a reprieve and slid back beneath the sheet and blanket. She surrendered to the embrace of the bed that was hiding place and refuge. Yet sleep was impossible as early morning raced toward dawn.

Two forty-five: the oven door slammed shut. Each evening before she went to bed she unplugged the microwave and the stove. Sharp knives were locked away in a drawer to which only she had the key, an action taken the day she found Gregory shaving with a paring knife, oblivious to the blood trickling down his neck. Three thirty: the gurgling, boisterous flush of the toilet down the hall echoed. This did not mean that Gregory had used the toilet. Four o'clock: the leather-slippered feet padded back to the den. She imagined rather than heard Gregory lay down. Half an hour later, sleep now firmly out of her grasp, she rose from her bed and walked barefoot down the stairs, past an array of photographs—their wedding in the sanctuary of Metropolitan AME Church; Lauren, back then bespectacled and toothy in her Girl Scout uniform; Sean at his high school graduation in black robes, his eighteen-year-old smile self-effacing and unsure, arms hugging Gregory's and Diane's shoulders; the framed *Washington Post* article about Gregory and his partner Mercer, standing before their award-winning signature building, the city's main library, only eight blocks from the White House; Gregory kissing Diane at the conclusion of her installation as a judge for the family court division of the D.C. Superior Court.

The photos trailed to the den where Diane opened the door and saw Gregory finally asleep, swathed in a wrinkled checkered shirt and khakis, an outfit he had insisted on wearing every day for the past week. She had consigned her husband to this room and slept behind a locked bedroom door ever since the afternoon he struck her, nearly giving her a black eye. The room's walls were filled with paintings bought during their travels, separate and together, masks from Nigeria and Ivory Coast full-lipped with feathers and carvings designed to evoke and invoke spirits springing both from heaven and hell. Mementos from Cuba, Turkey, and Israel filled the shelves along with the awards Gregory and Mercer had won over the years. A faded blueprint of the first building they had designed occupied one wall.

Diane padded over to the fold-out bed. Gregory lay asleep atop the rumpled sheets, mouth open, his lips caked with spittle. He snored, a volcanic staccato that seemed to threaten to choke him. His arms were wide—either in supplication or defeat, she could not tell which, for either captured what lay before them. She gently sat down on the bed, stunned as always, by the sight of his massive, thick shock of hair that had turned white in the four years since the diagnosis of early onset Alzheimer's. She buried her fingertips in the gray and white beard that she could not convince him to let her help him shave or trim. She gazed upon this stranger. This husband. Gazed at him in the early morning quiet with pity, love, revulsion, guilt, and shame, steeling her eyes shut for a moment to quell that reflexive storm of emotions that often singed her heart.

Scattered around Gregory like finds from an archeological dig were his "friends"—a small teddy bear with a checkered ribbon around its neck that had arrived last year with a bouquet of roses sent by a friend for her birthday, a pad of bright orange Post-it notes, an egg-shaped marble paperweight, an inch-tall wooden carved elephant, and a set of keys. During the day, Gregory obsessively moved the objects from windowsill to mantel to kitchen countertop.

The teddy bear was now odorous, dirty and soiled, with an eye and the nose missing, the Post-it notes on which Gregory had scrawled crude markings that resembled nothing more than a figurative nightmare, were scattered like crumbs around his body. Numbers and letters, the set of keys to his Lexus, his office, and this house were objects whose purpose he no longer knew.

The beginnings of dawn filtered through the curtains, warming the room. Diane sat and dared a long, courageous look at her husband. In several hours she would take him to Somersby where he would become a resident of the facility's memory care unit. She did not want to cry but felt the tears where they always began, in her groin, a tight-fisted, fierce tumult. She did not want to cry, was aghast that there were tears left, but just like that, her eyes were damp and she was bobbing in the undertow of a torrent of terror and sadness.

# Chapter Two

Lauren stood staring out the floor-to-ceiling window that showcased the Capitol dome captured against the gray sky. All morning, since she'd risen two hours ago to meet this dreadful day, she had been cold and trembling, yearning for a warmth that had nothing to do with heat or temperatures.

She'd been spending twelve-hour days at Caldwell & Tate followed sometimes by twelve-hour nights watching over her father, protecting and feeding him, to relieve her mother, who had already performed her shift. Tying a bib around the neck of Gregory Tate. Wiping spittle from the lips of Gregory Tate. Leaning on the man who had held her up. Helping Gregory Tate remember a plate from a fork.

It was through his eyes that she scaffolded and defined her place in the world. He had made her who she was. Who she wanted to be. Daddy's girl, the architect. By the age of ten, she'd possessed an intuitive sense of the beauty in structures, how to judge it, how to know when it wasn't there. At sixteen, her father had taken her on a trip to Chicago where he was to make a presentation for a mixed-use development in Hyde Park. It was spring in the city, but winter had been unyielding and the lake was pockmarked with small islands of ice.

A boat tour unveiled the elegance of the Chicago skyline, and as she sat beside her father, snuggling against him for warmth and love and approval, the skyline looked grand above and around them, each building in dialogue with its neighbor, their symmetry, color, width, and depth shaped into a perfect statement of intelligence and art. That was the happiest moment of her young life. A world of skyscrapers whose hold she never wanted to leave. That was the moment Lauren knew she would follow her father into his world.

A test in high school confirmed what she already knew, that she loved math and art and found them compatible and codependent. Her classmates read books, watched TV and movies; she drew floor plans for houses and rooms that bloomed in her imagination. Blueprints fascinated her—the minutiae, the hundreds of details on the page that represented everything from a door or a light fixture, to a wall or a screw an eighth of an inch wide. Creating them, she was intellectually fulfilled, sublimely lost and eternally found.

She told her father she wanted to be an architect and that's when they created a world of their own, in which she was daughter and mentee and he was father and mentor. A world that set them apart in the family circle. A world with its own language and vision, passions and rules. She listened quietly and studiously at the dinner table as her father talked about fellow architects, complained about shoddy workmanship, discussed the bids he and Mercer prepared. By her junior year in high school, he allowed her to sit inconspicuously in meetings at Caldwell & Tate where she watched him make presentations.

When she graduated from Cornell University's School of Architecture, the following evening over dinner at a restaurant in Manhattan's Little Italy, her father had leaned toward her, kissed her on the cheek, and whispered, "You aren't just my daughter now, you are my eyes, my memory, and all my hunger, too. Now you know who I am."

And who was he? She had indeed become his eyes, his memory, and everything else. And what she remembered about him from years before was hers alone, but what she saw now was too unbearable to claim. Yet she claimed it every day because he was her father. He gave her life. He'd given her his life. Eventually, she'd stepped into her father's shoes and joined his firm. She had to learn how to walk in his path.

Today, a phalanx of caretakers and strangers awaited her father at Somersby. This day was a severing that already felt bloody and raw.

Lauren reached for her cell phone on the kitchen counter, wondering if she had somehow missed her mother's call. When she checked her phone and saw that she hadn't, Lauren went into the living room and slumped onto the sofa. Her mind brought forth the day she found her father standing in the middle of the bedroom he and her mother then still shared. He stood urinating, staring in wonder at his flaccid penis, which he was shaking up and down to dislodge the final drops as they fell onto the carpeted floor. When he sensed her presence, he merely wiped his palms on his pants, left his member poking out of his unzipped pants crotch, and gazed at her in unmasked triumph. Lauren shook her head, but still remembered the twinkle in her father's eyes as he'd stood there, the puddle inching closer to his stockinged feet.

Closing her eyes against that memory, Lauren hugged herself tight. The feel of her own staunch embrace conjured thoughts of Gerald. She woke this morning alone but not *alone* like before. Her sheets, body, and bed were drenched in the perfume of what she had daringly begun to call love. Gerald had dressed and kissed her good-bye sometime around midnight. He was her lifeline. Until they'd met, everything had felt like the end. Every day an unwilling act of closure. In the past three months, he had given her the courage to think that nothing ever really ended. Every conclusion was finish line and launching pad. That's how he thought. That's how he talked.

"Call me as soon as it's done," he'd whispered last night as he kissed her good night and good-bye, leaning over her prone, sated, and sleepy figure.

"Even if I don't answer because I'm in a meeting, text me. I want to hear how it went."

The shaved gleaming head, the gold earring in one lobe, the musculature primed by hours in the gym. All that poise and sensual assurance had been the first line of his offense when they'd met in a smoky, dark club in Northeast. One of those cavernous places, all noise, sound, sofas, and table islands—a setting for fake intimacy. She'd been there with Whitney and Marla. He'd been watching her, staring at her really, from the crowded circular bar. What had he noticed? The black sequined top she wore, low-cut and inviting, or her eyes, which Marla had made up so dramatically that Lauren had not recognized herself in the mirror?

Gray suit, black shirt open at the neck. He was friendly, almost brotherly, as he slid onto the plush purple sofa and introduced himself, asked their names, and repeated Lauren's several times as though testing it out before he extended his hand and asked if he could buy her a drink, if they could find, as he called it, "their own oasis" somewhere in the club.

Gerald had taken her hand and did not let it go as he navigated a path for them through the wall of bodies. Their oasis was in a patch of open space on the crowded balcony overlooking the warehouses, budget motels, and traffic along New York Avenue. They were outside, beneath a dark sky whose face, Lauren noticed as if for the first time ever, was flecked with a multitude of stars. They sat at a table being cleared by a dreadlocked waitress.

She hadn't had a date, a kiss, or sex in over two years due to the demands of caring for her father and her increased workload at the firm. All the men at Caldwell & Tate were married or already taken and she lacked the nerve for online dating. It was easier to be alone. Lauren had thought all of this as she settled into the seat facing Gerald. She was parched, on edge, self-conscious.

"So you know since this is D.C., my first question has to be what do you do?"

"Does it have to be?" Her heartbeat thudded at the sound of herself, ironic and sassy. Who was this woman?

"No, but that's as good a place as any to start, don't you think?"

"My mother would probably say a background check would be better."

His laughter was a thunderclap. She laughed in response and uncrossed her legs beneath the table. The waitress appeared, anointing them both with an intimate smile. Had she heard their banter? Did the waitress know that Lauren was nearly whirling inside with delight?

"I'll have a bourbon—and you?" he'd asked.

"White wine."

The waitress placed tiny white napkins before them both and went to the table behind them.

"I'm an architect."

"Damn, I'm impressed." Gerald's eyes had widened and then narrowed. Lauren felt herself momentarily shrink and then she sat up in her seat, blossoming in the studied aim of his gaze.

"You're blushing. I can see you better now. I can see all of you."

"Really?"

"Really."

The statement, Lauren thought, was preposterous. If he meant, which she hoped he did, that he could see inside her, her longing for peace of mind, healing for her father, for love, for a connection with a man who could calm her perennial ache, then she hoped the preposterous words were true, even as she trembled at the thought. She hadn't wanted to talk about her father and how he founded Caldwell & Tate, but there seemed no way not to. And then she found herself telling him about her design work for a new children's museum at National Harbor, a contract the firm had finalized earlier in the week.

"I'll never look at D.C. the same way again, knowing you and your dad got your hands all over it."

"What keeps you busy?"

"I'm with an IT firm in Northern Virginia. We do a lot of cyber security work."

"If you told me the name of your clients would you have to kill me?"

He'd blessed her with a reprise of that laugh, a

storm of happiness. "Believe me, we're not that deep, but we do okay. You come here often?"

"My first time. My friends brought me. Actually I hate places like this. I was afraid I'd feel invisible."

"I hope you feel seen. I hope you feel discovered." Gerald's fingers brushed her hand. "Why'd you come with your friends if you hate places like this?"

"We've been friends since high school. I'd run out of excuses, and they asked how I could hate someplace I'd never been. So I took a deep breath and got dressed. And they're always saying I work too much."

"Do you?"

"I have to. My father's been ill."

"I'm sorry to hear that."

At that moment the waitress placed their drinks before them.

Gerald had raised his glass and said, "Let's toast to the fact that life still goes on."

"Are you sure?" she asked.

"You wouldn't be here if it didn't."

Maybe her father no longer had a life. Not the kind of life he would have thought was his due after the years of work, dreams, and family. But Gerald had told her over and over these past three months, when they made love—her appetite for him, an astonishment—when he visited her at her office,

21

that life went on, brutally, sullen with darkness and lit with grace. Life went on.

Just then she saw the call from her mother come in and answered it saying, "Mom, I'm on my way."

# Chapter Three

"Do you think this will be enough clothing?" Lauren asked skeptically. Lauren wore tight-fitting jeans, a Cornell University football jersey, her copper-colored locks shaped into a bun—an outfit Diane thought more suitable for moving someone into the dormitory of a college campus rather than into an assisted living facility.

Toiletries, a week's worth of underwear, socks, slacks, and shirts on wooden hangers lay on the sofa. There was Gregory's worn chessboard and the sturdy chessmen (he would never play the game again, Diane knew, but it had once meant so much to him), a photo of the family gathered for Gregory's surprise sixtieth birthday party, and a stack of blank writing pads. Armed with the blank sheets of paper, he could spend hours drawing, though the wobbly, childlike sketches he produced now looked nothing like the designs that had been a signature of his professional life.

"You were there when they told us not to bring much. The fewer choices he has to make about what to wear when he looks in that cubbyhole of a closet, the easier it will be for him."

"I want him to take this, too," Lauren said, as she walked to the mantel above the fireplace and lifted a picture of Gregory building sand castles with her on the beach on the Outer Banks in North Carolina. In the photo she was five years old, digging a moat around a sand castle in the shadow of Gregory's love-filled gaze.

Hugging the framed photo to her chest, Lauren said, "We still don't have to do this, Mom. I can move in here, work from home. Mercer and I have discussed me having a more flexible schedule." The words were a deflated life raft that inspired an annoyed shake of Diane's head.

"Lauren, we've been through this. You've done enough. I can't ask any more of you. I can't ask any more of myself."

"Daddy deserves better, he deserves more."

What *more?* And where would that *more* come from, Diane wondered, seething and offended. Would it spring from some secret reserve of resilience she had not tapped already? Turning away from Lauren, she began piling items in cardboard boxes and said, with an iciness designed to quell further discussion, "We all deserve better than this. We all deserve more."

"I know it's been hard on you, Mom, I . . ."

They heard Gregory's footsteps and turned to see him standing at the bottom of the stairs clutching the nicked and scarred leather briefcase Diane had given him as a wedding gift, which he had carried to work every day. Barefoot, his corduroy jacket on inside out, the legs of his pajama bottoms inexplicably rolled up to his knees, Gregory's face was luminous and expectant. He looked like a boy ready for the first day of school, a boy who was over six feet tall with white hair.

The incongruity and absurdity of what Diane saw set off a seizure of flashbacks: finding Gregory's shoes in the refrigerator and a gallon of ice cream stored in the microwave. The sight of Gregory watering a large boulder in the backyard as though it were a flower. Suddenly laughter engulfed Diane, filling her chest, bursting through her throat. She sank to her knees, the raucous mirth astonishing her daughter but giving her a chance to breathe. *On my knees.* Perhaps that was the best place to be, she thought, vainly attempting to quell the outburst and wondering why she felt it necessary to derail what had suddenly steadied her. *On my knees. Maybe I should pray,* she thought and then decided that the laughter was more than enough.

"I'm fine, I'm fine," she whispered as Lauren helped her up from the floor. Diane walked to her husband, held him in her arms, and kissed him. She then stood back and gazed at his elongated face, the prominent, slightly crooked nose, and that damned beard. A face beautifully battered. A face bland and blank.

The tan corduroy jacket and striped pajama bottoms had been removed, and Gregory sat naked on the bed. The white tufts of hair on his still broad chest bloomed thick and unruly. At sixty-eight, Gregory's arms and shoulders had maintained a sinewy musculature. His member lay tucked between thighs beginning the descent into a benign flabbiness. And his legs and feet, which Diane had always found beautifully tapered, had grown somehow smaller. Those strong legs, those thighs had carried him so far.

Once they had walked early mornings and early evenings down Montague and the lovely surrounding streets. They'd walked for exercise—Gregory striding slightly ahead of her—for solace and relaxation, on springtime evenings, holding hands as Diane shared the details of a particularly thorny case or Gregory fumed about the impact of micromanaging neighborhood councils or bungling city agencies on Caldwell & Tate's projects. The streets of their neighborhood had called to them. How many hundreds of miles had they walked together over the years? Now, for Diane, the thought of walking with Gregory conjured the fear of him being swallowed up, evaporating into thin air if she turned away from him for even a second.

Kneeling before Gregory, Diane opened the legs of his boxer shorts. Gregory stepped into them, holding on to her shoulder. *Thank God he doesn't need diapers yet,* she had thought more than once, envisioning herself wiping Gregory's butt. And each time she allowed herself the thought, both brutally honest and shameful, she beat it into submission with the knowledge that she would wipe her husband's ass if she had to. Standing up, facing Gregory, Diane lifted his arms and helped him into a white T-shirt.

"Gregory, today we're going to a place where they'll help you feel better," she told him as though he could understand her lie. Running his hands over his chest, Gregory suddenly pushed past her and headed resolutely and for no apparent reason toward the bedroom door. She pulled him back into the room with the combination of force and gentleness she had now mastered. This was the tightrope she walked: communicating in a way that did not condescend, show anger, or impatience. Remaining poised because she had to be prepared for absolutely anything to happen—to be pushed aside, hit, squinted at, or walked away from, because those actions now substituted for a verbal response.

She handed Gregory a black shirt and watched him investigate the collar and the buttons for several moments before correctly slipping it on. As she watched him meticulously button the shirt and saw him gazing at his hands performing this act, she silently prayed that this ruse would work. What else could she say? What lie or half-truth would suffice to voluntarily get Gregory to leave this house for good?

Gregory had successfully stepped into his pant legs and now, with her help, was buckling his belt. As she held him around his waist, Gregory grabbed her hands in a suffocating grasp. His gaze was deep and empty and she flashed back to the moment when he had struck her.

He had burst into her study as she sat reviewing case files. That voice, that anguished, guttural scream, she sometimes still heard its echo:

"What did you do with my memories? My memories, what did you do? Why did you take them away?"

Then the blows, the slaps, her horror. Lauren miraculously entering the house in time to pull Gregory off of her. And the crater of distance that had engulfed them in the aftermath, a distance that led her to sleep behind a locked bedroom door. Since that day, every moment in his presence had been a breath-holding negotiation of unfamiliar, eerie emotions that had crept into the seams of their marriage. It did not matter that a sinister apparition now occupied Gregory's body, a force that tortured and enslaved him. Those blows had been the first ever between them.

"I'll be there," she assured Gregory now, looking away before the words had left her lips and Gregory freed her wrists. She was a lawyer and so had parsed the truth. Never once had she told him she would stay. But this was her husband, not opposing legal counsel. This was her bedroom, not a court of law.

"You look very handsome," she beamed, trembling, as her hands brushed Gregory's cheeks.

And he did. Looking at Gregory Tate, no one would suspect for even a moment what was happening to him.

Diane sat in the driver's seat of her car watching Lauren walk with Gregory to the entrance to Somersby, their figures receding across the small parking lot. Lynette, a certified nursing assistant, waited for them in the lobby of the assisted living and memory care facility. While Lynette cared for Gregory, Diane and Lauren would unload the boxes and clothing. Diane placed her head on the steering wheel, eyes closed, and surrendered to this self-imposed moment of solitude. She breathed in and out, slowly, counting each breath, a trick she had learned to calm herself. Sometimes it worked.

But not a single breath quelled her fury at Sean. Sean, who had called last night and told her that today would be more than he could handle. More than he could bear. He couldn't and wouldn't go with them to take Gregory to Somersby. He simply couldn't do it. Tearfully, he had admitted and confessed everything. He was selfish. He was a coward. He was as terrified as she was, as was Lauren. But he wasn't there yet. Not where they were, able to face this day. But now sitting in her car, encased in a shell of anguish, breathing in, breathing out, there was nothing left of Diane's shattered heart to break.

Four years from the first signs, to the diagnosis,

to this place—an odyssey of denial, drugs, "alter-native treatments," dashed hopes, and unanswered prayers. If she could drive away now and not witness what her yearning had wrought, she would.

A blast of cold air startled her when Lauren opened the passenger-side door and asked, "Mom, are you okay?"

"I'm fine," she lied.

Somersby masqueraded as an upscale hotel with its décor: walls in calming, soothing earth tones; wide windows that flooded the floors with sunshine and light. Somersby was nestled in a residential neighborhood near Silver Spring, Maryland, and Diane had been charmed by the name that inspired images of a country estate or manor. The movie theater, private dining room for families and guests, the library and computer lounge, and the cozy living areas with fireplaces all provided comfort and a quality of life designed, it seemed, mostly to assure the families of those who now called the facility home that at Somersby, elderly fathers, mothers, and siblings would not waste away.

When Lynette, a tan woman of commanding girth and compassionate bearing, opened the door to Gregory's room, she said brightly, "Here we are," as though ushering them into a palace rather than a room so small it resembled a cell or a dorm room. Diane had forgotten how small the rooms were, how pitifully tiny the bed seemed, and how inadequate the desk and bureau appeared to store the material objects of a life.

Lauren sat gently on the uncovered mattress, as though afraid the bed might break, and looked at her mother.

"It looks small, I know, but he'll spend a lot of time in the dayroom, the dining room, on trips. We keep them busy." Lynette's apologetic smile did little to lift Diane's sudden gloom.

*Busy,* Diane thought. Busy performing tasks that meant little to the residents but provided the framework for a reasonable facsimile of life, rather than a mere existence. She had been told about the memory exercises residents performed designed to stimulate what remained of memory, to beat back the disease even by an inch. But in the end, Alzheimer's always won.

Gregory's life had shrunk to the width and breadth of this room, the length of the hallway outside his door, the space of this three-story building. The anger and sadness Diane felt was as much for herself as for Gregory, because her life had shrunk into the tight parameters of this room as well.

Gregory peered into the room from the doorway, and Lynette said, "Let me take him down the hall, I'll introduce him to some other residents while you get the room ready."

Lynette gently steered Gregory away from the

room and rested her arm on his shoulders, saying, "Mr. Tate, I'm going to do everything I can to make you comfortable here."

"So this room will be his life," Lauren said, the moment her father and Lynette were out of earshot.

"You heard what she said; he won't be in this room much. They make every effort to keep them out of the room, active and socializing with others."

"You sound like a brochure. Mom, this is a prison."

"What do you think our home was for me? For him? I can't do it anymore. I can't do and be everything he needs. I no longer even know what he needs."

"I was ready for this when I woke up this morning," Lauren said. "Sure, I could do this. Now it feels even worse than I imagined."

She marched into the hallway and began bringing boxes into the room. They took refuge from each other in silently unpacking clothing and filling the closet and drawers. The chess set and the photo of Lauren and Gregory on the beach sat atop the chest of drawers.

"Now it looks like a cell masquerading as a bedroom," Lauren concluded once they were finished, looking around in dismay.

Lynette and Gregory walked back into the room. "I was showing Mr. Tate the library. I think he'll like it there." Diane heard the soothing neutrality in Lynette's voice, designed, she was sure, to mask what was taking place.

Lynette's cheery aplomb set Diane's stomach roiling. She feared she would throw up, and took a deep breath, willing her body to halt its incendiary rebellion at the thought of what in this dreaded moment they were actually doing.

"Where is everyone? I haven't seen any other residents," Diane asked.

"They're in the dining room. Let's head there."

The memory care unit was both hermetically sealed and spacious. Residents' rooms lined a carpeted hallway that opened up at intervals to reveal dens, meeting rooms, an area with an open kitchen space, and several islands where residents often practiced setting a table as a test of memory.

*This is where we will break bread,* Diane thought, holding Gregory's arm as they entered the dining room. Here he would stay, among absolute strangers. People stranger than even she and Lauren and Sean were to him now.

A faux fireplace sat against a wall, plants hung from the ceiling, and a wide swath of floor-to-ceiling glass doors framed the facility's dormant garden. Autumnal beauty—mellow, radiant, and still—was rooted on the other side of the glass. She surveyed the faces, clothing, and demeanor of those sitting at the tables. Only a few people looked up as they entered; most seemed enmeshed in their own worlds.

Gregory gazed curiously around him and, at Diane's urging, slid into a chair beside her. Looking around the room at the wheelchairs, walkers, and faces that revealed everything and nothing, Diane told Lauren, "This is his new family."

"How will we fit in?" Lauren asked. Diane did not even attempt to answer the question.

"Hi. Welcome to Somersby. I'm Miss Shirley." The woman seemed to appear from nowhere, suddenly standing beside the table at Lauren's shoulder in a bright orange dress, cream-colored apron, and hairnet. Miss Shirley's voice was craggy with a smoker's velvet trill and she squinted through thick-framed glasses, smiling at them.

She handed them each a menu and explained that the residents were always given a menu from which they ordered their meals. Diane showed Gregory the menu and pointed to her choice for them both.

At a nearby table, four women sat chatting coherently and she could hear snatches of their conversation. Leah Temple, the director of Somersby, had told her that some residents had been placed here not because of severe mental decline but because they had wandered away from home, nearly been lost, and family wanted them in a facility that could ensure their safety.

Their trays appeared before them, brought by

two young women in blue uniforms and hairnets. The meal was broccoli, baked haddock, and sweet potatoes. Diane reached over, cut Gregory's food into small pieces, and handed him a spoon. She watched him eat and felt a stab of doubt, second thoughts, but did not know why.

Lauren ate slowly and held Gregory's hand even when he repeatedly pushed her away.

"Daddy, I love you," she whispered over and over to Gregory, who sat contentedly chewing, wolfing down the food with a vigor Diane had not seen in weeks.

After lunch, Lauren left, telling Gregory, "I'll see you soon, Daddy. Be good."

Gregory waved good-bye and whispered the words, "Be good, be good," as she left the room.

Diane and Gregory walked the carpeted halls, passing the doors of the residents. Taped on each door was a photo of the man or woman who lived in the room and included a list of their hobbies and professions (teacher, fireman, bank vice president, social worker) in the lives they had left behind. After they strolled the halls, they napped. Diane lay spooning with her husband, grieving what they had lost, trembling at the thought of what lay ahead.

Three hours had passed. *Everything in place,* she thought. Everything except her emotions. What was there to say that would not upset the fragile web of subterfuge? Diane sat beside Gregory, watching a rainstorm beat against the window. The words in her mind were weights she was too weak to lift. She wanted to leave. Guilt made her want to stay.

Diane stood up. Gregory, roused by her movement, pulled Diane back onto the bed.

"Don't go. Don't leave." He had sat beside her quietly, nearly comatose, but now his banked bewilderment and terror inspired the plea that was a contagion seeping through his hand and fingers into her arm, which he now held tightly.

"Gregory, I have to go now."

"No," he demanded, yanking on her arm for emphasis.

Now she was afraid. Of him hitting her. Of her striking back.

"Gregory, I said, let me go."

He said nothing but tightened his grip in response. With her free hand, Diane pushed against his shoulder, but Gregory had morphed into a wall. Each push, each shove, lodged him more firmly in place. He sat beside her angry and implacable.

Exhausted, she whimpered, "Let me go, Gregory, please. I'll be back," she promised, though Leah Temple had asked her not to visit for three weeks, to allow Gregory time to realize that the facility was now his home.

"No." The tiny word was uttered with childlike, unreasoning truculence.

"I'll be back."

"No."

Diane managed to stand up even as Gregory held her arm. With one final push, she shoved him onto the bed. Now she would run. Looking around for her purse and jacket, she felt his hands on her shoulders pulling her back onto the bed. That's when she heard the knock on the door.

"Come in, help me, please," she shouted.

Lynette swiftly entered the room, cooing in disappointment. "Oh, Mr. Tate, what're you doing? What're you doing?" She placed her body between them, helping Diane stand up as she firmly but gently pushed Gregory down on the bed.

"Go, go, go now," she whispered to Diane, who gathered her things and ran from the room, from her husband.

Standing before the entrance door to the memory care unit, Diane remembered that it could only be opened with a security code Lynette had told her earlier in the day, a code that she could not now recall. A howl erupted from room 4B. The rank odor of guilt rose from her skin as she felt the warm palm of Jessica, one of the nursing assistants, on her shoulder. Jessica's fingers speedily punched in the numbers that set her free. A last look backward revealed that Gregory's door was now closed, but his moans rumbled down the hall-way.

Diane raced to the parking lot, bumping into a couple walking toward the entrance. She opened her car door and sank into the driver's seat, breath-less, her pulse a knotty drumbeat. Her frightened breath was the only sound she heard as she sat wondering at the bitter taste of this bewildering, terminal, new beginning.

# Chapter Four

Looking at his watch, Sean saw that it was twelve thirty. His mother and sister had probably done the deed by now. He'd been looking at his watch all morning, hating himself for not reporting for the real duty that had called him today. The real work he knew he had been put on this earth to do. All morning he had been ambushed by thoughts about his father. But he had forced himself to remember where he was. He was at work, in a basement he was renovating, at work on a job already a week past its deadline.

This was construction as a work of art, he thought, looking at the bookcase Manuel and Steven were polishing. The shine of the finish on the case and shelves seemed sunlit. The bold, broad molding was flush with the ceiling of this three-story Victorian that dated back to 1912, and gave the impression that the stately, deep-hued, wall-length bookcase had grown like a sturdy limb from the innards of the drywall. Three more bookcases to go in this monster-sized basement. Sean looked from Manuel and Steven to the pile of wooden planks stacked in a corner near the steps. Planks that had to be cut, sanded, finished, and handled at every step of the process as though they were building bookcases in their own homes.

Manuel, a five-foot-four pit bull of energy and focus, stepped down from the ladder and dropped his rag on the floor. He turned to Sean and smiled. His English was rudimentary, but he understood everything Sean told him and was so skilled that Sean called him "the house whisperer."

Steven, rangy and bearded, with a soiled painter's cap on backward, stepped back and said, "Man, I wish this was my house."

Sean's cell phone vibrated and he reached for it in his jacket pocket.

Archie's voice came in a sorrowful blast: "Hey, man, look, I'm sorry."

"Don't gimme that bullshit, Archie. We've been here since eight o'clock. I been calling you since eight thirty. Where you at, man?"

"Ima be there. Ima be there. Hold tight. I'm on the way."

Sean heard the familiar Monday-morning-just-came-off-a-bender slur in Archie's voice, a croaking whine that made everything Archie said sound like a hustle or a lie.

"You got one hour. I'm not s'posed to be doing your job."

"Okay, okay, I'm on my way."

Sean hung up and stuffed the phone back into his pocket.

"Sean, he can't keep doin' this. Why you let him get away with this? You gon' let *me* pull that bullshit?" Steven asked, hunching his skinny shoulders, throwing his cloth down, and storming past Sean out the sliding doors into the backyard.

"No good. No good," Manuel said, shaking his head. He walked to a table near the fireplace and grabbed his keys. "I go for lunch now."

No, it wasn't good. And he didn't need Manuel or Steven to tell him that. A week ago, thieves had broken in and stolen all their tools. Now they were finally back on track.

This was his crew, and he was their boss. He got them work. He found the clients. And he was supposed to handle their shit, no matter what it was. Hell, he knew this wasn't good. But it was better than where he'd been a couple of years ago. Better than knowing what he wanted and being afraid to go after it.

Everything he knew or thought he knew about contracting he had learned from these guys. Steven, the young brother he'd taken on as part of a city-wide effort to connect ex-cons with jobs, had done five years for trying to be the marijuana kingpin of Simple City. Archie, the old head of the group, had nearly thirty years in construction working on some of the city's biggest projects. But when he got paid at the end of the week he dove into a fifth of scotch.

Usually it was just Mondays. What was it about Mondays that made them blue, bleak, and impossible for Archie to face? That made him resist the call to come back to the world?

Still, Archie was the boss when Sean wasn't there, and it was Archie who had taught all of them to honor a house, not to just repair or build it, but to work on it as though they were working on a cathedral. Guys who had fired Archie for drinking still gave him a good recommendation.

Manuel and Steven didn't know it, but it was Archie who had introduced Sean into the tight-knit, competitive world of the city's black contractors. He'd taken Sean around to work sites where Sean had observed how the men who'd been at it for years worked with their crews, managed a job.

Sean had been a contractor for three years now but remained in start-up mode, doing the same "see-me-hire-me" jockeying he'd used when trying to get his first jobs: driving by a work site, looking for whoever was in charge, asking for subcontracting work, anything—plumbing, floors, demolition, clean-up, painting. He had a crew or could get a crew to do any of it. All of it. Trusting he'd get good word of mouth when a client was satisfied. Giving out business cards at the Home Depot; calling real estate agents; tracking down city government contracts; bidding on jobs, calibrating what was too high, what was too low.

He'd never before been more aware of the power—and powerlessness—of money. Getting nearly ten thousand dollars for a week and a half of work, and out of that having to pay salaries and deduct supplies. He dreamed about money at night.

Nothing was for sure. Everything was a possibility he had to nail down into a certainty. But this was the price he paid to turn houses into homes, and in rare moments, turn craft into beauty as the backdrop for living a life.

Once in the early, lean days, sitting in Archie's truck in an alley behind a house his crew was demolishing, Archie had told Sean, "Youngblood, you can do this thing. Ain't nothing to it but to do it." Archie had leaned back against the driver's seat, adjusted the rearview mirror as though he was expecting a bill collector or an ex-wife to round the corner, and said, "You just got to keep doin' what you doin' that's all. Keep being hungry. Being broke is inspiration. Hell, that's the story of my life."

"Yeah, but look at your life. Archie; you could be somebody's boss. What the fuck happened?"

Archie had turned his rheumy eyes on Sean and said, "Sometimes the knockouts, everything you didn't see coming just happens to you and all you can do is try to get back up every time it knocks you down."

Archie was a conundrum, a shadow. Sean knew all about Manuel's family in El Salvador, the wife and children he had left behind and who he hoped would join him in America one day. Steven had told him about his two baby mamas and the boys he'd grown up with in Simple City, half of them now dead. But it was Archie whose story he didn't know, who had given him a way to imagine his own.

Still, he'd have to let him go, he knew that. Monday was as valuable a day of the week as any other. He'd let him go and soon. But not today.

Pissed, Sean slumped onto the basement floor, removed his jacket, and dipped a paint brush into the half-full can of finish. He stacked several sanded shelves and painted each one with the brilliant yet toxic gleam. Painting, he forgot Archie and his breathing slowed. Painting, he was encased in a zone impenetrable to even his own reliable, vexing worries. Painting, he had never told anybody, was how he prayed. But the brushstrokes merely kept pace with the onslaught of questions, embers glowing at the edges of his thoughts. How had his father reacted when his mother and sister said good-bye? What had his mother told him to get him to stay?

The good thing about living with Alzheimer's, Sean sometimes allowed himself to think—because he lived outside its grip—was that you had no idea when someone had failed you. The bad thing about having Alzheimer's, he knew—because it had stolen his father from him—was that you had no idea when someone had failed you. This was all bullshit rationalizing gleaned from the books and articles his mother collected and pressured him to read. To understand the ultimately inexplicable. To dive into the freezing waters of all this loss and somehow reach the surface, step onto the shore, and stand shivering but strong.

His father was moored in a world where he thought he was thirty-one or thirty-two years old, a bachelor, with all that he would achieve still a heartfelt desire. Was the fact that Sean found it harder and harder to look at his father a verdict on his love? Sean had allowed himself to conclude, unlike his sister and mother, that there was nothing left of the man he wanted to love, honor, and respect. But that void, and his insistence on it, offered Sean little he could use in acknowledging the man who remained and always would be his father. A ghost, a shell of himself, but still his father.

It had cost his mother all the love she had to decide to put his father in Somersby. He knew that, but all he could do on this day was pay his own price, his devil's due by bailing out.

As a recovering prodigal son, letting them down had become a reflex.


Caught in Georgia Avenue eight o'clock traffic, Sean checked his phone and saw a text from Valerie, a curt, four-word inquiry: *How did it go?*

Sean dreaded telling Valerie the answer to her question, even as he meditated on the reality that he was a grown-assed man in a grown-up relationship. It didn't get more grown than living with a twenty-seven-year-old widow whose husband had died in Afghanistan. He loved her, and that unfortunate soldier's son, too.

Sean had just passed the contractor's exam and given notice to the big-box hardware store where he'd been working when he met Valerie. She'd strode into his aisle, unsure what she was looking for, but she'd needed his help.

Valerie was a big-boned woman who wore her weight as an embellishment, her size a sensual promise. She smelled of jasmine and both her reddish brown hair and freckled cheeks were girlish. Somebody he already knew he would want to take home. Her giggle was music, an invitation, when she became confused about her purchase.

When she came back two days later to return the bolts, washers, and faucet she had bought for her plumber, she was coy, lingering long after they found what she actually needed. Sean had asked for her number, but she'd shaken her head no and instead asked for his. He actually dreamed that night that she would call. In reality, she made him wait three days.

Initially, Valerie put her son Cameron between them. Their dates usually included the boy, as if she was testing Sean to see if he could love her and her son.

"I don't come unencumbered," she'd said. "We're a package."

She'd told Sean this as though she had practiced using the declaration as a scare tactic. But now, almost three years later, he'd moved in and they had begun to talk about marriage. No one in their families knew yet, but they considered themselves engaged. Even his dad, now forgetting everything, would be happy for him.

When Sean entered the apartment, he dropped his keys in a ceramic bowl on a table near the door.

"I'm home," he called. Greeted by silence, he was enveloped in the aroma of garlic and tomatoes. The living room had the look he loved: Valerie's shawls and the caftans she was knitting were piled on the sofa. Cameron's soccer ball, several Spider-Man comics, and video games lay on the floor near the television. He saw Valerie's and Cameron's plates on the table, littered with remnants of garlic bread. The kitchen stove and sink were a puzzle of pots, pans, and dishes. This wasn't disorder, Sean thought. This was a place where you could tell people lived.

Walking down the hallway, Sean passed the closed bathroom door. Behind it, he heard Cameron splashing and engaged in a muted but fervent conversation with himself. Or was he giving orders to action figures? Valerie was in the computer room manipulating a spreadsheet on her desktop. Sean placed his hands on her shoulders to claim her and to steady himself.

"How did it go with your dad?" she asked, turning around to face Sean, and in that swift movement severing his touch. Her eyes rested on Sean's face with an electric expectancy that would accept nothing short of the truth.

Sean turned from those eyes and walked a few feet away, sitting on a leather hassock. He sat examining his clasped, tense fingers, not looking at Valerie.

"You didn't go with them?"

"I couldn't. It seemed too much like saying good-bye."

There was her silence. Then his silence. What more did she want him to say?

"Sean, we talked about this last night." The words came in a whisper he had not expected.

That's what he loved about her and what he hated about her: the way she charged in, refusing to let a thing rest until it had been solved.

Gathering his will and his wits, he aimed the words at her. "You mean *you* talked about it and tried badgering me into saying I'd do something I knew I couldn't." He stood up in self-defense, to explain why he lost his nerve.

"What are you afraid of?" Valerie looked up at Sean from her swivel chair. The disappointment in her eyes stunned him like a blow.

"When I finally get my life together, he's gone. He can't see it, can't comprehend it. What I am supposed to do with that? You saw the last time we went to the house—that rigid, vacant stare. The stories he tells that make no sense and go on forever. Asking me over and over if I'm his son?

That's what I'm afraid of. And it makes me feel like shit that you and Lauren and my mother don't seem to be as afraid as me."

He had said it, and now his heart bulged with regret and relief. His eyes glistened. He blinked back the onslaught. He didn't deserve the anointing they promised.

"I can't speak for Lauren or your mother. Sean, I know what it means to lose someone. To really lose them. Your father isn't gone. Love what's left."

After that, he had no appetite. Valerie shepherded Cameron through the rituals of preparing for bed before escorting the boy into the kitchen where Sean sat at the table studying the food on his plate rather than eating. The six-year-old climbed onto Sean's lap and hugged him good night. Watching Valerie and Cameron walk to the boy's bedroom, Sean plunged into all the thoughts that the searing moment of truth with Valerie had unleashed.

He had never told anyone how the impact of Alzheimer's on his father reminded him of his own continuing struggles with dyslexia. His father had lost the ability to read. *Reading.* Even now Sean saw numbers and words backward. Sometimes reading felt as exhausting as lifting weights. He knew in some sense what his father must be going through, how frightened he must have been the first time he looked at a page and saw nothing he could comprehend.

In elementary school, Sean had been teased for his halting, stuttering attempts to read. The words they'd used were branded into his psyche, and even now those wounds radiated their own special heat: *slow, different, special.* Words he had heard his parents use when he held his ear to their closed bedroom door. Cold, clinical words that sounded like the opposite of love.

When he looked at the pages of the books that filled every corner of his room, he saw shapes and sequences of letters appearing to move, disappear, or shrink, sometimes actually dancing across the page. The sight of all that induced a nausea that sickened him.

Eventually, he was enrolled in a pioneering school staffed by specially trained teachers, psychologists, linguists, and tutors with all the time in the world, all the time he needed, who crafted lessons just for him. There, he wasn't broken. He wasn't a problem. They told him his brain was healthy, it just took him longer to make the connections reading required. The walls of the bright, sun-filled school were plastered with posters of the pioneers of science, math, the arts, and culture who were dyslexic. He learned to read, write, and spell. But it was always laborious, and he still needed help, extra time on tests, and the forbearance of those in the real world beyond the borders of the special school. He was convinced deep down, in the place that was his alone, that he was a problem. The optimistic, experimental school couldn't stop him from thinking that.

He was still a Tate, the son of a man whose buildings were part of the landscape of the city, whose mother judged and decided the fate of others, whose sister became the son, he knew this, that his father had always wanted.

Visiting Caldwell & Tate projects with his father, Sean had been mesmerized by the sight of the craftsmen at work. How a wall was built, how a buildings' frame grew over time, became a massive skeleton that in his mind he compared to something spawned by the hands of Hercules or Goliath. This was the greatest show on earth.

One summer, he'd spent a part of every day watching a high-rise being constructed. He sat in a park in McPherson Square, across the street from the K Street building for three or four hours at a time, munching on the lunch his mother had packed for him.

He could read this; construction was a language he understood. Working with his hands had always felt like salvation. He was the handyman his mother never had to hire. Wood and brick, cement and stone were not inanimate but had sprung from the same soil that had given him life. But he wasn't like Lauren, who could tell their father all this and thereby seal the lock on their father's respect as well as his love.

If you were a Tate, you went to college, even if you

didn't learn a damn thing. While Lauren studied architecture at Cornell, Sean had sweated it out at a junior college in Maryland. He'd graduated but he still had trouble spelling and writing.

After college, for nearly a decade, he'd done it all—even selling pot, until a close call with the cops had reminded him that he could end up in a courtroom next door to his mother's. He'd been a security guard in a building his father had helped design, worked on a construction site, washed cars, bartended, and driven a limo—anything where his weakness would not be exposed.

He had let the family down and he felt it every time he went to an obligatory holiday dinner, funeral, or wedding—rituals that even he could not avoid. None of them had told him he was a failure, they hadn't needed to. His own mocking chorus was ever-present in his mind. The checks his mother wrote when he was broke, the pep talks from his father to help him find his way, the encouraging calls from Lauren. So much love. So much faith in him. And for most of his life he hadn't felt he deserved any of it. Every family his mother reunited in court and every building Caldwell & Tate designed dragged him into the foaming undertow of self-doubt. It was hard to know which was worse: his father's nagging that he had to do more, be more, or his mother's seemingly patient acceptance of the leveling-off of his life. Both made him feel like shit.

Sean could hear the television in the bedroom

he and Valerie shared but he chose to tackle the kitchen. At least he could do that. But neither rinsing the pots nor scraping the plates halted the rush of the longing for his father, the intrusion of the past.

"Haven't you learned anything from me?" his father had asked once.

Sean had been working then at the big-box hardware store. He'd actually liked some parts of the job: helping customers find bolts, screws, lumber. Tangible items they needed to repair, fix, and build. Working with his hands, he was secure.

But on the day his father asked him this, he'd been thirty years old, making thirteen dollars an hour. If he ever wanted to get married, have kids, exist, and be visible to others and himself, how would he do it? Some days he was lodged in cement, other days sinking in quicksand.

His father had come by his apartment that evening without warning and when Sean opened the door, he'd known Gregory could see the sink full of dishes, could sense the creeping despair in the boxy, drab efficiency apartment in a complex where there had been two murders in the last year.

"You could've called," Sean had said sullenly, sinking onto the dark-brown corduroy couch, picking up the remote, and turning up the volume of ESPN. Gregory had grabbed the remote from Sean's hand and thrown it across the room, the instrument grazing Sean's cheek.

"What the hell?" Sean sprang from the sofa, buzzed, belligerent, more angry at what his father saw than at what his father had done.

"So this is your life?"

"I guess it is."

Gregory slumped onto the matching corduroy love seat. "I'd slap you if I thought it would do any good. Your mother's worried about you. We both are. She wants to know why you don't call. She expected to hear from you on her birthday at least."

"Sorry, it's not about y'all. It's me; I need my space," he said, in a muffled voice directed at the television screen.

"You don't get to fire your family because you can't handle your life."

Sean had watched his father stand up and almost hoped he would hit him. He was ready to bleed. But his father had merely looked around the apartment and shaken his head.

"You think you're damaged goods. You believe life is hard for you because of dyslexia. Sean, dreams are blueprints, dreams are first drafts. I didn't raise you to be small. I'm expecting more. You're expecting more. You're just scared you can't hold it in your hands."

"You're ashamed of me because I don't wear a suit and tie to my job like you," Sean had shouted weakly, knowing the words were a blatant lie.

"I'm ashamed of you because you've sold yourself short. You're running from nothing instead of standing still and letting the thing that could ignite you and the talents you have catch up and claim you."

Sean laughed contemptuously. He watched his father turn to look at the television screen and saw a new and unfamiliar pall of age on his face.

"What do you want me to tell your mother?"

"Tell her I'll call her soon. Tell her I love her."

"And I'm supposed to make her believe that? You don't realize it now, Sean, but life is short. Whatever you do, you don't want life to get away from you. Nothing is guaranteed. Not your health, not even the next day."

"Dad, what's going on?"

"I'm just saying, I mean, I don't know what I'm saying. It's just that . . ."

The confused timbre in his father's voice. The withered, drawn look on his face. The shadows in his eyes . . .

"What's wrong?" he'd asked, although he did not want to know, was afraid to know.

"Nothing, nothing. It's just that I'm starting to forget things."

"Are you okay?"

"Health-wise, sure." He had shrugged. "It's my mind, my thoughts."

"Dad, you're strong. Whatever it is, you'll beat it," Sean offered, embarrassed by the hollowness of his pat response. He'd sat looking at his father wishing he had the nerve, the courage, to ask more.

Gregory had taken a deep breath and said, "Stop being a stranger."

Sean stood up and walked his father to the door. A space yawned between them that neither chose to close. He watched his father walk down the stairs and called after him, "Tell Mom I'll call her. I'll call her soon."

His father had not answered.

And Sean didn't call his mother that day. He couldn't. He knew he would have had to ask about his father. He would've asked and his mother would've told him what his father could not. His mother would have told him the truth.

Sean sat in the kitchen flush with all the emotions of that encounter. All the longing for connections he had been too fragile and fearful to make. They'd been through so much as a family since that day with his father, nearly four years ago. Alzheimer's had brought Sean back into the fold, stumbling, resisting as he was even now.

"You coming to bed?" Valerie called.

"In a minute. I gotta do one more thing."

Sean wiped the counter with a paper towel and surveyed the order he had brought to the kitchen. Then he pulled out his cell phone. He dialed his mother's number.

"Hello, Mom. How'd it go?"

Another sleepless night. But this time, night was frightening, nearly foreign. Diane had not imagined

that on this, the first night of Gregory's absence—
or was it exile?—that she would feel their house,
their home, cast upon her so brooding and heavy. So
accustomed was Diane to her husband's rambling
expeditions through the house as she tried to sleep,
that this new solemn silence was disquieting. The
bedroom closet still held some of Gregory's shirts
and slacks, the drawers were layered with excess
socks and underwear. The sum of the life they had
lived together pulsed in the air she breathed, lying
in bed, in the dark, unable to sleep, able only to
remember.

Sean had called as she sat downstairs in the living
room watching the ten o'clock news, asking her,
timidly, how the day had gone.

"We got through it."

In truth, the day had drained her: leaving Somersby
and going to the superior court for two afternoon
meetings, preparing for the next day's docket of
cases, opening the door to her empty house at eight
thirty. So although she had rehearsed a soliloquy
that would vent her disappointment, at the sound of
Sean's voice, the rage she had harbored and stoked
felt inelegant and unnecessary.

"When you go see him I want to go with you,"
he said.

"I won't see him for three weeks. He needs that
time to adjust."

"Mom, I feel like shit."

"Sean, you've spent too much of your life, too

much of your time feeling that way. Your father wouldn't want that to go on."

"I let you, all of you, down."

"We've got an unforeseeable future of days ahead with your father. Days on which you can do what you couldn't do today. Give Valerie and Cameron a hug for me. Hold them close. Now you get some sleep."

Forgiving her son felt like the one thing she had done right today. The one thing that unequivocally made sense.

And now she lay in the dark. Unable to sleep. Too tired to read. It was three a.m. In the quiet, alien confines of her house, Diane's mind sifted, conjuring who she once was. How she had created and become Diane Tate. She found relief in the flashbacks that rained down on her in place of dreams. Who would she be without Gregory? How could she let him go and usher in even the barest outline of the woman she was bound to become? If she could not sleep then she could remember.

# Chapter Five

## 1960–1977

Loving Gregory Tate had helped Diane reinvent herself, yet in some ways she would always still be standing in the doorway of her mother's bedroom, watching her apply makeup as if she were an actress preparing to go onstage.

Ella would glide over to her closet to choose the dress she'd wear to go six blocks down the street to Jim Dandy's, the neighborhood bar. Ella's skin was the brazen, polished color of a raven. She had high cheekbones and small eyes that were wary, unbelieving, and distant.

Ella's brittle laughter would rip open Diane's and Ronald's sleep when she'd come home with an "uncle." They'd enter the apartment like burglars, knocking over chairs and lamps, their hushed whispers and giggles erupting in the small apartment's darkened gloom. Her brother Ronald, two years younger but with a body that spoke its own language, more than once—pajama-clad and raging—had stepped between Ella and one of these men's fists. It took Ronald longer to learn his schoolwork than Diane, but he could size up the men their mother brought home in a glance—a skill that turned into a steady surveillance.

Then there were the days and nights when Ella went without sleep and whirled through the apartment washing, cleaning, smoking, talking frantically to Diane and Ronald, and chatting on the phone for hours, her antic, frenzied voice signaling the cliff on whose edge she teetered.

But Ella Garrison was more than those crazed days and desperate rendezvous with men whose names she could not the next day recall. She was a nurse at Freedman's Hospital, and over dinner, Ella often told Diane and Ronald about her patients, the ones she helped the doctors save and the ones they could not. Over time, she said, her patients told her everything: that they were afraid to die; that until this illness, this disease, they had been terrified to live; and that if God gave them another chance, they would live a full-blown life.

Ella witnessed the patients whose beds were surrounded by a steady flow of family and friends and those for whom no one came. And it was the lonely ones who sank into despair and refused to eat, that on her days off Ella would visit with Diane and Ronald in tow, bringing a get-well card purchased at People's Drugstore on the way and signed by each of them.

When Ronald protested that they didn't even know the people Ella made them visit, she scolded him, saying, "But *I* know them. I've emptied their bedpans, taken their temperature, and comforted them when their sickness made them mean and hateful. I haven't met a stranger since I became a nurse. You all are my children and no matter what you do when you grow up, I want you to take care of somebody."

Diane possessed faint yet stubborn memories of the father who had left them when she was five years old. She often rummaged through her mother's drawers trying to find a picture, anything that would give her an answer to the question of why he went away, to which her mother simply responded, "He didn't love me or you and your brother anymore."

But Diane would never be released from the childhood terror she'd felt after her father had left. Stationed at the living room window for hours, looking for him to round the corner. Wetting her bed, refusing to eat, throwing toys at her mother. All to make her daddy come home. And then as the days and weeks passed, Diane had surrendered to her mother's silence, her mother's riddle-like explanation. She surrendered to the only person who was left. Over time, the anger and sometimes hate her mother inspired in her congealed in equal measure. What could her father have done to deserve to be so stoically erased?

Loretta Epson, Diane's best friend in the fifth grade, visited her father at Lorton Prison in Virginia once a month. He had stabbed a man to death during an argument over a game of craps, yet Loretta was not denied the father who had committed what Diane learned in Sunday school was the greatest sin. Loretta's mother told her that her father was the only father she had, so she had to love him no matter what. Diane convinced herself that it was Ella and her fearsome, wild moods that had made her father leave. Maybe there had been "uncles" too, who drove him away. Her anger was neither childish nor transitory. When she grew up, she vowed, she would find her father, and just like Loretta Epson, love him in spite of his sins.

If her childhood was one of concealment, her adolescence offered the equally searing pain of discovery. When Diane was thirteen and Ronald was eleven, Ella was hit and killed by a car speeding along Florida Avenue. The 1963 Volkswagen had been stolen half an hour before by the three teenagers and then barreled through a red light as Ella stepped off a curb just blocks from where she nursed the sick and the dying.

Aunt Georgia, Ella's older sister, swooped Diane and Ronald up and brought them to live with her. On Friday nights, Uncle Harold and Ronald would sit in the living room together watching boxing matches on television while Diane and Aunt Georgia folded clothes, warm and tingling with static, from the dryer. For Diane, there was a closet full of new dresses, and for Ronald, a Schwinn bicycle and skates. For neither was there any mention of their mother.

But when Diane was a senior at Roosevelt High School, Georgia finally felt it was time. Diane was parting her hair and pinning rollers tightly against her scalp when Georgia entered her room that night. The stricken look on her aunt's face brought Diane from the mirror to her bed where Georgia sat.

"You're almost grown," Georgia said, "and I promised myself I would answer your questions about your mother and your father when I thought it was time."

"Is it time?"

"I think it is."

Georgia cupped Diane's chin in her fingers, gazed at her niece, and said, "You look so much like her, you always have. I should've told you this years ago. I just didn't know how."

"I'll go get Ronald."

"No, I want to tell you first. If I can tell you, telling him will be a bit easier." Georgia took refuge again in Diane's face for several long moments and then said, "You were four and Ronald was two when it happened. I was watching you both for Ella that night. A man broke into your parents' apartment. He had a gun. He tied up your father in the kitchen and raped Ella."

"My mama was raped?" Diane clutched her stomach to still the queasy invasion of a lava of sickness slithering into her groin.

"Then he stole what little money they had in the house, the radio, and the television. Ella and Samuel reported it to the police, but they never found the man." Her aunt's voice, crisp, bloodless, charged on. Diane would do anything to make it stop.

"They were never the same. Neither of them. Your father started drinking, wouldn't come home at night. Ella came home from work one day and found a note from Samuel saying that man had taken everything. He had to leave. He couldn't stay."

Diane had always known there was more than the unadorned explanations her mother had offered, but this history, so intimate and so monumental, made her wish that she was mute so no words would be expected. All her young life, she had felt branded and did not know why. How had her aunt hoarded this story all these years? How had she said it aloud now?

"I was there the day she tore up every picture she had of Samuel and swore that she would never forgive him."

"Did you know about all those other men?"

"Yes, I did. I think she was looking for your daddy in them."

"And my father, he just left us?" Diane asked, her voice stiff and incredulous. She had lived through the loss but until this moment had not known its depth.

"Yes. He did."

"What about his family?"

"I've run into them sometimes and they don't

seem to know much about Samuel anymore. I know he had a sister who just after a while got tired of Ella telling her she couldn't see you and Ronald."

"So she kept us from knowing about my father and the rest of my family?"

"Diane, she was hurt."

"If she was raped, why did she act like a whore?"

"That's the wrong question. How did she get up every morning and give another new day a try? I was her sister, and I could never figure that out."

"Why didn't she tell me what happened to her? Why he left?"

"You were thirteen when she died. Maybe she was waiting till you got older. Maybe she didn't want to risk losing you, too, by asking you to carry what she could hardly bear."

Her mother had been mangled and nearly destroyed by one man. Forgotten by another. Still, Diane could not quell the yearning for her father even as the lingering promise of even more discontent was embedded in it. Now she knew why her father had left. He was weak. He had let them all down. He had fled from her wounded mother and what had remained, Diane was now certain, of her mother's love.

Diane was an A student whose English teacher had given her paperback copies of *The Street* by Ann Petry and *Go Tell It on the Mountain* by James Baldwin, stories that they did not read in class. Miss

Daughtridge, a silver-haired, long-legged, white woman who walked the aisles of class like a field marshal, asked Diane one day after class, "Tell me, what will you do with your gift for words?"

The question, like all the questions Miss Daughtridge asked, assumed that she was instantly due a reasoned and deeply considered answer. Clutching her books as she stood before Miss Daughtridge's desk, Diane had stammered, "I don't know. I can do lots of things."

Miss Daughtridge handed her the two books. "I think you can handle these."

The books filled her hunger not only for story but for a replica of everything that, at seventeen, she knew life could be.

She soon realized, however, that she did not want to use words like Ann Petry or James Baldwin, to tell stories that she knew were half lie and somehow all truth. She wanted to make words achieve what they never had for her mother or her father—to make things right. The joyriding teens who'd hit Ella with a stolen car had served three years in a juvenile facility, a punishment that embittered everyone Ella had left behind. Diane's favorite TV show was *Perry Mason*, and although she had never once seen him defend a person who looked like her, she loved his stoic yet unquenchable commitment to finding the truth, to law and order.

After high school, she ran, but never fast enough,

from her mother's life and her mother's death. From her father's disappearance and his weak-kneed cowardly love. At Spelman College in Atlanta, Diane learned from her professors that she was there not just to get a degree but to figure out how to crack open a resistant world for her people. She imitated the confident demeanor and style of the black girls of privilege who were her classmates, yet snuck off campus to serve free breakfasts provided by the Black Panthers to children in the projects of Atlanta.

Then, in the middle of the fall semester of her senior year, Aunt Georgia called and told her Ronald had been killed in Vietnam. She'd come home from Spelman tight-lipped and controlled. At Arlington cemetery she sat beside Aunt Georgia watching her nervously pat the folded American flag that lay inert—and to Diane, obscene—on her lap. During the repast following her brother's burial she accepted everyone's condolences and the hugs of Ronald's friends—one or two headed to college and several to Vietnam themselves—and then walked upstairs to her room and wrecked it, tossing sheets, blankets, clothing onto the floor, ripping up the paperback books, the poetry of Gwendolyn Brooks, Maya Angelou, Nikki Giovanni, and yanking the posters of Gil Scott Heron and Angela Davis off the walls. If she'd had a match to strike, she would have immolated what was now debris, as well as herself.

Diane graduated salutatorian from Spelman and then she ran to New York University School of Law. The law, she was sure, would make her someone with more answers than questions. On her best days, she walked through the world remembering that her mother had told her to take care of somebody, pleased that she had chosen a profession dedicated to doing just that.

Yet the nightmare raging within her whispered, *Men leave, men rape, men die.* When Diane watched her lovers leave, she watched them go as Ella's child. Ella, who had shattered at night and gathered up her remains in the morning because she'd had bodies and souls to heal.

Diane returned to Washington from New York to work as a legal aid lawyer in D.C.'s public defender service, unique in the country for hiring graduates of the nation's top law schools to represent indigent clients. The courts were clogged with so many young black men on trial for everything from mayhem to murder that the black court-appointed lawyers began calling the pool "the chain gang."

She was by then a woman who saw her mother's face in hers, all the time and everywhere, for she had the same smooth, seamless dark skin, the same look of doubt that made some think that she could never be satisfied. But the look of calm certitude that gave her eyes a probing, meditative glow—

that was her own. Those eyes made her clients feel that she was on their side and assured her friends that she could be trusted with their secrets.

She sat face-to-face with her mostly young clients and listened to their stories of innocence, guilt, wrong place, and wrong time. Sometimes they had murdered, but Diane often learned that they had killed because someone was out to kill them or they'd taken a life to prove a decadent sense of manhood seeded in the very soil of their lives. They had stolen but also had nothing to lose. They sold drugs not just for greed, but for respect. Of the scores of those she was assigned to defend, only a few, she concluded, were sociopaths, criminals with no hope of salvation or redemption. Most of their stories circled back to barren and bleak childhoods that ensured they would end up just where they were, staring at a lawyer, considering a plea deal and wondering which of their friends they would be reunited with in jail. Until they sat across from Diane for the first time in the basement of the superior court, many had never ventured out of their decaying and forgotten neighborhoods— Anacostia, Barry Farms, Ivy City, Sursum Corda, Trinidad—never seen the White House or the Capitol, and couldn't imagine either of those buildings having anything to do with their lives. More than once, she had wondered if, sitting across from her at the nicked conference table, was the son of the man who had destroyed her parents' lives.

She wondered if she would extend to her mother's rapist the compassion she found herself bestowing upon her clients. She was haunted by the knowledge that defending her clients was so much more than legal procedures and bargaining with prosecutors. The essential meaning of life, of crime and punishment, for her clients, for the society that had made them, were the questions and obsessions often obscured by the grind of never-ending cases. Only rarely did she have time to breathe in the renewing essence of those inquiries.

Increasingly burdened by a sense of futility as she plea bargained more cases than she tried or got a client off on one offense only to have him show up in handcuffs again months later, Diane began to think of changing to family law. Surely there she could make a difference, defend these young men as juveniles, steer them into rehabilitation services and treatment for the learning disabilities, post-traumatic stress, and emotional abuse that was the ticking time-bomb pulse of their criminal acts. If she couldn't do that, then the choice of law made no sense.

# Chapter Six

## 1978

The night Diane met Gregory, he was an architect at a party full of lawyers, wore a dashiki—though, by then, even the Reverend Jesse Jackson had begun shopping at Brooks Brothers—and he interrupted a boring conversation Diane was having with a justice department lawyer. He dismissed the lawyer just by thrusting his hand at Diane, standing his ground, and saying, "Hi, I'm Gregory Tate."

"That was rude," Diane scolded him, astonished, as the lawyer quickly and quietly skulked away.

"Not really. I call it survival of the fittest."

"You're wearing a dashiki and throwing around an out-of-context Darwinian quote that's been used to justify racism, colonialism, and war. Is this nerves or balls?"

"Both." Gregory smiled, too confidently for her comfort.

She was a tall woman, exactly six feet, used to entering a room and allowing everyone to catch their breath, evaluate her, get comfortable with her height and what they imagined it might portend. Gregory was a few inches taller, though she was not sure why that mattered. His light skin, those gray eyes with a flicker of blue, the keen features and straight hair texture made Diane wonder if Gregory was one of those racial dinosaurs, more proud of and interested in the white ancestor who had bequeathed him that hair, those features, than of the scores of blacks whose blood flowed more generously in his veins. She knew him—or thought she did—could look at him and know what kind of neighborhood he had grown up in, what his parents looked like, what his values were. She had him down pat. Diane heard and felt the creak of a familiar curtain lower between them. She was on one side and he was on the other. Gregory Tate, she suspected, was the product of a world where skin tone and class were sometimes interchangeable bloodlines.

On her side of the curtain, Diane remembered Jeff Darlington, a boy from that world who she had met at fifteen in the D.C. Youth Chorale. They'd stood at the bus stop after the rehearsals and talked about folk singers like Odetta and Bob Dylan and the colleges they wanted to attend. He'd call Diane in the hour or so after she had finished her homework and before she had to go to bed and they'd talk in whispers and hushed laughter about the cliques at their schools which they hated, not because they had never been invited to join but because they knew there was so much more to the world and to them. Diane waited for Jeff to ask her out to a movie. She dreamed about going to see *Dr. Zhivago* with him. And then, one night after they had talked about his membership in the chess club and an article she'd written for the school paper, he'd said apologetically, "I like you a lot, but you're too dark. I couldn't have you as a girlfriend."

Those words changed everything Diane had felt for Jeff. He had defined her with a lethal casualness that was a stake she felt pulsing inside her flesh even now. In the weeks that followed, her growing coldness toward Jeff baffled and angered him. His indifference to the impact of those words for Diane drew blood. Was he joking? Was he stating what was in his world a fact? How could she possibly call him a friend? Fantasize about holding his hand? In the world she was now a part of, Diane often looked around the restaurants and boardrooms for Jeff, having practiced in her imagination striding over to him and asking coldly, "Am I still too dark?"

But the fact that Gregory had approached her, a six-foot-tall, dark-skinned woman still flouting a big afro when all her girlfriends had cut theirs down to a "sensible" height or begun once again perming their hair, made this man suddenly interesting, although she was certain she was not his type—and he wasn't hers.

Gregory formally introduced himself, asked Diane her name, and told her that he was a cousin of the guest of honor who had just graduated from Howard's law school. The party was held in one of the rambling Victorian houses surrounding the Howard campus, houses full of "character" that rarely hid the disrepair. It was August and the tiny sweltering living room where she and Gregory stood was packed. The tie-dyed covered sofa for six held at least nine and the steps leading upstairs were home to bodies prone and hunched over in intense, seemingly conspiratorial conversations. The drinks of choice were sangria and malt liquor. The drug passed from hand to hand was marijuana.

"So now that we've established you've got nerves *and* balls, Gregory Tate, please tell me there's more to you than that."

His laughter broke open his face, washed over her, and was so loud and joyous those around them turned to look. Gregory reached for her hand, leading Diane into the den where in the blue-light tinged room, couples were slow dancing to Heatwave's "Always and Forever."

"Actually . . ." she began, looking him dead-on as he positioned his palm on her lower back and moved in close.

"Shh," he whispered, gently pushing her head onto his shoulder against the musky, warm material of his dashiki. Diane relaxed and found that she was made for his arms to hold her like this, the instinctive movements of their thighs, pelvis, and arms entwined, and the gentle drag of their footsteps across the floor, lulling and delightful. When the song ended, she released Gregory, bothered and charged, a quiver of mindless laughter whirling in her throat. After dancing, they moved to the front porch among a procession of partygoers leaving and arriving, other couples leaning on the banister, huddled on blankets on the grassy lawn. They sat in a corner, sipping sangria, surrounded by others but both feeling entirely and happily apart.

He was the son of a "Gold Coast" family, one of the black families that lived along Washington's Sixteenth Street, home to the president of Howard University, black members of the president's cabinet, and the city's black upper crust. Gregory had not used the term "Gold Coast," but in the southeast neighborhood of her childhood, Congress Heights, and even in Petworth where Diane had lived with Aunt Georgia, Sixteenth Street was often referred to as though it were an Alpine principality, a mythical land whose black population breathed a rarified air.

Diane grilled Gregory until he told her that his father was not just a doctor but the head of surgery at Howard University Hospital, once called Freedman's Hospital, where Ella had been a nurse. And he told her he was an architect. His mother, Margaret, taught social work at Howard University.

"I won't stereotype you if you don't stereotype me," Gregory said after they had traded personal histories, his with references to summers on Martha's Vineyard and graduation from Wilson High School, hers with stories of growing up in southeast and Petworth.

"All that, and you don't want me to stereotype you?"

"Actually, no, I don't. Can you do that?"

"I don't know," she told him, the statement quelling the reprise of an unruly desire. "Why architecture?"

"I loved math and art and that's what architecture is. I looked at empty lots and wondered how the space could be filled." Gregory leaned back in the plastic folding chair, his gray eyes aflame with remembrance and satisfaction. "One of the most thrilling moments of my life was a midnight tour of the ruins in Rome a couple of years ago. My dream trip? Egypt. Now *that* was architecture." He sighed, like an unabashed lover.

"Do you know," he continued, "there's not a single building downtown, in the city's power center, designed by a black architect? I'm going to change that. My heroes are men whose names too few people know: Paul Williams, John Brent, and Louis Bellinger, early black architects whose lives and work I've studied."

Gregory's ambition and confidence was bracing and seductive and Diane felt the need to match his gift for revelation with more of her story. He went into the house to refresh their drinks and when he came back to the porch she took her cup and haltingly began, "My parents divorced when I was young. Then my mother died. My brother and I went to live with my aunt." The lie came easily. She had told it so often a part of her believed it was true. Couldn't you consider it a kind of divorce, what her father had done? Rarely could she admit how much it mattered what people thought of her. Of her background. Of her family. Of her beginnings. Law, with its specialized jargon of offense, defense, boundaries, and arguments, had schooled her in the art of creating and controlling her narrative. The truth promised conflagration if she ever spoke its name.

"I'm sorry, but I know you're more than what you lost. Tell me more. Now I'll ask you, why the law?"

"It seemed to promise a way to set some things right. For me injustice isn't theoretical.

"I went to law school and worked a year or two as a public defender, and now I'm with a firm specializing in family law."

"Will you promise to tell me one day why injustice isn't theoretical for you?"

"I'm black. I'm a woman."

"But there's a deeper reason, and I hope one day I earn the right to hear what it is."

Gregory drove her home from the party and on the way they stopped at Ben's Chili Bowl on U Street and ordered hot dogs laden with a soupy stew of cheese and a mountain of fries. They sat in a booth in the crowded diner and gorged on the food and each other. Gregory pointed across the street and told her that he had an office in that building, which his family owned, though the rest of U Street was ghostly and treacherous, still scarred from the riots sparked by Martin Luther King Jr.'s assassination a decade earlier. The streets had been dug up and in daylight resembled the aftermath of a bombing, all as part of the work on the city's first-ever subway system.

They talked about the end of white rule in Rhodesia and the prospect of majority rule. Diane was optimistic. Gregory, as he lathered his fries with ketchup, wondered if black despotism would replace white tyranny.

"In the end, Nkrumah became a dictator," he reminded her.

He thought America had lucked out with Jimmy Carter as president and didn't deserve him and predicted one term. They both confessed with whispers and laughter to watching the nighttime soap opera *Dallas*.

Parked outside her apartment on Newton Street, Gregory asked Diane for her phone number and she scribbled it on the back of one of his business cards. When she reached for the door he lifted her hand away and kissed her, long, hard, and convincingly.

Diane had dated fellow attorneys, an ex-client who she'd gotten out of a charge of embezzlement, and a lot of men who were separated, unavailable, or brought with them messy emotional baggage. She was skittish, felt supremely orphaned as she carried grief for her parents and brother in her bones, despite the resolute face she turned to the world.

Gregory Tate was dangerous. He had stirred in her an original and unfamiliar desire not just for him but for a new version of herself. And besides, she thought, as she slipped into her nightgown that night, she was probably too dark for his family. He was Sixteenth Street, she was southeast. Still unsettled by Gregory's kiss, and by the memory of how her hands had held his cheeks, wedding his lips more firmly to hers, Diane fumed.

He was so sure of himself. That confidence, she decided as she brushed her teeth, was vanity and arrogance. The ghosts of her mother and long-gone father would surely walk with her into any room she and Gregory entered and upset everything. By the time she slipped beneath the sheets and plumped her pillow, Diane had convinced herself that she hated Gregory Tate.

The first call came on Sunday afternoon, twelve hours later. Elusive, fitful sleep had confirmed Diane's desire to overturn the decision to give Gregory her phone number, and with it, entrée into her life. When he asked her, in a voice full of expectancy, if he could take her out on Saturday, she simply said no.

"No? Why not? We had a great time last night. I know we did. I wasn't faking and I know you weren't either."

"I've had time to think about it and I'd rather we didn't go any further."

"I'm not proposing; I'm asking you out on a date."

"I have a right to my feelings."

"All right, if that's what you want." And he hung up.

Implicit in Gregory's parting words was a promise that he would not call again. But he did. He forced her to lie, to tell him she was preparing for a trial, that she had to go out of town, and he trapped her in the lies saying, "So it's not really that you'd rather not go any further?"

"Just leave me alone," she told him the last and final time he called, and then broke down in tears as she sat looking at the inert phone.

He had not called in two weeks. Now Diane wondered what she had done.

"Put that little girl, the one scared to be loved, in check, Diane," Paula Briscoe said, leaning forward forcefully across her desk. "She's not who you need to be listening to right now." As usual Paula was multitasking, lecturing Diane with a withering stare, then standing to search for a law book on the shelves behind her desk.

"Spare me the psychobabble."

"Spare me the bullshit," Paula said, turning to face Diane, book in hand. "You asked me what you should do and I told you. Give the brother a chance. Unless you don't think you're good enough for him, that is."

"I never said that and you know it."

"I know what you said, and I've seen what you do. You're all tied up in knots. That little girl whose mother was raped and died too young and whose father disappeared, she gets no vote on this. If I can still believe in love, you can, too."

"I told you that in confidence, Paula, I wish you wouldn't use it against me."

"I wish you wouldn't hide behind it." Paula's secretary, Louise, entered the office and told her a client had stopped by unannounced. Paula, a small, wiry woman with her hair brushed back in a bun, cast one last long stare at Diane before she followed Louise, pointing a finger at her. "Don't move, I won't be long."

It was times like this that Diane resented Paula. Paula had established her family law firm in a house in Logan Circle, one of the first female-headed firms specializing in cases of spousal abuse and incest. Diane had mentioned to a friend, who had mentioned to another friend, that she wanted to leave the public defender's office, and they had arranged for Diane to meet Paula.

Paula had grown up in West Virginia, married at seventeen, and endured a decade-long marriage of brutal abuse. She'd finally gotten the courage to leave the marriage and move to Richmond, Virginia, where she stayed with an uncle and attended Virginia Commonwealth University and law school at the University of Richmond. It was a brilliant and inspiring story, one that Paula often shared with women's and judicial groups.

Eventually, Paula won a three million dollar judgment against the D.C. government on behalf of a group of girls abused in a juvenile detention facility. She wrote articles, gave speeches, and worked with a national group of lawyers to create the language and laws turning spousal abuse from a "family matter" into a crime.

As Diane sat waiting for Paula to return, she thought how amazing it was that this woman, eight years older, had become her colleague, mentor, and friend. It was Paula who had finally made her a lawyer.

Working with Paula had helped her to fully embrace family law not as an occupation but as a mission. What else could you call standing up for children who had been abused, neglected, or forgotten? She had wanted this. To make an end run around the misery. To staunch the slide into disaster at its source. Not to get a client off, but to secure a space where the courtroom would not become a second home.

It was demanding work, navigating the nexus of bureaucracies designed to salvage children in need and children in danger and to connect those children with foster care, mental health programs, good schools, counselors, and support for their parents. As guardian ad litem, Diane would represent some children's interests in the courts for years, along with handling divorce and custody disputes, bloodlettings as awful as some abuse cases.

Paula's entrance broke into Diane's thoughts about a ten-year-old she was representing in court in two hours and about how she had come to Paula to lay down the weight of the enormous desire and fear Gregory had inspired.

"Where were we?" she asked. "Oh, that's right. I remember. You forget, I was at that party, Diane. I saw the man. Witnessed the chemistry between you, heard snatches of your conversation with him. I saw your face. Don't make him pay for something he didn't do."

Several weeks passed. One day, as Diane got off the bus and watched it groan noisily down Fourteenth Street, she looked across the street and there he was, sitting on the steps outside her office. Crossing the street, she clutched her briefcase and marshaled a formidable stride that belied her emotions.

"What are you doing here?"

"You left me no choice. I couldn't forget you. If I have to stalk you I will. I don't usually jump through hoops, but you have brought me to my knees. I'm not ashamed to say it."

There was only longing and desire etched on his face. It was the same longing and desire raging inside her, the same longing and desire so different than any other she had felt.

What was she afraid of? Whatever it was, she stood before Gregory fully in its grasp.

"You aren't used to being rejected, are you? To someone telling you *no*. Not in that safe, secure world you come from. Because of what you look like, who your parents are, who you know."

Gregory's skin flushed, anger warming his face. "I own a business, so forgive me, but I hear *no* all the time," he shouted. " 'No, your firm doesn't have enough experience. No, you don't know the right person in the mayor's office. No, we can't trust you with a project this big.' What are you talking about?" Gregory stood up and gazed at her in befuddlement and disgust. "You *are* stereotyping me, putting me in a box, when I swore I'd never do that to you. And you don't even give me a chance to make my case. What kind of lawyer are you?"

As she watched Gregory walk away, Diane corralled her fast-fading strength, reached in her bag for the keys to the door, and entered her office. This was where she belonged. This was where she was in charge. Her desk was stacked with folders, and she tossed her briefcase into her swivel chair and placed her hands on the desk. She suddenly felt sick. She thought of his laugh—that big, bright, bold laugh—and the feeling of his arms around her waist and suddenly bolted out the door, nearly twisting her ankle running down the front stairs. But he was gone.

The next day, Diane called information and asked for the phone number of Caldwell & Tate.

"I want to see you again. Really, I do. I'll understand if you say no, if you think I'm crazy. It may not seem like it, but I couldn't forget you either." This was what she said instead of hello when he picked up.

"Should I tape this conversation in case I need it in the future?" Gregory laughed.

"I'd like you to come over for dinner this weekend. More than anything I'd like to start over."

"Why should I come? Are you sure you don't plan to poison me?" She heard the jest in his voice and nearly wept with gratitude.

"I have to tell you something. It's about my mother and my father. The night we met I didn't really tell you the truth."

The story was actually a simple one, and as she told Gregory what little she knew, and how long it had taken her to know it, the waters parted between them.

"Sometimes I feel like I'm the scar left from all that," she said. "The evidence that remains."

"And the man was never found?"

"No. I've talked to some local cops about the case but it's ancient history to them, a cold case no one's trying to solve."

"I don't know what you're thinking, but I'm not that man who hurt your mother and I'm not your father. I just want to get to know you."

# Chapter Seven

## 1978–1979

When she stopped blockading her emotions, Diane fell in love easily. Love like this was an unknown quantity. She had long assumed she would be an amateur in an expedition like this but soon proved herself a hardy explorer. Gregory and everything about him seemed so expansive. The way he had pursued her. The way he walked into a room with an unsettling flair. The large-scale smile. The handshake that felt like a confidence and a caress. The voice, deep, rich. One that, Diane soon learned everyone told him, belonged to a radio DJ or a crooner of "baby-making music." When Gregory introduced her to his friends, his arm around her shoulders, Diane stood with him beneath their private spotlight.

Still, she wondered if Gregory saw the flash of surprise on the faces of some of his female friends when he introduced her. Despite her credentials—Spelman, which counted for a lot because it was a famed HBCU, and NYU, because it was a prestigious white university—Diane despaired of ever possessing the sense of entitlement that Gregory and his friends possessed. They were black like her but their parents and kin had prepared them for the leadership of the race and ownership of their private worlds. It was only in Gregory's embrace that she did not feel like a tourist.

Still, in time, Diane settled into loving Gregory as though she had finally crossed the finish line of a marathon. *Maybe,* she thought, *I can be happy.*

Happy like Gregory, beloved by his accomplished family, certain that he would blaze a trail as an architect or die trying, and blessed with a friendship with his partner that he had told Diane had enlarged and ennobled him.

Of his partner, Mercer Caldwell, Gregory told her, "He is my brother." And although Gregory told Diane that they shared responsibilities in the firm, he also told her that he felt Mercer was the stronger designer. Mercer was a small man, almost petite, with large, languid eyes. While Gregory was often dressed with a casual ease in tie-less shirts, worn but expensive jackets, and scuffed shoes, Mercer was fastidious, in a business suit each time Diane saw him. His moustache clipped and shaped to give depth to his long chin and sculpted face, Mercer could listen so closely it would seem as though he was deep in meditation.

One day, Diane stood in the shadow of the steel loins of a Caldwell & Tate project. The new municipal office building would stand at the crossroads of one of the city's busiest neighborhoods. The showcase building would house the new offices of the city council, and the mayor had decided that he wanted it to be located in the city's once vibrant black core, as a precursor of what he promised were good times to come. A tailor shop, shoe shop, diner, boutique, jazz club, record store, beauty parlor, and liquor store all occupied the street where this building would stand.

Gregory had told Diane that he and Mercer were chosen from a pool of over two dozen architects. "We don't have a crown yet, but so far this is the jewel in it," he'd said.

Watching Mercer and Gregory consulting with the project manager a few feet away as workers drove cranes that hoisted beams into the air, Diane now felt a swell of pride knowing that someone she knew, someone she loved, was responsible for all this.

Gregory had unfolded the blueprint for th building on the hood of his Volkswagen Beetle and explained how what she saw on that paper would become a building. But it was unclear and unfathomable to her. All she knew was that a building would soon stand on this corner and that a sign on the site read: A PROJECT OF THE DISTRICT OF COLUMBIA AND CALDWELL & TATE ARCHITECTS.

Afterward, the three of them walked across the street to a soul food restaurant. Today Diane had come with an agenda. She had met Mercer before, but they had not talked much and she wanted to find a way for him to tell her who Gregory was. As an attorney, she spent a great deal of time listening to her clients for what their words, their silences, and their expressions told her about their cases; to judges, whose eccentricities and personalities dictated their decisions as much as the law. She knew how to listen, and today she wanted to find a moment when she could ask Mercer questions only he could answer about Gregory.

They were just about to settle into a booth in the back of the restaurant when Gregory bounded out to visit with a friend he spotted parking his car outside.

"How did you and Gregory meet?" Diane asked. "He told me his version, but I'm a lawyer so I know there are always multiple versions of the same story."

"Am I under oath?"

"If you want to be."

"I studied in the architecture program at Howard a couple of years before Gregory. I had graduated by the time he came in, but I met him at an AIA convention. He and I were damn near the only black faces in the place, and believe me, there were a couple of thousand architects there. Somehow Gregory and I latched on to two other brothers and one night, the four of us skipped the panels and sessions and went up to my hotel room and played poker and ordered room service. We were doing our own networking, not just connecting with the white boys. We were trying to find a way to make a different set of connections. I liked the way Gregory played poker. He played it brash, yet smart. I liked his hunger. Wasn't too many men I knew who talked about what they were gonna do like they had already done it.

"I had a little architectural company in Philly I was struggling to make work when I met Gregory. After we met at AIA, I packed up and drove to D.C., stayed with him a couple of weeks till I found my own place, and we set up shop. Caldwell & Tate. I liked that he didn't just want to design and build, but that he wanted to make a mark, wanted to play in the same sandlot as the big boys. I'd felt the same way for a long time, but I gotta tell you, I hadn't gotten to the place where I could say it as smooth as Gregory, say it and not give a damn if other Negroes thought I was 'smelling myself' or thought I was better than them.

"Some black architects feel like they got to stay in the community and improve it one building at a time. They act like if you focus on major projects in a city center you're turning your back on *the people.* But Gregory could see that if we could get our name on a major project in the high-rent district, that would reverberate back in the places where our people live. Gregory didn't see any Mason-Dixon Line in the city. Except to cross it. He's got that 'I belong here, wherever here is' air and potential white clients like that shit. He's a glad-hander. I come in, slide in really, to close the deal, sign off on everything. And *he's* the better designer."

"He told me you were the better designer."

"I guess that's the hallmark of a good partnership. All I know is his motto is, 'Get the job. Get the job. Get the job.' He's made it mine. If you can't get the job, you ain't got a damn thing. I saw my daddy work for other people all his life, and he told me to be my own boss. Gregory Tate helped me put words to what I was feeling. What I wanted."

Mercer leaned forward animatedly, a wry, battered smile flickering across his face. "We decided when we set up shop we weren't gonna be only Georgia Avenue architects. We plan to leave our mark on this whole city, and especially on the real estate downtown. There's easily a billion dollars' worth of boarded-up housing and property in this city right now. All the decay and filth you see downtown, it won't be like that for long, and we want to be positioned for the turnaround. After being locked out of the action for generations, now we're getting some of the major building work in this town."

Mercer settled back against the booth and eyed Diane closely. "You gave him a real run for the money, sister. At one point, he was talking about *me* coming over to your office to plead his case. Vouch for him with references and such." Mercer laughed.

"I had some issues that really had nothing to do with him."

"Sister, we all got issues."

"Tell me something, just between you and me, that I should know about him."

"He's hungry. Hungrier than me. Like that building we're doing. That's a big deal. A big *fuckin'* deal for us. In four years this is our biggest contract. Normally it would have gone to a white firm, although our design was solid and our bid low, that's just the way it has been. But Gregory's got something to prove. He's the youngest son, chose a profession you got to study and intern for almost as long as to be a doctor and without the guarantee of a steady clientele. Medicine's the family business. He wants to prove he made the right choice."

"What's he told you about me?"

"Damn, you're shameless," Mercer said, reaching for his beer. "That you're a beautiful woman of substance. But you don't believe that do you?"

"Is it so obvious?"

"Only to someone really looking closely. But he's right, and you've got the brother, long as he's what you want. And if he don't treat you right, my foot goes up his ass."

"Whose foot goes up whose ass?" Gregory asked as he rejoined them.

"I was just telling Diane here that I got her back."

"She'll be well taken care of."

"I just told her I'm gonna see to that."

"My goodness, young lady, you are quite . . . *tall*," Margaret Tate observed when she met Diane. Tall, that was the word, innocuous and harmless. But Margaret Tate, a slender woman with an olive complexion and dressed that day in tailored slacks and a white silk blouse, looked at Diane with a pinched smile that merely enhanced the disdain Diane was certain she saw settled in her eyes. She had said "tall," yet "orphaned, damaged, dark," was what Diane heard.

"Mother, this is Diane, the woman who has stolen my heart," Gregory said after Margaret had opened the front door and hugged Gregory as though she had not seen him in years (he'd told Diane he visited his mother and father every Sunday). Margaret then turned regretfully away from her son to look at Diane, who felt herself *looming* in the vestibule, waiting her turn, for what she was not sure. After the comment about her height, Margaret consumed every aspect of Diane with a practiced, glacial glance. In a few seconds, Margaret's eyes studied Diane's natural hair, her large hoop earrings, and her face, then receded.

The living room resembled a stage set, open and sunny with a profusion of plants and fresh-cut flowers in the windowsills and on settee tables. The sofas and chairs were overstuffed, startlingly white with deep brown cloths draping the cushions for contrast. The room felt open and closed at the same time as Diane sat in one of those white chairs and watched Gregory sit beside his mother on the sofa. Gregory had told Diane that Margaret and

Ramsey Tate had hosted fund-raisers for Walter E. Washington, the city's first presidentially appointed black mayor, and for Marion Barry, the first elected mayor. *Probably in this room,* Diane thought, hearing in her mind glasses tinkling and the buzz of animated conversation.

"Help yourself," Margaret told Diane, pointing to the coffee table burdened with a full silver tea se , crystal teacups, and an array of small sandwiches cut in triangles.

"Thank you," Diane whispered, reaching for a teacup as Margaret filled it, suddenly uncomfortably aware of how tall she was.

"Where's Dad?" Gregory asked.

"Napping on the sun porch. Go wake him. He's been sleeping since noon, and he should come and meet your friend."

Watching Diane sip her tea, Margaret placed her hands on her thighs, leaned forward slightly, and said, "Gregory tells me you're a lawyer." Diane now noticed the layer of pancake makeup and the rouge flowering on Margaret's cheeks.

"Yes, yes," she stuttered.

"And you're from Washington originally?"

"Yes, southeast, Congress Heights."

"And your parents?"

"My mother was a nurse at Howard Hospital back in the days when it was Freedman's."

"Was?"

"She died when I was a child."

"I'm sorry. I know that must have been difficult for you. My husband was once head of surgery there. I wonder if he knew your mother."

To that suggestion Diane said nothing, she merely reached for a sandwich for which she had no appetite. She imagined if her mother had known Ramsey Tate, if he might have been one of the many "uncles" she brought home. The thought made her place both the sandwich and the cup of tea on the coffee table in order to steady her nerves.

"And your father?"

"He and my mother divorced when I was very young and I never got to know him."

"You poor dear," Margaret said, her face creased with what seemed to be genuine concern. "That makes all that you've achieved that much more significant, considering where you came from. Come here sit beside me," she offered expansively, scooting over on the sofa to make room for Diane, who sat reeling from the sting of Margaret's condescending conclusion. She could hear Gregory talking to his father, and she wished she could telekinetically transport the two men into the living room.

Margaret coaxed out of Diane the story of her journey to Spelman and law school. Sipping her tea, Margaret nodded in approval.

"Come, come closer," Margaret urged her as she reached for a photo album on the side table. "I want to show you some pictures."

The leather-bound album was a cavalcade of the history of Margaret and Ramsey Tate's families: An ebony-hued dark-skinned drummer boy who looked no more than twelve or thirteen, dressed in a Union army uniform and white gloves. One of Margaret's aunts wearing a high-necked dress of brocade and lace. She was president of the local chapter of the National Negro Women's Club organization. A photo of Ramsey Tate examining a little girl in a clinic in Greenwood, Mississippi. Margaret and Ramsey on the beach at Martha's Vineyard.

"Family is so important, and we're very proud of ours," Margaret said gently closing the album. "There are other pictures in that album I didn't show you. Pictures of my uncle who was lynched in Memphis because he owned some land and a grocery store and refused the money a white man offered him to buy it, pennies on the dollar for what the store and the land was worth."

The bitterness in Margaret's voice as she revealed this chipped away at the glazed veneer of welcome Diane had felt rising between them. If this was what sufficed for warmth, Diane decided, she would take it. Without warning, she found herself admiring this titanically self-possessed woman.

"So you're a lawyer. That's a good start. Where do you want to ultimately land?"

"Land?"

"Yes, what have you set your sights on? A judgeship?"

Diane was satisfied with where she was but felt to say that to Margaret Tate would reveal an unforgivable defect. "Well, I have time."

"Do you? Are you sure?" Margaret shook her head in dismay. "That's the thing about *whites*. They never sleep, they're never satisfied."

"Mother, are you harassing my girlfriend?" Gregory asked as he wheeled his father into the room.

"No, it's just that I'm so impressed with her I could talk to her all day."

Over the weeks and months that followed Diane's visit to Gregory's parents, she and Margaret built a kind of détente. One question from Diane and Margaret would launch into interlaced memories of her role as coordinator for a fund-raiser at their church for the work of Dr. Martin Luther King Jr. and the Southern Christian Leadership Council, her doctoral research on the political impact of black sororities, or the challenges and frustrations of chairing the department of sociology at Howard. Diane felt somehow anointed when, as the two women cooked dinner together for the regular Tate gatherings, Margaret would say as a way of learning about Diane's work, "I read about the most awful case in the *Post* this week. Are you working on that?"

Over the required second-Sunday dinners that brought Gregory's brothers, Bruce and David, to the house—Bruce with his wife and son, David with a procession of attractive girlfriends—Diane was slowly inducted into the Tate clan.

Ramsey Tate, at seventy-five, was twenty years older than Margaret. The vigorous, influential head of surgery at his hospital had, to everyone's surprise, begun showing signs of dementia several years earlier that eventually forced him to resign. Two years later, he suffered a stroke that left him, despite rehabilitation, wheelchair-bound with only partial speech.

Over those Sunday dinners, Gregory's father sat amongst his family, despite the twin challenges of dementia and the stroke, his eyes glazed with brightness, holding up his left hand when he wanted to speak, his voice hoarse and cracked and nearly unintelligible but still stubbornly vibrant as he weighed in on family gossip and discussions of politics. Diane watched as his wife and sons listened with patience and what seemed like gratitude to his halting, treasured words. She watched Gregory help Margaret place Ramsey in the lift chair that took him upstairs. She saw Margaret read him articles from *Ebony* and *Jet*, whole chapters from murder mysteries.

This was what families did, Diane thought. They cared for one another, loved even more fiercely the weakest among them.

Diane helped Gregory care for his father, laying out clothing for him as Gregory helped him bathe, sitting on the sun porch beside him when Gregory helped Margaret with errands, touched to the core when Ramsey Tate squeezed her hand and struggled to mouth and utter the word, "Daughter."

By Christmas, she and Gregory had begun talking about marriage as the assumed next step. Marriage would give her a whole new history; no one except Gregory need ever know how loss and abandonment had stained her. She had not been raised to walk the tightrope stretched across the terrain of Gregory's world and she shivered at the thought, wondered if she would fit in with grace and comfort. Her past told her she did not belong here but her heart told her she had come home.

They married a year to the day after the August night they met and Diane became a Tate, a member of a world that from afar had seemed ceremonial and self-absorbed. Dinners and dances, fund-raisers, galas, and more. In the summer, they'd spend two weeks in Oak Bluffs, a village on Martha's Vineyard. There was the beach and the round of parties, the salons hosted by the island's most celebrated black lawyer, doctor, or banker, or the next presumed black winner of the Pulitzer Prize.

She felt like an imposter. On guard for any words or deeds that confirmed her belief that she was an interloper in this world. Vigilant for slights, hiding behind disdain to prevent any unexpected strike against her or the ghost of her parents who stood invisibly by her side.

One night in the ladies' room of the Hilton Hotel, where Margaret was being honored by her sorority, Diane had taken refuge from her table of twelve. Suddenly, Margaret opened the door and strode over to her daughter-in-law. Margaret's gray floor-length gown hugged her curves and revealed a swath of her neckline and chest. A pearl choker clung to her neck and the matching earrings shone like surprised, tiny eyes. Neither woman spoke as they drifted over to the mirror.

"You're so sure we think we're better than you, but you've already decided you're better than us."

Before Diane could respond, Margaret forged ahead. "My son married you for a reason. He loves you. I'm glad he did. We have welcomed you into our family. But I feel your resistance to truly accepting us. Out there you see the final product. You don't see how all that was made. The grandmothers who were domestics and saved to put somebody through Howard or Fisk. The fathers who were Pullman porters and on-call, all the time, but who grinned and bore it. And yes, we like to think we've made it. Because we have. But we know we're black, and we hit the glass ceiling every day. My son loves you. We all want to love you. Let us. Get over it."

Diane stood, strangely relieved by Margaret's injured soliloquy. It had slashed the skin of the barricade she had erected, that separated her from the world she had married into. That wall she knew, held off a famished longing and desire.

She wanted to ask but could not, "What part, Margaret? What part do I get over first? The father I didn't really know or the mother who was raped?" The whirlwind of Margaret's words had left her with a throat parched and aching and her eyes wet with stifled tears.

She wanted to tell her mother-in-law, "It's less about who you all are than who I'm afraid I'll always be." Orphaned and alone, no matter the depth of Gregory's love. That is what she tried to will herself to say. The words she mustered instead were plaintive, a stripped-down plea: "Just give me some time Margaret. Just give me some time."

Diane had brought it all into the marriage with her like some rancid dowry—her mother, her father, the grief sown into her fingerprints and her cells, and the fear that she would never be at ease in Gregory's world. That she could never make his world hers. Clumsily, callously, Margaret had called her out. How long, Diane wondered, had Margaret been preparing that speech, waiting for what she deemed to be the opportune moment? Was her discomfort tonight so obvious? Why had Gregory said nothing? *How could he have said anything?* It had to be Margaret; she was the only one who could have said those words. Perhaps, the only one in the family who had the right.

Margaret's palm touched Diane's cheek. "I didn't

want to offend you, but I had to say something."

Flushed with a brokenness that was unexpectedly healing, Diane said, "Let's go back to the ballroom. There's an extraordinary woman who's about to be honored."

Diane and Margaret settled back at their table with Gregory, Ramsey, Bruce, David, and several of Margaret's sorority sisters. When the program began again, Margaret was introduced and walked to the stage to accept her award for her work mentoring younger members of the sorority and for heading the organization's community outreach programs. Margaret spoke of joining the sorority while an undergraduate at Howard.

"All the things that have come to matter most to me happened to me on that campus," Margaret said, clutching the crystal statuette. "I met my husband who gave me love and a family. And I joined this organization and found a sisterhood that ensures I will never, ever be alone."

Margaret gracefully wound her way back to her table through the ballroom full of women and men who had stood to give her an ovation, accepting the hugs and handshakes with a practiced generosity. When she reached her table, Diane was the first to stand, the first to reach out for her, the first to offer an embrace.

Three days later, Ramsey Tate had a heart attack while napping one afternoon and died in his sleep.

Diane joined Gregory and his brothers in handling the multitude of preparations for the memorial and funeral. Planning for the kind of "home-going" befitting the life of Ramsey Tate allowed them to sideline the act of grieving. The memorial service took place at the Tate family church, Metropolitan AME, and was standing room only as fellow doctors, former medical students, patients, friends, and the scores of people who knew Ramsey Tate from his work with professional, civic, and political groups honored his memory.

That night, after she and Gregory returned to their home, to the house that Ramsey had made the down payment on, after a long day that had begun with the memorial, then was followed by the internment at Lincoln Cemetery, and a repast at Margaret's house that lasted until nearly eight p.m., they went to their bedroom and wordlessly undressed. Beneath the sheets, they held on to each other, silenced by the arrival of the mourning that had been stalled and by the presence of death that had entered the house with them.

"How was it for you when your mother died?" Gregory asked, releasing Diane and turning on his side to face her.

"I was so young. It somehow wasn't real to me. My aunt and uncle took my brother and me in and they felt the best thing was to go on. To not say much about what had happened. There was no one really that I could talk to about whatever I was feeling. I recall feeling disconnected from what I knew would be emotions like nothing I had ever felt before. So I tried to erect a wall between those feelings and the rest of me. I got pretty good at that."

"Well, this is real. And I feel it. The grief but not the sadness. My father was such a presence in my life, in all our lives. During Freedom Summer in 1964, he took me and Bruce and David to Mississippi with him to provide medical treatment for sharecroppers. He let me watch him perform an operation one time. He told me that he wished I'd become a doctor but that he envied the adventure I'd have as an architect."

"I wish I'd known him before. So we could have talked. Really talked."

"Y'know, in his spare time before he got really sick, he wrote poetry. He was no Langston Hughes, but reading it gave me another way to know who he was."

Her husband had lost his father and because of who his father had been, what his father had evoked and inspired in them all, Diane knew this moment would open and seal them, bound and bond them.

She kissed Gregory and told him, "Maybe this is the best moment, the only moment to tell you this. I'm going to have a baby."

"Thank you, thank you," Gregory said, holding Diane close, kissing her face, cheeks, lips in an unabashed display of pleasure. "He would've been so happy."

"We'll tell our child all about their grandfather."

"Who knows, maybe he'll meet your mother in heaven."

Diane laughed at the thought, so generous, brimming with a sincere innocence that made her want to love Gregory forever.

# *Chapter Eight*

## 1980

Now that she was pregnant, Diane hungered for her paternal family. She was ready and willing to try to find her father. The day Georgia told her that Ella was raped, she had pressed into Diane's hand a phone number of another aunt, her father's sister.

Over the years, Diane had stapled that slip of paper to a page in her diary, under lock and key, and placed it in a music box given to her by a lover on Valentine's Day. She then put it in a safe deposit box in a bank downtown.

Her joy at being pregnant was clouded by thoughts of all the questions she would not be able to answer for her unborn child. Questions that revealed the emptiness of the family inheritance she had to offer. There was all that she did not know. And there was what she did: in the years that had passed since her father left, he had not reached back for her, and the aunts, uncles, even the grandmother and grandfather that she was owed had been rendered nonexistent.

The child she carried needed answers, perhaps even more than she did. Yet the knowledge that seemingly no one from her father's side cared to know her, search for her, was a blatant injury.

Invisible to whoever remained of the Garrisons, Diane strained to be seen by the world. She owed this child answers, even if the search for answers only led to more questions. Friends had told her that having children filled you with focus and direction. Her baby wasn't even born yet, but it had already made her think that she could stand up for herself as she had stood for others.

Nearly all those she had represented as a public defender and in her family law practice had been erased by someone. Guilty or innocent, abused or neglected, her job was to give them a voice, to remove the cataracts of prejudice and indifference from the eyes of judges and juries. No one had fought for her, so she fought for those who had been disarmed.

And so one evening, she decided to tell Gregory all of this, slipping into a chair beside him in his office at home, where he sat making initial sketches for a home for senior citizens to be built in Rockville, Maryland. He finished a few marks, and when he looked up at Diane, what he saw on her face made him put down his pencil. "What's wrong?" he asked.

"I want to try to track down my father."

"Are you sure?"

"Why wouldn't I be sure? All these years, I've allowed myself the luxury and the lie of believing it didn't matter. That I could go on not knowing at least something about him, where he went, who he is. But with the baby coming, I feel like it's now or never."

"He and his family never reached out to you. I just don't want you to get hurt."

"Gregory, how could I get more hurt than I already am?"

"I'm afraid to answer that question."

"You've got family to give our baby. I only have my Aunt Georgia and Uncle Ray. How will I explain that?"

"Our baby won't need explanations, excuses, or apologies for things you couldn't control."

"But I can't be a mother to our child until I at least try."

The next day on her way to court, Diane stopped by her bank and retrieved the slip of paper from her safe deposit box. Later that afternoon, she returned to her office, closed her door, and made the call. Her aunt's name was Marcia. Was her aunt still alive? Was this still her phone number? What would she do if the number had been disconnected? If no one answered, would she call back? The onslaught of questions gave her a momentary reprieve. Then Diane felt the movement of the baby in her abdomen, a slight, gentle roll, a shift that brought the child closer to her heart. She picked up the receiver and dialed the number.

"Hello?"

The voice was hoarse and resonant with age. She

knew this was her aunt Marcia. And Diane, who had not thought of her father in a specific, concrete way, who had only imagined him as a figure fleeing her mother, her brother, and her, realized that her father would now be a man in his late fifties or sixties. He might be sick. He might be dead.

"Hello?" the voice asked again.

"Hello, my name is Diane. My father is Samuel Garrison, and I'd like to speak to my aunt Marcia."

"You Sammy's girl?"

"Yes. Yes, ma'am."

"Lord have mercy, I was hoping this day would come. My brother run away. Left town like *he* was the criminal. Like he was the one who done wrong. And then he did."

"Yes, ma'am. I know it's been a long time but I'm trying to find him."

"He ain't never tried to find you, did he?"

"I don't know."

"I get a call or a card from him every couple of years. If you looking for him all I can do is give you the last address and phone number."

"I would like that. Could we meet somewhere? I'd like to meet you, connect with you."

"I ain't seen you since you was three or four years old."

"Where do you live? Could I come to your house?"

"Naw, honey, you don't wanta do that. I live in Sursum Corda."

Just the name conjured images of drive-by

109

shootings and open-air drug markets. On its streets, children were regularly killed in the crossfire of bullets aimed to settle scores, to exact revenge. During her time as a public defender, Diane had several clients who had lived in the complex which sprawled over several blocks, resembling a barracks or a prison. The place had its own police station.

Instead, she met Marcia in Chinatown. After arriving fifteen minutes early, Diane was so nervous she vomited in the restaurant bathroom. She sat sipping a tiny cup of jasmine tea when Marcia came through the door. It was a blustery day and Marcia told Diane she'd be wearing a red leather jacket. The ferocious winds that whipped along the streets propelled Marcia through the door. Diane saw her aunt, a small, shriveled woman the color of nutmeg, look around the room and finally meet her gaze.

Her wide smile erased years from her face as she closed in on Diane, who stood and leaned forward and hugged the woman. She was tiny, her face was ruined, the only question was: *Had it been crack or heroin?* Addiction and ill-health had ruptured her skin, pockmarking it with scars and leaving her brown eyes overcast with a milky film so thick that Diane wondered how well she could see.

Marcia removed her jacket and revealed a linty black turtleneck sweater, the sleeves of which she pushed up her arms. She folded her bony fingers and settled her hands on the table.

"You turned out beautiful, just like your mama."

"Thank you. I'm glad you came. My mother's sister said my father had other siblings, too."

"Your two uncles are twin brothers. One's in jail, the other got an auto repair shop in Oxon Hill, Maryland," she said matter-of-factly. "You look like you made something of yourself. In fact more than something."

"Well, I guess I did. I'm a lawyer. I have a family law practice."

"Family law, huh? I guess that makes sense, all you been through." Marcia smiled again, momentarily lifting the mask of age and decay. "Your daddy would be proud."

The waitress came, and they both studied the menus, holding them before their faces as though seeking respite from each other.

When the waitress left with their orders, Marcia asked, "How far along are you?"

"Four months."

"You married?"

Diane held up her ring finger.

Marcia smiled, bigger this time, revealing three missing teeth. "Is he a good man?" she asked.

"He is a good man. Tell me about my father."

"What do you want to know?"

"Anything. Everything. Now that I'm pregnant, family, whatever I have left, means more to me than ever."

"That's a tall order," Marcia said, rummaging

111

through her pocketbook and pulling out a battered cigarette that she began to twirl in her fingers. "I'm still trying to kick the habit. When I get nervous, if I can't smoke one, it helps anyway to just hold one."

The waitress brought their small bowls of wonton soup and both women retreated from the moment by lifting their spoons.

Marcia had dropped her cigarette onto the table and after her third spoonful of soup, placed the spoon on her napkin and said, "Even when he was a child, Sammy acted like he'd been born into the wrong family. We lived over in Barry Farms. Back in those days, in the thirties and forties, it was a nice place. People had whole families. Daddies were around. People had jobs. Wasn't always much, but it was honest work. You could even leave your door open at night. Mama cleaned government office buildings. Back then, even the black college girls did domestic work, cleaned offices to get extra money. That was the easiest work for a black woman to get then. Sometimes the only work she could get. Our daddy was a junk dealer. I bet you don't even know what that is."

Marcia laughed, no doubt pleased by the thought that she knew something Diane most likely did not. "He'd collect old stuff people had thrown out, fix it up, repair it, or polish it so it looked like new and then ride around different neighborhoods selling it off a truck. Our mother couldn't read, and our daddy sold junk, and that shamed Sammy. Don't look surprised. Back in those days it wasn't so unusual to find black folk who maybe could add and subtract a little bit, but who couldn't even read a book their second grader brought home from school. The rest of us, me, Tyrone, and Tyler, we were satisfied with the life we lived, and thought in some ways we were lucky."

Marcia paused and indifferently placed her spoon in the bowl of soup, stirring the liquid and gazing into the bowl as though inside she saw the story she was telling beginning to unfold. "Sammy was always reading something—the black newspapers, old books, and magazines that Daddy brought home. He'd ask Daddy why he sold junk. Ask Mama why she couldn't read. And it was like he asked the question just so he could look at 'em with a cold look in his eyes. Daddy told him that junk put food in his belly. But Mama, something in her just shrank up whenever Sammy asked her why she couldn't read."

Marcia leaned back in the booth and looked at Diane unflinchingly and said, "He thought he was smarter than everybody in the family and because he thought he was smarter he thought he was better. He left us a long time before he left us. Mama and Daddy used to say they just wanted to live long enough to see us graduate from high school. Well Sammy didn't even tell nobody and he got hisself accepted into a small Negro college in North Carolina. He left and never really looked back." Curling her lips in distaste, Marcia said, "He'd write now and then. We had relatives in the town where the school was but they never saw him either. He'd come home for Christmas talking about his classes. I wanted to see my brother, but it was like a professor had come home instead. In his senior year, Sammy got a girl who went to the school pregnant, told her he was gonna marry her, and then just left."

"So he was always an outsider?"

"I guess that's one way to put it. You asked me, you want me to go on?"

Before Diane could answer, their orders came: Diane's stir-fried vegetables and Marcia's General Tso's chicken.

Diving into the food, Marcia said between mouthfuls, "He come back to Washington and worked over the post office. He had a college degree, but so did half the black men working with him. I heard some of 'em even had PhDs. That was in the days when the joke was, 'What did you call a Negro with a PhD?' And the answer was 'Nigger.' I'd run into him sometimes on the street and he would just complain about the black folks he worked with.

"Daddy died and then Mama died right after him, I think mostly 'cause she missed him. Sammy came to visit us whenever there was an emergency, mostly so he could make the rest of us feel like we were too stupid to know what to do. I was married to my first husband when Sammy brought Ella around and showed her off. He did all the talking, but all you had to do was look at her and you could see she'd fallen hard for Sammy. I ain't never had too much good to say 'bout my brother but I will say I'm sure he loved your mother. They'd been married about four years when it happened. Sammy called me middle of the night and said a man had broken into the apartment, tied him up, and made him watch him rape Ella and stole a bunch of their stuff."

With each new revelation, Diane lost more of her appetite. Now, she gave up any attempt to eat.

"You don't want that? Well, let me take it home," Marcia said.

"Sure."

"I went by to see them that night. The police had gone by the time I got there. If you looked at them, and looked in their eyes, it was like they had both been raped. All his life Sammy had wanted to be big, had wanted to be in control. That man busted in his apartment and *he* took control. Then Sammy got so he was over my house all the time. He'd sit on my sofa and just start crying. I saw a brother I'd never seen before. I wondered about your mama and told him he needed to go home and cry with his wife or at least let her cry on his shoulder and then he could cry on hers and they would be okay. He'd tell me he couldn't go home. He felt like he couldn't live in that apartment no more.

"About a year after it happened, I heard he and

your mama had separated. Then he was gone. It was all too much for me. I lost a brother and that poor woman had been destroyed. When I heard about her getting run over, I swear to God I didn't know what to do. I felt too ashamed to come to the funeral. That man raped her, but then I think what Sammy did killed her long before them boys driving that car."

"Where is he now?"

"He comes to D.C. now and then, but he lives out in Las Vegas. Married some woman from Argentina."

"Does he ever ask about me?"

"Honey, I wish I could say he did. Back when your aunt called and told me Ronald died, I let him know about that. I was sure that he'd call you then. No, honey, in all these years he ain't never asked about you or your brother."

Diane left the meeting with Marcia making a promise to stay in touch, a promise that she knew she would not keep. Outside, the wind was still strong as the two women parted.

"You didn't ask me for his phone number and address but I wrote it down for you," Marcia said hesitantly, offering a slip of paper. Diane looked at the paper, still reeling from the story her aunt had shared. As the wind whipped up bitter gusts and pedestrians bustled against them, the two women stood as though frozen. When Marcia had entered the restaurant two hours earlier, Diane had not imagined the power she possessed. Now, Marcia reached for Diane's hand, pressed the slip of paper into her trembling palm, and closed Diane's fingers around it. Then Marcia lifted the collar of her red leather jacket, turned away, and walked toward the corner.

Diane hailed a taxi. During the ride home she settled in the backseat and instinctively rubbed her abdomen. "I did this for you," she whispered and then wondered, *But what have I done?*

Samuel Garrison came back to D.C. over the years but he had never asked about his son or daughter. She rolled down the window. The wind remained as furious as it had been all afternoon. She longed for its bruising touch on her skin, longed for it to lift what she now knew on its wings and take it unto heaven. They would have been so easy to find. She hadn't known where he was. Told herself that she didn't want to know.

*Gone* had become a destination, an actual place with dimensions. Over the years in her imagination, Samuel Garrison lived in New York, in Canada, or Chicago, and always there was some insurmountable obstacle that kept him away from them. Now the truth sealed her off from forgiveness. If she undertook the task of forgiving, her father would have to stand in a long line.

Gregory came home that evening and found Diane in the nursery, placing baby blankets and clothing in the four-drawer mahogany chest they had found at an estate sale in Arlington. They had compromised on the color of the room, settling on pale blue walls dotted with pink clouds on the ceiling and the wall where the crib sat, overflowing with gifts from the baby shower Paula had hosted a week ago.

"I'm sorry I went to see her. There's such a thing as knowing too much," Diane said, closing the drawer.

"What did she tell you?"

"That he always thought he was better than the rest of his family. That he walked out on a girl he got pregnant. And that in all these years, he's come back to Washington and he never even tried to find us."

Diane sank into a cushioned chair beside the crib. She closed her eyes and took a deep breath.

"Are you okay?"

She took a slip of paper out of her jacket pocket and held it up as though offering it to Gregory. "She gave me his address and phone number."

"Isn't that what you wanted?"

"Not after what she told me."

Diane crumpled the paper, and Gregory bent on his knees before her, pried open her fist, and snatched it out of her palm.

"I won't let you do that," he said, rising from the floor, his voice final as he slid the paper into his pants pocket. "You wanted to talk to your aunt and you wanted her to give you a perfect father. A father you knew you didn't have. We just buried my dad last year and I'm not going to let you cut yourself off from yours."

Her face was hidden behind her palms, and when her hands slid slowly down her cheeks Gregory saw the tears. "I hate him."

"Of course you do. And you love him."

"I never want to see him."

Gregory pulled a hassock before Diane, sat down, and clasped her fingers. "I'm disappointed in you."

"In me?" She sobbed, befuddled, and sniffled, her face now a glistening mask.

"Yes, you're bigger than that. Bigger than him. At least hear his side."

"He never asked about us. He never tried to find us. I wanted to give our child a grandfather, not a monster."

"There had to have been a reason. A reason for what he did. A reason for what he didn't do."

"How can you take the side of a man you don't know?"

"Because I don't know him. And neither do you. This isn't over and for now that paper belongs to me."

"He's a coward who turned his back on one family after another. Why would I want to reach out to him?"

"You don't get to choose your parents."

"Sometimes, Gregory, sometimes, maybe you do."

# *Chapter Nine*

## 2011

*The past is never dead. It's not even past.* Gregory didn't remember who had said that. He'd tried to, but he didn't, or couldn't. And he was sick of searching the Internet for all the things he used to know. If the past is never dead and not even past, then their three decades together would outsmart the forces aligned against him. Against them. Massive, mercurial, but precise, the thing that had upturned his life wouldn't win. But it still felt like it had crossed the finish line, like it was already smiling, holding the trophy aloft.

He and Diane had been together all these years. Together through his battle with cancer. Together through the diabetes he now had. A warm-up? A trial run for this? *Together.* Not until Diane had he known the real meaning of the word. Marriage wasn't a contract. It was a bond of caring. Caring. Another word she had made him know, deep, inside and out. All those words that had joined them, made them: Wife. Husband. Ally. Friend. He was afraid one day he would forget them, too. They weren't afraid to talk about anything. But this? She, the litigator, the judge. He the designer, the builder. He hadn't figured out how to draw a blueprint for this. He still remembered reading his father's poetry, about broken bodies he struggled to heal, about life and death, and what those he saved and those he could not bequeathed him. Those poems had given his father something, added dimension to what appeared to be a full-to-the-brim life. Now *he* was using words, writing to himself what he did not want anyone else to hear or know.

### February 10, 2011

I keep getting lost when I'm driving. Forgetting where I'm going. Arriving some-where and not knowing where I am. So far, I've managed to keep it from Diane, from Mercer. But these days I'm always running late. Running behind. Running to catch up to where I'm supposed to be. I don't know what is happening to me. I should want to know. I do want to know. But if I find out I am afraid of the cost I will pay for that knowledge. Losing my company. Everything I've worked to build. Shattered.

### March 3, 2011

I don't feel the earth is assured anymore beneath my feet. This must've been how my father felt. I cared for him. I pitied him. I loved him. But I never asked how he felt, how *it* felt.

## April 16, 2011

I have two jobs now. The second being the work of masking this thing. Extending my business card to people I think I know but don't recognize. I'll offhandedly extend my card saying with as much casualness as I can muster, "Give me all your information; I think I lost it." If I'm lucky, they have a business card. If I'm not, I'll say, as I extend the back of my card, "Oh and write down everything, to make sure I spell your name correctly."

## June 20, 2011

There are two of me. Which one is real? I'll go days where I'm fine. Living the way I used to, not thinking about my thoughts, not wondering if around the corner of the next moment, I'll run into myself as a sham and a fake. Days when I'm fine. But the memory loss always come back. It comes back to take a little more than last time.

## July 2, 2011

Writing about it makes it better. Writing to whomever I am writing to, suddenly, I am not alone. But the writing makes it real.

*So this is how it begins,* Gregory thought. Forgetting over and over. All day long. Forgetting and then remembering, and because you suddenly remembered, convincing yourself that the forgetting was a lapse, a series of lapses, not your soon-to-be-permanent mental state.

He and Mercer were reviewing plans for a retail and condominium complex, sitting elbow to elbow at Gregory's cluttered desk. He sat listening to Mercer talking about the cost overruns and constant calls from the owners, staring at the squares on the whiteprint, the lines, the boxes, the squares that he knew, yes, he knew were rooms, doors, light fixtures, stairs, skylights, windows, floors. He knew that even though there were moments, sitting beside his partner, when he had no idea what he was looking at, what the lines meant. This in and out, this feeling of being insubstantial, a breathing question mark, had his armpits drenched in sweat.

"When we go to the meeting, you talk about the changes in the design. I'll cover the new costs, okay?" Mercer asked, looking at him.

"Where is the meeting again?"

"What'd you mean? Where we always meet, in their offices."

"I've been swamped with emails, distracted. Where is it again?" He asked this with a nonchalance he was certain Mercer heard as utterly false.

"Mount Vernon Square," Mercer snapped, his brows clenched in concern. "Across the street from First Congregational Church. Don't tell me you need the address. Damn, Gregory, we've been going there once a week for the last six months."

"Gimme a break, I've got a lot on my mind."

"Well, clear some of that shit out of your brain, so you can think. And remember the meeting's at four p.m. I'll meet you there."

When Mercer left his office, Gregory pulled out his cell phone and searched for First Congregational Church on the phone's GPS. The map of the city popped up, and he could suddenly read and understand these lines. He saw Mount Vernon Square on the screen. Then he searched the pile of what looked like rubble on his desk and somehow found amid it a card with the address of the company. Finding the address stalled his fear. He now knew the name of the company. He knew the address. But as he recalled the landscape of the city, when he said out loud, "Mount Vernon Square," when he whispered, "Mount Vernon Square," there was nothing. His mind was hollow and bereft. Empty.

Gregory fingered the blueprint, a design done on crisp white paper, the kind he had been looking at all his life. His office wall cases were stacked with rows and rows of the paper, rolls and rolls of it, overflowing. All those lines and squares on the paper were now buildings where people worked, played, and lived. Those lines were the bread and butter of Caldwell & Tate, but there were days when the lines meant nothing.

How would he get through the meeting this afternoon?

He could still access his passion for talking about design, master all the jargon when needed, the language of his calling. He'd get through it, he'd muddle through. He hadn't blown a meeting yet. But the forgetting, the dislocation that plagued him, promised, he was sure, an awful day of reckoning. On that day, he would lose himself. On that day he would lose his thoughts. Would he lose Caldwell & Tate a contract?

Through the glass door to his office, Gregory watched Mercer heading toward the elevator. He saw the young designers they had hired in the last year—Martin Kim, Darren Jackson, Josh Watson—lounging in the kitchen over coffee. This was his company, his and Mercer's. *Mine to lose,* he thought, as he stealthily reached into a bottom drawer for a flask full of bourbon. With his head below his desk, he took a swig. The taste, so familiar, steeled him, erased the edge off of his terror. He returned the flask to the drawer and opened a pack of gum, cramming two sticks into his mouth.

Gregory leaned back in his high-back swivel office chair and closed his eyes. He hadn't designed anything in two years. After more than three decades together, he and Mercer now devoted their time to bringing in contracts and managing them. Looking for money to pay the staff. Slaying dragons. There had never been enough time to design, to feed his appetite for art and math. It got lost, so much of it, in the minutiae of keeping Caldwell & Tate afloat.

Odd things, things he knew by heart, he couldn't now recall. But he could somehow always remember the shame, the screw-ups. Last week at the Department of Regulatory Affairs solving a series of bureaucratic mix-ups on permits for the complex on Mount Vernon Square. When the site manager had no luck, Gregory himself had gone to the office.

He had walked up to the Plexiglas window when his number was called and the woman behind the window with a short blond haircut and light brown eyes began joking with him.

"How've you been?" she had asked, with a broad and inviting smile. "Been a couple of weeks since I've seen you down here. I met your daughter; she looks just like you. She's sharp. Your son still want to be a contractor?"

The steady, jocular stream of questions had assumed a relationship he had no knowledge of. He was certain he had never seen this woman before in his life. Yet she knew about Sean and that Lauren worked for his firm. And that would be like him, within ten minutes, to know her life history, to have shared his. But because he was polite and all-business in response to this onslaught, the woman had taken offense, making him stand before the Plexiglas window for forty-five minutes while she "researched" the problem in a back area where he could see her at work, leisurely and begrudgingly, stopping to chat with coworkers, nailing him to an unseen crucifix every few minutes with a bruised and bitter stare.

Gregory opened his eyes and saw Lauren in the outer office, her arms filled with blueprints as she headed upstairs. Next year she would take the licensing exam. She would be one of only three other female African American architects in the city. Smart, ambitious, focused. His twin.

She witnessed his days, his increasing mistakes. He explained them with a shrug and an excuse of a sleepless night, but Lauren had seen the flask in his desk and said nothing, out of love. She had slipped him a bottle of Visine for his red-rimmed eyes and interjected in meetings when she heard the faltering of his voice and sensed the flight of his memory. From bulwark to burden, that was the trajectory Gregory feared he was on, all that was left for him to bequeath his daughter.

Had his father given him this illness? He carried his father's awful journey within him. First there was the forgetting, the confusion, the day he had accused Gregory bitterly, shouting, spittle hitting Gregory's cheeks, of stealing his wallet. And the skeptical, long, and untrusting look that preceded the first time his father asked him, "Tell me, again, whose boy are you?"

"Dad, it's me. I'm your son, Gregory," he'd tell him.

Gregory's own muddy emotions had sunk him down into a soup of despair, until he learned that just telling his father his name momentarily cleared the gloaming fog choking his father's mind—for a half hour, fifteen minutes, until he asked him again: "Tell me whose boy are you?"

The dementia made a victim of his mother, too. Did she and his father make love during all that? Ever jointly revisit a past that was coherent and beloved for them both? He'd witnessed her stoic care of his father, knew the love was still there, but just like David and Bruce, Gregory never asked how she bore his father's day-by-day vanishing act. He never asked because he could not fathom how he would handle it if Margaret told him the truth.

Gregory had seen close up who and what he feared he could become.

A decade ago, cancer had been harder to fight, harder to beat than he had ever been able to tell anyone. He'd had a team of talented doctors, the love of his family, and the will to live, but his body never recovered from the brutal efficiency and side effects of the chemotherapy and radiation.

The cancer, Hodgkin's lymphoma, went into remission after ten months of treatment. He'd been in remission ever since. He had told Diane everything he could, but there was no way to describe the pain of cancer, how it depleted and deformed every ounce of fight and resilience, how it felt some days as if he were being devoured. After he was "cured," he developed diabetes. He had it under control, but still it was a new, invasive, and unsettling element of his body and health.

But he'd made it, kicked cancer's butt. Had even told friends that it had been a blessing because it reminded him how lucky he was to be alive, how gratified he had been by the outpouring of love and concern and support for him and Diane from colleagues and friends.

Cancer had quenched any dread he had of death, but this loss of memory, its stubbornness, its resilience, if it was what he feared . . . he could not even name his trepidation.

Gregory sat in the cafeteria of Washington Hospital Center waiting for his brother Bruce, a general practitioner. He had left the office early. As he stood outside the offices of Caldwell & Tate, he realized he would have to pretend he was a tourist and ask a stranger on the street how to get to Mount Vernon Square, a ten-minute drive from their offices. On his way to Washington Hospital Center, he'd gone out of his way and found the Mount Vernon Square office and thankfully it all came back to him. All the meetings with the investment company. All of it. A comforting tidal wave that baptized him in confidence.

He was facing the entrance so Bruce would see him. He was ravenous and had already filled his tray with a turkey sandwich, potato salad, a large cup of coffee, and a slice of apple pie. He'd need the energy for the meeting. He felt more in control, less fragile when he'd had a good meal.

Gregory gazed at the doctors and visitors wolfing down lasagna, soup, salad, and throwing their heads back to drain cans of soda, bottles of water. Which of them, he wondered, was there waiting for someone to die? Which of the doctors had a patient for whom they could do no more?

Gregory saw Bruce enter the cafeteria, look around, and nod to him. He then headed to the food court. His brother was at least thirty pounds overweight and had just stopped smoking a year ago. His black hair was thinning rapidly, leaving strands of sheer white covering his balding pate. Bruce arrived at the table with a cup of lentil soup and a vegetarian casserole on his tray.

"I'm finally taking my own advice," he said, pointing to his meal.

"About time," Gregory chided. "How's Aaron?"

"Coming home from rehab next week. It's costing us a small fortune."

"What do they say, third time's the charm?"

"Hell, it better be. My son is killing my retirement fund." Cutting into the casserole with a plastic fork, Bruce said, "Fucking drugs. Why would a kid like Aaron, with all his advantages, need to take drugs?"

"It's an equal opportunity curse. Diane says 80

percent of the cases she hears are rooted in drug abuse."

"So what's up?" Bruce asked, his eyes weary and indifferent, contradicting the intent of the question. Bruce could never wait for the end of a story, was nearly allergic to eye contact, a doctor with the world's worst bedside manner. Gregory watched his brother stuff the vegetable casserole into his mouth, studying his plate, avoiding Gregory's querulous stare.

Gregory wished then that David were alive. Their brother David had died three years ago in a small plane crash, returning home from a medical convention in Philadelphia. That's who he would have rather gone to with these questions. David might have given him some hope. But Bruce would have to do.

"Do I seem different?"

"What do you mean?" Bruce looked up, apparently finally interested. "You don't seem different to me," he concluded with a shrug.

"Do you see forgetfulness in your patients much?"

"What?"

"Symptoms of dementia, Alzheimer's."

"Why do you ask?" Now his gaze was riveted to Gregory's face, those brown eyes taking stock of him with a new intensity.

"I wonder if I'm getting what Dad had. I can't remember things. Addresses and people."

"I haven't seen any changes in you."

*Of course not,* Gregory thought silently, bitterly. *We're brothers who see each other four or five times a year.*

"I wonder if I have Alzheimer's. Dad had it. Dementia. That means it's in our DNA. My kids, your kids."

"But we don't know that's what you're experiencing." He paused. "Alzheimer's is a bitch. We can't screen for early symptoms. Even if we could, there are no treatments that make a significant difference. Patients come to us for answers and there is nothing we can do. What medications there are relieve some of the symptoms but can't stop the progression of the disease. Alzheimer's erases all our education and training. It renders the hundreds of thousands of dollars we spent on becoming doctors useless. We hate Alzheimer's more than cancer. David used to say, 'Cancer fights fair compared to Alzheimer's.' And African Americans? We've got a 50 to 70 percent greater risk of developing it than anybody else, because of our higher rates of diabetes, high blood pressure, and high cholesterol."

Gregory laughed uneasily, looking around to avoid the resignation—*or was it defeat?*—he heard in his brother's voice. He looked anywhere but at the man who had just spoken those words.

"Still, I can give you the name of a specialist if you're concerned. Shit, man, Alzheimer's. Dad also had that stroke, diabetes, and high blood pressure. How's your health?"

"Fine. Diane and I are in the gym regularly. My diabetes is under control. I bought some software online to help my memory, but Bruce, I'm scared. I haven't said anything to Diane, but she notices all this and I don't know what to say."

"Yet you still drink?"

"Sociably."

Bruce shook his head dismissively.

"And you're still a pompous ass. Look I came to you—"

"For answers and for encouragement, I know, but you just asked me about a disease that won't allow me to offer you any of that. Bullshitting you would be worse than dashing your hopes. But you may be overreacting, Greg. You're still young. Hell, we both are. Haven't you heard sixty-five is the new forty?"

In response, Gregory stood up, reached for both their trays, and took them to the conveyor belt. He sat down again as Bruce leaned forward across the table, preparing to say more. Thrusting an armistice into the bloody campaign of truth his brother had waged, Gregory asked, "Do you remember the summer Dad took us to Mississippi?"

"Hell, yeah." Bruce's smile broke open his face. "The summer I decided to be a doctor."

"You mean the summer you almost got killed and not by the KKK?" Gregory laughed. "That night the three of us snuck off to that black juke joint on the edge of town."

Bruce blushed, his eyes lighting up in merriment. "Yeah, and I almost got cut by some crazy nigger named Blade for dancing with his woman. A fact I didn't know till he came out of the bathroom and saw us slow-dragging in the middle of the floor. Damn, she was all over me."

"Yeah, and Blade was about to be all over you, too."

The laughter bubbled up, an oasis between them.

"You got off lucky with just that black eye," Gregory teased.

"Till we got home and Dad was waiting on the porch for us with Reverend Reagan and his shotgun for emphasis." Bruce shook his head.

"Freedom Summer made you a doctor and me an architect, looking at the shacks those sharecroppers lived in."

The mellow satisfaction of the laughter settled like a mist as the two men rose at the same moment.

Instead of saying good-bye, Gregory told his brother, "All we are is memories, Bruce. That's all we are. Even more than flesh and blood."

Just before the four p.m. meeting, Gregory sat in his car in the hospital parking garage, as cars slowly passed by looking for an open space. He sat cradled by memories that felt on loan, battered and suspect.

Gregory watched several cars slowly drive past, drivers shooting him impatient sign language and looks that asked, *You pulling out?*

*No, I'm not,* he mouthed. His brother, the doctor had just told him there was no hope for what he feared was imminent. He sat in his car soaked through his skin with sweat and drowning in an unfaithful and mocking memory.

When they met in 1978, Mercer was driving a Crown Victoria, a whale of a car that pushed everything else off the road, back when everybody was switching to Japanese cars. Mercer's tape deck was full of Buddy Guy, James Brown, and Lou Rawls, who he had declared were actually priests walking among the savages on Earth. It was them, those men, Mercer swore who were the real holy trinity.

How many thousands of hours had they spent together, plotting, planning, conspiring to build a company that would leave a footprint in the city? Mercer, like a brother. Gregory felt him in the car with him.

And Diane was everywhere with him, all the time. Diane, who he had wanted so badly when he laid eyes on her. Gregory had dated what Mercer like to call "the United Nations" by the time he met Diane and had passed into that zone where a man is ready to make his next step with a woman beside him. The time when he prays at night that luck will wipe his slate clean and that he will recognize the woman when she appears. Caldwell & Tate was five years old and the small contracts, one after the other, had begun to widen their network, had gotten people who mattered talking about them. When he saw Diane at the party that night, he'd seen a woman without whom he could go no further. Yet there had come a time when he'd wondered where all that love had gone.

She had been a judge for a year when they stood facing off in the living room—this time, Diane accusing him of failing her and their children.

"The one thing that matters to me most, family, that's what you make a mockery of. I might as well be a single mother. When will you look around and see the family you've left behind? Is there a finish line for this race you're running?"

"Actually no, hell no. I have to go out there. Mercer and I have to go out there and slay a dragon—a fuckin' dragon—every day. You've got families in trouble lined up, filling your courtroom. You'll never run out of a job to do. We've got a payroll that we magically have to meet. If we don't have a dozen contracts signed off on or ready to be signed off on, we're screwed. And you wonder why I leave here at six a.m. and fall through the door at midnight. Nothing we do can crack that damned glass ceiling. We can't be more than a boutique black firm no matter how good our designs. Diane, you say I should be with you and the kids more, but if I'm not out there scratching and clawing, hustling, I can't come home to you at all. Not empty-handed."

Without their determination, they never could have gotten some of the deals they landed. Caldwell & Tate was always competing against big white firms with track records of building half a dozen huge projects in any given year. There was too much money, too much ego and prestige bound up in the major projects for many black firms to ever be considered. They were always paying what Mercer called "the black tax."

Mercer reveled in recounting a presentation in the conference room and imitating the reaction of the corporate stakeholders. He would lean forward, narrow his eyes, and lance one of the designers with a look of withering disdain and ask, "Nigger, what makes you think you can handle a project worth this much money?"

Of course they had all laughed, for such raw, naked racism would never be expressed. Most often it came wrapped in condescension or paternalisms that could still land a bruising knock-out punch. The more he'd proved, the more he'd had to prove. How many ways could he tell Diane that?

But now there was nothing left to prove. That night on the Beltway had changed it all.

"Look, Gregory, we've got to face it. Something's wrong. Maybe you should give some of your duties to the other designers. We've got a company to run, employees to pay. Too much is at stake," Mercer had told him that afternoon.

Who was this man, ordering him around, he had wondered in astonishment. Mercer, schooling *him* on the company that was *his* idea. Gregory had looked at his friend's smooth, unlined face, the tailored gray shirt and crimson silk tie. Not a wrinkle or ruffle in Mercer's demeanor. So smooth, not unraveling like him.

"Lauren will handle the City Center visit tomorrow evening. I can't risk you taking the lead on that," Mercer had said. Gregory was expected to accept this conclusion.

Marshaling a calmness he did not feel, Gregory said, "Let me go with her. One last time. One last client. I promise I won't say anything, I'll let her do all the talking."

"This is a no-win, don't you understand? If you say nothing, don't answer questions, they'll wonder why."

"You can't just throw me out. Take the company, my work, away like this."

"Gregory, you can't remember a damn thing anymore. You're always lost or late. Throw you out? We've both got the devil at our back. I'm listening to myself saying all this to you. This is breaking my heart."

Mercer had stood before him talking about a broken heart when all Gregory saw was a man aging like some gleaming, hardy wood. Not being chipped away, eaten from the inside like him.

Before he'd slipped away from the conversation,

for that was how he thought of *it,* he'd said to himself, *The hell with Mercer. The hell with them all.*

The next evening, he was on the Beltway, headed to the City Center meeting in Silver Spring, Maryland. He would get there ahead of Lauren, remind them that he wasn't dead yet. He'd popped in a CD, Donny Hathaway's "Valdez in the Country," a soothing assurance that he would be all right. Music helped. It grounded and calmed him.

The Beltway was a tidal wave of cars. How many thousands, he wondered, were at this moment creeping along the cement girdle that wrapped like a snake around the DMV as it was called now—the District of Columbia, Maryland, and Virginia.

The music and his thoughts, like normal, like before, working together, seamless, automatic.

Then he had no idea where he was. He felt himself oozing, slipping, and sliding, down a hole he couldn't outrun or outthink. On the other side of the glass, a nation of automobiles and trucks and the occasional motorcycle. Headlights, with accusing, blistering eyes. His hand had frozen on the steering wheel. Was there an emergency? An act of terrorism? A trickle of wetness and then he was sitting in a puddle of his own urine, the smell of it hot, pungent, filling the small space with his disgrace. The huge green-and-white exits, where would they take him? If only he could stop and ask someone in one of the thousands of cars in front, in back, on his left, on his right.

He'd dared to blow his horn once, then twice, at a woman in a car on his right. She looked at him. Frantically, he waved at her, not to say hello but for help. She smiled then sped to cut off a car in front of her.

By the time he finally had the nerve, the will, to exit the Beltway, he was in Pentagon City, swerving off the exit ramp. The lights of a gas station quenched his fright. Parking near the air pumps and car vacuums, he felt his spirit, something inside him that he could not name but could only thank God for, take hold of him and set him crawling up and out of the darkness.

He could breathe. Think. Remember.

At a Burger King up the road, he had pulled into the drive-through and ordered fries and a cheeseburger, parked on the lot and consumed the food as though it were both his last meal and his first. Half a mile up at a Dunkin Donuts drive-through, he ordered two cups of coffee, which he was certain would help him find his way home. The client would have to wait.

He staggered through the front door at ten p.m. Diane was away at a conference. Slumping on the sofa, he checked his cell phone and found a dozen messages from Lauren. There was only one thing to do.

In the basement, in the rear of the top drawer of

his filing cabinet, behind yellowing papers and old photographs and documents, his hands found the bottle. He'd sworn he would never go back. Back then he had stopped on his own. Hadn't needed twelve steps. But if there was ever a night when he needed a drink . . .

This meeting with clients would be his last. He had finally agreed with Mercer, with Lauren that he would work from the office. Today, his last hurrah. He couldn't sit here any longer. As it was, he figured he'd just make the four p.m. meeting. At the first stoplight, he reached for his phone, punched in his GPS, and reminded himself where he was headed: Mount Vernon Square.

He entered to see Mercer and the investors gathered in the cavernous conference room around a horseshoe-shaped table studying blueprints. He caught Mercer's eye, winked, and gave him a thumbs-up. Mercer's wary, worried eyes gave him nothing back, so Gregory walked over to the sideboard and filled a cup with coffee from a silver urn before turning to the wide picture window that looked down on Mount Vernon Square.

*Remember who you are,* he thought. *Remember what you have done.*

They'd beaten the odds and left an indelible mark on the city and the region, even with the insane deadlines, the clients who paid late or pulled the plug on contracts, the weeks and sometimes months that staff salaries were late. They'd worked on monuments and office buildings in Washington, Fairfax County, and Silver Spring. A sports stadium in Prince George's County, shopping and recreation centers, and schools. His wall at home was filled with awards, and he had served a term as president of the American Institute of Architects.

Their signature project was a new library in downtown D.C., the nexus of historic buildings. The building had heralded the remaking of the city's architectural identity and demographics.

The library was airy and spacious, a confident and nearly playful glass tower in a city of squat buildings which, even in contemporary design, were still paying homage to Greece and Rome. The library bore the imprint of the best of their design-teams' skills, with Mercer and Gregory fine-tuning and adding defining touches. That was the last time he'd had fun, been excited about the work.

The library had altered the city's landscape in a way that inspired imitations. The building received rave reviews and went on to win awards, but when the congratulatory dust settled, white developers told Gregory—while shaking his hand in admiration—that they liked the design so much they had hired another firm, a white firm, to design a building just like it for them.

There was the glory of the library, and then in

2009, falling off the economic cliff along with everybody else. The depression they called a recession. Rolling up their sleeves to let go of designers they were as close to as family, getting lean and mean, determined to rise again. It had taken a few years, but they were back.

Soon after, Caldwell & Tate partnered with another firm to put in a bid to work on the planned Museum of African American History and Culture on the Mall. The memory of the months spent planning for that presentation still buoyed him. A building was a story etched into stone, so there was as much discussion about the philosophy and beliefs that would inspire the design as anything else. Movement. Evolution. Those words had been the foundation of the design. In the end, Caldwell & Tate and their partners made the short list, but they were not chosen.

The lead investor tapped Gregory on the shoulder and engaged him in a conversation that he heard on a distant loop, only remembering that this man, with his white-blond hair and football-player girth and neon, self-assured grin, merely required that Gregory answer "Yes" to every request. He and Mercer told him "Yes" and then did what the project needed, not what this asshole wanted. It had worked so far. But today they had been called on the carpet.

Mercer walked to the head of the table and launched into an overview of the project's first six months. Then he signaled for Gregory to come to the front.

*Just go ahead. Go on,* he thought, walking to the podium before a screen that would soon fill with a PowerPoint presentation. For several moments Gregory said nothing, just looked at the six men around the table. How could he make them fall in love with the project again, he wondered, despite the delays and cost overruns. He clicked on the first slide, an image of the finished project. Sleek, modern, but they would be keeping the brick walls and high ceilings of the original building, preserving what had made it unique.

Finally he told them what he, in his heart, believed: "This building will make anyone who lives in it glad to come home."

# *Chapter Ten*

## January 3, 2012

We've never argued about anything like we're arguing about this. Diane says I'm in denial. That my pride endangers me. Twice I skipped, just didn't show up for doctor's appointments. "Don't you want to at least know what's happening?" she keeps asking. There's too much at stake. Too much to lose. But even this denial, this resistance. It's not me. I know it isn't. But neither is the other person inside me. Or is that really me now?

Gregory touched Juliette Beamer's ass. Standing behind her at the water cooler as she leaned over to fill her cup with hot water, Gregory touched her backside. First his fingers brushed the silky floral cloth of the dress he had been admiring all morning. Then his fingers tensed and grabbed her, feeling the easy give of flesh beneath his fingers. Her scream bludgeoned him into wakefulness from what felt like the grip of a hallucination. Juliette abruptly turned around. Then he saw the disgust and fear in her eyes.

"You touched me. Gregory, why would you do that?" she shouted.

"I—I didn't."

"Yes, you did."

Afternoons when he was bushed and needed a break, it was the image of Juliette's wide, sensuous face framed by a neat, tight cap of reddish brown curls that he'd dive into. But he had never crossed the line. Had never even thought to. Juliette had worked with Caldwell & Tate for fifteen years, had started as secretary and was now senior administrative manager.

Gregory shrank beneath the outraged gleam of Juliette's eyes where he saw the depth of his trespass and the breadth of her pain.

"It wasn't me, I mean, it wasn't me, it was . . ."

"Who, Gregory, who? There's only two of us here, and I didn't turn around and grab my own ass." Juliette's anger swelled her with a fierce righteousness as she stood her ground, her face thrust into Gregory's so close that he could not see, sense, or feel anything else.

"I swear, Juliette, I'd never do something like that. It wasn't me."

"What's going on?" Lauren asked coming down the stairs from the second level. Everyone else was out to lunch.

Juliette stood now gazing at Gregory, shaking her head. Befuddled pity had overtaken her anger. "Your father," she said, the words a damning indictment.

"I'm sorry, I didn't mean . . . If you say I did, but I, I didn't know . . ." Gregory stammered, sweating,

146

pinned between the curiosity of his daughter and the loathing of the woman who was the linchpin of his company.

"Lauren, your father touched me inappropriately. I don't know what's going on, but something's wrong. Maybe you should take him home."

As they stood at the water cooler watching Juliette stalk away, Lauren hugged her father and led him into his office, whispering, "What happened? What happened?"

Gregory slumped into his chair. He felt whipped, near tears. "I don't know. Why would she lie? Maybe I did what she said."

"Don't worry about that now, Dad. You're probably just hungry, tired maybe. Let's go get something to eat." Lauren comforted him. "Let's go get some air, you'll be fine."

"What if Juliette tells Mercer?"

"I'll talk to her, tell her that you haven't been feeling well. She knows you, knows how out of character this is."

"What if she tells Mercer?"

"Dad, come on, calm down. Let's go get something to eat."

That evening he couldn't tell Diane that he had touched Juliette. But who was he kidding? His need to keep secrets had made everything a lie, confusion. He had spent the first few minutes home pensive and brooding, and now he was complaining about a designer he and Mercer had hired several months earlier.

"We got punked," he said, while cutting the roast chicken breast. "His recommendations were great. He works well with his team, and his portfolio was one of the best we'd seen in years. Now, it's like some other person comes in to work every day. Just yesterday I told . . ." He chewed the sliver of chicken, stopped, swallowed, and reached for his glass of water.

"I said to . . ." he began again, placing his knife and fork noisily on his plate.

"Who did you tell, Gregory? Was it Mercer?"

"Yes, yes, of course. Who else? Who else would it be? We interviewed him together. I remember that. Who else would I be talking about?" he asked irritably, pushing away from the table and heading to the kitchen. "Don't say anything. Please don't say a damned word," he sneered, leaning against the kitchen counter, watching Diane as she rose to stand in the entrance to the kitchen.

"You don't get to say that to me."

"I'm tired, that's all."

"Gregory . . ."

"We're past deadline on the school in Landover."

"Gregory . . ."

"I forgot my best friend's name."

An hour later Diane moved close to Gregory beneath the bedspread and turned the plasma television to a jazz channel. The voice of Abbey Lincoln oozed into the room.

"Gregory, how does it feel?" she asked. "When the memories leave you? When you can't bring them forth?"

How could he create for her the sensation of the past, of all that he knew, was sure he knew, evaporating like steam, like thoughts turning to ash? When he tried to turn his mind into a hand, a fist that could retain the words and thoughts? Only to find that too often, he was not fast enough.

"I look at my driver's license twenty, thirty times a day to remember who I am, what my face looks like. I can't stand to drive anymore. What if I get lost, or go over the speed limit and get stopped, get arrested all because I can't answer a cop's questions?"

He can't tell her that he has imagined a way out if it is what he fears and what he dreads. Would he even be able to do it? He might start the process and in the midst of it have no idea how to finish. He could never say the word to Diane. He couldn't be that selfish.

Diane turned on her side and moved closer to him, closing her eyes, lying against his chest. Gregory clutched her arm and thought about how he had—yes, he had—touched Juliette, *touched* her. Even now, in this moment he remembered the feel of her strong hips beneath the silky softness of her dress, and how he had wondered at the color of her slip, her panties. He trembled, fearful and shamed that he had done that. He lay beside his wife remembering that moment, when so many other things he wanted to call forth were now gone. No, he couldn't tell Diane. What she had seen was more than enough. He couldn't tell her everything.

He reached for the remote and punched in a channel for classical music.

"Mercer," Gregory said, whispering his friend's name over the sound of the Brahms symphony. "Mercer," he declared, vowing never to forget it again.

He heard Diane's gentle breathing as she slept beside him. The Brahms symphony couldn't block the shame that warmed him. Gregory held tightly to Diane, both solid and fleshy beside him. His agitation woke her. She yawned and then her fingers rested on his penis, gently probing, fondling. Her tongue rimmed his earlobe. His hand pushed her gown up.

"I'll never forget how to do this," he murmured, words which fell warm and true against Diane's neck.

"I love you, Gregory."

"I'll never forget that either," he said as his fingers parted her thighs.

"I'm not begging. I'm not pleading. Not anymore. Bruce gave me the name of a neurologist and we have an appointment on Tuesday."

Diane made the announcement, a stern satisfaction in her voice as she poured Gregory a cup of coffee. He tried to block out the words as he sipped his coffee—black with a touch of sugar—its warmth filling him with a salutatory sense of healing.

Sunday morning and they had finished breakfast. Sections of the *Washington Post* and the *New York Times* were scattered between their plates. A member of Congress was being interviewed on *Face the Nation*, which filled the TV screen in the living room. Outside it was raining.

He didn't want to resist. He didn't want to fight. Not anymore. Not about this. This thing had encroached on every part of his life. There was no hiding, no possibility of subterfuge. One morning Diane had come into the bathroom and seen him shaving with his toothbrush. The next day she woke up to find a gallon of ice cream melted in the microwave. He had put it there because he thought it was the freezer.

He knew it made no sense, his fear of a diagnosis. But he also knew it made perfect sense. The news that awaited him, and he knew it was bad, would obliterate his identity and gradually make everything, from drinking this cup of coffee, to loving this headstrong, determined woman, meaningless. And that would be his cross to bear alone.

"What if I refuse?"

"Gregory, you aren't a child. Stop talking like a

three-year-old." The impatience in her voice stung him, stung him as though he *were* a three-year-old. All of them now, Mercer, Diane, his children, eyeing him like he was an alien or a broken object they couldn't decide whether to repair or throw away.

"We know something's wrong," she insisted.

"Nobody—*nobody*—knows how much is wrong as well as I do," he shouted.

"How can you stand this . . . *not knowing?* This isn't you."

"How do you know what's me anymore? This is me now."

Diane plunged into a bristling quietude, an absence, he thought, of even the sound of her breathing, a pulling back of her presence and energy as she looked out the kitchen window at the rain. *Over three decades together and now this,* he thought. There was no name for this betrayal. Her face had melted with age into a soft, certain beauty that reflected what she now possessed inside. She refused to dye her hair, and the gray and white strands framed a face of vulnerable, shimmering strength.

"You're not alone," Diane said, turning to face Gregory.

"You can't be there for all of it. Not inside my mind."

"I won't let you do this to yourself. To me or our family."

"So it's about you?"

"It's about all of us. Maybe you are afraid to know. But we all deserve to."

Dr. Lance Ogden had been a neurologist for forty years. In the initial visit, during which Gregory and Diane shared the changes in Gregory over the past year and a half and discussed his general health, he was compassionate and accessible. Today, Diane and Gregory sat facing him across his desk as he casually reviewed Gregory's test results.

"The MRI didn't reveal any strokes or tumors. It was perfectly normal. But the PET scan results are a different story."

*PET scan,* Gregory thought; the name sounded so innocuous and harmless. The procedure was an imaging test of his brain using a radioactive substance called a tracer to look for signs of disease and injury. It revealed how well or how poorly his brain was working. That's what Dr. Ogden had told them. He'd taken the test in a room down the hall, sat before a computer and was asked questions. He'd been so nervous he could barely think. He was being analyzed, judged; how could he possibly do anything but fail? If he couldn't think of an answer or took too long to respond, or couldn't remember something that had flashed on the screen a few seconds or minutes earlier, all that counted against him. Against him and his brain.

"Mr. Tate, are you listening?" Dr. Ogden asked

gently. Gregory stared at the tiny brown spots on the doctor's balding head, his drooping yet oddly alert eyes, and wondered how he could stand telling people bad news all day long.

"Yes, of course," Gregory said, squeezing Diane's hand.

"The results of the PET scan reveal significant decline in your cognitive and logical thinking."

"Logical? I'm forgetting things, not going crazy."

"Gregory, please let him finish," Diane said.

"Mr. Tate, this is an objective measurement of what you have been experiencing. And in your initial visit, when I asked you dates and places and tested you for recall in our conversation, your performance was haphazard."

"Haphazard?"

"When I look at the MRI results, which revealed nothing abnormal, the PET scan results, which do, and factor in your accounts, this tells me that you likely have early-onset Alzheimer's disease."

Gregory felt himself upright, sitting beside his wife holding her hand, and simultaneously choking, drowning. All with his eyes wide open.

"What do you mean *likely?*" Diane asked.

Dr. Ogden paused and leaned back in his chair. He swiped the top of his bald head as though brushing back strands of hair. "Actually, the only method of definitively diagnosing Alzheimer's is with an autopsy or biopsy. It's a clinical diagnosis. It's too early to see on an MRI."

"My father had it," Gregory said mostly to himself, but loud enough to be heard. "It wasn't called Alzheimer's then. I think they called it old age or dementia."

"Neither dementia or Alzheimer's are a natural part of aging. As its prevalence has increased, many think of it as result of living longer, but it's not normal."

"Early-onset, what does that mean?" Diane asked.

"It's not strictly a disease of the elderly. I have worked with patients as young as fifty who have it."

"I'm sixty-five," Gregory said.

"It's still early-onset."

"Well, at least now we know," Diane whispered. She turned and faced Gregory, enfolding him in an embrace that enclosed them in a world of their own making. They sat breathing in the sanctity and solemnity of the moment.

"Do you two need time alone?" Dr. Ogden asked.

"No, no," Diane said, releasing Gregory. "We've got work to do. Tell us what's next."

"I want to put Mr. Tate on Aricept. It's not a cure, but it will help with the symptoms and slow their progression. You are diabetic, but seem to have that under control. You aren't overweight and your cholesterol is good."

"Why, Dr. Ogden, why?" Gregory asked. "Because of my father?"

"Not necessarily. Some people in the field argue that it is heredity; others think members of the same family can develop it for different reasons. Telling you I don't know why is almost as difficult as telling you that you have Alzheimer's."

"How long do I have?"

"You don't need to try to answer that, Dr. Ogden," Diane cut in.

"Mr. Tate, I want you to continue all the healthy things you've been doing, eating right, exercise. I don't advise alcohol. It's also important that you keep up your social networks. Engage in work as much as you can. Spend time with friends. Practice a hobby. We want to preserve every neuron and synapse possible."

Friends. Gregory thought of how isolated he and Diane had become, how friends and acquaintances had begun to drift away, embarrassed by something he had said or done or just by their being healthy and strong, not knowing what to say.

"How long have I had it?"

"Generally, the disease can take years before symptoms are apparent. It could have begun developing a decade ago. I don't have a patient for another half hour. If you want to sit here for a while, you can," Dr. Ogden said, rising from his chair. "Zoe will have the prescription for you at the front desk and will make an appointment for another visit in six months."

They both watched him leave, Gregory thought, as though he was exiting the scene of a crime he had stumbled upon.

The image of him touching Juliette rose up like the sparks of a flame. If he could do that, if he could think about her what he had thought, what else could he do? Turning to Diane, he whispered, "If I ever hurt you, I want you to do what's best for you. I don't want to be a burden."

"Gregory, I'll never—"

"Don't make any promises," he said, his fingers gently pressed against her lips. "The treachery of this disease will make liars of us both."

They walked to the parking lot of Washington Hospital Center still holding hands, as they had been holding on to one another since entering the physician's office.

*"We have work to do."*

Sliding her key into the ignition, Diane repeated the words to herself. That was how she had managed to talk back to the diagnosis they had received. But now she did not want to go home. She was parched for the sound of laughter, a sighting, however brief, of joy. Surely they could not lose that. They had to fight for it. They had to find it. Somewhere in the city on this sweltering July afternoon.

"I want an ice cream cone," she declared, pursing her lips and braving a smile, casting it upon the still waters of her husband's face. "What about you?"

"Why not?"

They drove to Georgetown, parked in a lot, and entered their favorite upscale ice cream boutique.

She could not speak for Gregory, but reading the blackboard, which listed thirty different flavors, Diane savored the return of childlike anticipation that had her mouth watering.

"Let's try a flavor we've never had before," she told Gregory.

"Yes, your honor." He winked at Diane, a minuscule action that after what they now knew she accepted as a miracle.

Gregory ordered a double scoop of banana split and Diane, Oreo cookie. Busily, greedily licking their cones, they left the store and walked into the rays of a broad-shouldered sun. They crossed the street and sat in the park facing the waters of the Potomac River. For nearly an hour, they sat watching tourists board the boat that would take them on a ride across the river to the islands on the other side, children squealing in surprise and delight as they were drenched in water beneath the waterfall in the center of the park, and cyclists, lean and strong, whizzing past them.

"You asked Dr. Ogden how long you have. It's not over yet. I'm not through loving you. *That's* how long we have."

"Let's go home," he said. "I want to be alone with my wife."

At midnight, in the dark, Gregory said, "I want to say it. I want to tell them."

"Are you sure?"

"It's important for me to try." This was the first night she would hear him weep, without restraint. It would not be the last.

Two days later, the family convened in their living room. Margaret, accompanied by Bruce, Lauren, Sean, and Mercer, all entered the house and hugged Gregory. None had asked what the family meeting was about.

"We have something to tell you," Diane had told each of them during the call.

Margaret settled in their midst, still feared a little by all them. She sat in the high-backed, royal blue taffeta-upholstered chair she had given Gregory and Diane as a housewarming gift when they moved into this house. Over the years, Diane had come to think that Margaret had purchased the chair for herself. She could not recall a time when the family was gathered in this room that Margaret had not sat in the chair, which made whoever sat in it resemble a monarch. Her salmon-colored, cowl neck blouse revealed a swath of Margaret's wrinkled neckline, and her auburn hair was pulled back in her signature bun, now thinner and marbled with swaths of gray. She gazed at her family with a face that was lightly rouged and largely unlined.

Gregory leaned forward and released his grip on Diane's hand. He looked at each one of them, lingering on their faces, faces Diane now knew one day he would not recognize.

"Diane and I went to see a neurologist, and I have Alzheimer's." Gregory exhaled a hollow, despairing breath, as if exhausted by the declaration, which he had offered as a kind of confession. He looked at his hands and when he lifted his eyes he told them, "One day I won't know who any of you are. I'm sorry."

"Are they sure?" Sean asked.

Diane was relieved when Bruce, sitting on a hassock beside Margaret, began to explain all that their internist and Dr. Ogden had told them about Gregory's illness.

"So he has to die in order for them to know if it was really Alzheimer's?" Sean shouted, storming into the kitchen where they heard the refrigerator door open, cabinet doors slamming. "Bullshit, bullshit!" The hoarse screams came from the kitchen, along with the sound of Sean's shoes scraping the floor.

Mercer shifted uncomfortably from his perch near the mantel. "You can come to the office as long as you want, Gregory."

"For what?" Gregory asked, looking up at his friend in surprise.

"I want to apologize," Diane said. "We suspected . . . we know you all have known there was something terribly wrong. We couldn't figure out how to face it."

"I hoped that if this showed up again in our family it would take me, not any of my sons," Margaret

160

offered wistfully. "What can I do, Diane, how can we help? Was there something that we could have done earlier? My goodness, one day he called me and asked to speak to Ramsey. I didn't know what to say, but when I heard that tremor in his voice—the one I heard sometimes when Ramsey asked for the impossible or inquired about things he should have known—I told him that his father had gone out of town for a few days. What was I to do? Bruce, you told me he came to you and asked for help. Why didn't you do more? Wasn't there something you could've done for your brother?"

"They went to see the specialist I referred them to," Bruce said defensively.

"Listen to all of you, talking about him as if he isn't even here," Lauren shouted. "Mom said there's medications Dad can take. He's agreed to participate in a study that Hopkins is conducting. Isn't that right, Dad?"

"When did I say that? Study my brain? Why, there's nothing wrong with me." Gregory stood up and threw his arms open in supplication and reassurance. "It's the drug companies. They want to get us all doped up, that's all. Sure, I forget sometimes. But I'm not sick. Ask me anything," he shouted, bounding over to Margaret, his face bright with a terrifying lucidness. "I know you, you're my mother. I know today's date. I know my phone number. I know who you all are, you're my family."

When Sean reentered the room, Gregory looked at him pleadingly. "Tell them, David. Tell them there's nothing wrong with me."

The next day, Gregory was lucid and clear-eyed when he came into the office. He eased into the ergonomic chair that faced Lauren and said, "I wanted us to talk before I lose everything. While I can tell you what I want you to know about the business, about other things, too."

"Dad, there's no need. You've been a great teacher."

"It may be their building but it's your vision," he said ignoring her words. "Never work for anyone who doesn't respect you. We've had clients who thought our job was to just draw lines on paper. We're hired for our ability to give the client what they didn't know they wanted until we designed it. They can fire us, but we can also fire them."

Lauren watched her father look out the glass wall in her office at the designers at work, waiting for him to turn back to her, the moment between them feeling so tender, she dare not touch it.

"While I still have a mind, I get to say what's on it."

Lauren walked to the other side of her desk and fell onto her knees and held her father's hands. "Daddy, please don't go."

"Honey, that's the one thing we all gotta do. And we don't get to say how."

# Chapter Eleven

Diane was in community court—an effort by the city to place judges in the neighborhoods where lifestyle and life skills issues festered, creating breeding grounds for the most malignant forms of neglect. Parents who had dropped out of school in the tenth grade and now considered school to be optional for their children. Parents who had grown up hungry and now served Fritos and a Coke for breakfast. Parents who had never been to the dentist and couldn't make or keep a doctor's appointment for their child. This was how it started and ended in everything from teen pregnancy to murder.

Jacinda Reed was not sending her two daughters to school and she sat facing Diane across a conference table in a small room located in a recreation center on Minnesota Avenue, a room rank with the odor of cheap government carpeting and the nondescript furnishings to match. The weave that haphazardly crowned the woman's head was matted and lint-filled. A dark space behind her lower lip that signaled a missing tooth enticed Diane's gaze each time Jacinda parted her lips and reflexively brought her hand to her mouth, too late to hide the sorrowful gap. Diane smiled at Jacinda to quell the judgment roiling in her mind, judgment that she had trained herself to keep at bay but that was becoming as unmanageable as an untrained pet.

In Jacinda's eyes, there was the dullness. This was where the seeds of the story often lay, Diane knew. Often, in women, the light had been extinguished by a loved one, or there was a steely, icy glare— evidence of a conscience frozen, compassion unknown. When she saw either gaze, Diane knew that all manner of neglect and abuse was possible. What chilled her was when she saw either gaze in the eyes of both parent and child. Looking in Jacinda's eyes, she saw the slack, glittering evidence of drugs and knew that the woman was high or coming down from a high. In Jacinda Reed's case file, there were reports on her throughout the foster care system and her later arrest for prostitution. But Jacinda, buzzed and unkempt, had initiated this current process and asked for help after receiving a warning from her daughters' school.

Nora Tolliver, Jacinda's social worker, red-haired and matronly, sat beside Jacinda, her fleshy arms resting on several files pertaining to this case.

"Ms. Reed, your daughters have missed thirty-five days of school since the beginning of the school year. You've been working with your social worker, Ms. Tolliver, on strategies to address this situation but she's told me you haven't been cooperative."

"How can I be cooperative? I'm on welfare, Judge Tate, your honor."

"Do you realize how much your daughters have missed in *thirty-five days* of absences? I will give you credit for contacting social services before they contacted you, but we're here today because you've been inconsistent in responding to the assistance of Ms. Tolliver."

"I'm on welfare, and by the time I get my check, pay the rent, buy food, and pay the other bills, it's hard for me to wash our clothes at the Laundromat, and I can't send them to school in dirty uniforms. I sure ain't gonna do that and have people thinking they come from a dirty home." Jacinda spoke confidently and sat up straight, her eyes now raging with defiance.

Diane slid a legal pad across the table and told Jacinda to write down all her monthly bills. As she watched her labor over the figures and the spelling of words like *electricity* and *Laundromat,* Diane wondered if Jacinda was even functionally literate despite, according to her case file, having graduated from Cardozo High School. Graduates of the city's school often read at a ninth-grade level. Over a third of the city's black population was classified as functionally illiterate. She once had a client who signed a legal document with an *x*.

"Judge Tate, your honor, like I told Ms. Tolliver, a load of clothes costs a dollar and a half to wash and seventy-five cents to dry. On what I get in my check I have to choose sometimes between clean clothes and a meal on the table. Guess which one wins?"

Diane vetted the list of expenses three times, each time coaxing fuller disclosure out of Jacinda. Finally, the grubby sheet of paper that now served as a binding contract designed to alter Jacinda's expenditures and behavior was completed. Jacinda Reed was followed by two other cases.

Two hours later, as Diane drove to the superior court, she thought of the cases awaiting her. She'd been appointed to the family court in the early nineties, when D.C. was a graveyard. Back then the number of murders in the city annually averaged four to five hundred. The city was gripped by years of bloodlettings fueled by the epidemic of crack cocaine, but the deeper root was the dark legacy of generations of neglect and indifference for people and neighborhoods that no one cared about until there was an election.

The emotional toll of working in the family court was often harrowing and so, twice, Diane had rotated out to serve three-year stints on the bench in civil court. But she had always felt her mission was on the bench in the family court. The families—mothers, fathers, and children—pulled her back again and again to a docket whose challenges and misery were often more raw and dramatic than those in criminal court.

Diane thought the Carl H. Moutrie Courthouse was an ugly building. It squatted like a giant gray lunch box in the center of Judiciary Square, the city's nexus of local and federal law and order.

The FBI's Washington field office and the US Tax Court were among the buildings that occupied the six-block area. The National Gallery of Art and its spectacular east wing, guarded by the iconic sculpture of Henry Moore, was three blocks away. Each weekday, long lines of people snaked out the glass doors of the superior court, headed inside to get married, mediate a dispute, file for a divorce, seek child support, testify in a trial, or serve on a jury.

"It's a building where people go to find justice, only to find that it looks like a stockade," she'd often said to Gregory.

He'd explained that the superior court building was a classic representation of federal and judicial buildings designed in the 1930s and 1940s, which emphasized architectural stoicism, a style challenged in the city's more recent designs.

"Granted it's an expression of its time, but I would think you'd want the public's first sight of a structure to be an invitation, not a threat," Diane had said.

"Architecture is used to send all kinds of subtle and overt messages," he'd said. "Some people might argue that a courthouse *should* instill trepidation."

When Diane got to her office, she looked out her window and thought of how, more and more, she preferred the chaos of her work to the slow dismemberment of her life at home. As a judge, she had a reputation of being strict but caring, and she prided herself on her ability to listen to everything a person said—and sometimes could not say.

On this day, however, she shuddered at the thought that she would have to see Jacinda Reed again next week, and felt her temples throb at the thought of the cases she would have to hear after lunch. Gregory's illness had accelerated a burnout that had been seeping into the lifeblood of her work. The insubordinate reality of her own life had Diane wishing for a judge of her own. A judge who would set her free. Her courtroom had become a hard-edged refuge from which she longed to flee, and she had begun to think about early retirement.

Diane heard a knock on her door. Her assistant, Rudolph, reminded her of the family treatment court graduation ceremony taking place in half an hour.

In the conference room, decorated with balloons hanging from the ceiling and vases filled with plastic flowers on the tables laden with food, she hugged the judges she had not seen in a while and gossiped with them about pending cases. She thanked the stakeholders from the private and city agencies in attendance.

All of them in different ways had shepherded the women of the program through a grueling and strict process of therapy, drug counseling, job training, and parenting classes. Each woman had lived for six months in a residential treatment facility and earned the right to be reunited with her children by successfully completing the program. Unprepared for the rigors of the program, each year, nearly a third of the class found it easier to allow their children to remain in foster care or give up their parental rights than break the drug habit.

The room hushed as the six women walked to the front to sit near the podium. Kirk Franklin's gospel anthem, "Imagine Me," filled the room from a boom box in a corner. Each woman had charged the beaches on their own private D-Day in the past year and a half. Now each woman was clean. Each woman was sober. Walking down the aisle, they looked startlingly innocent, staring straight ahead, concentrating on a perfect march to the stage. Each woman carried a white rose.

Diane opened the program and realized that her thoughts had diverted from the welcome offered by the chief judge of the superior court and the remarks of the presiding judge of the family court. And then she heard her name and walked to the podium. Diane gazed at the family and friends filling the rows of aluminum folding chairs. This ceremony always made her emotional, and she gazed around the room to settle herself and to take in the full measure of what was about to take place.

"We call them ladies," Diane said, turning to look at the six women. "When we first meet them in our courtrooms, they have lost their children and all that makes a good life, yet beneath that often frightened—and sometimes belligerent—demeanor, they are ladies. *Ladies* is an old-fashioned term that we don't use much anymore, but we use it in the family court as a way of showing respect, because too often in their lives, these ladies were not accorded respect. They didn't respect themselves, their children, or the gift of life. But now they do. They have followed the sometimes tough-love rules laid down by me and my fellow family court judges, and when they've fallen down, they've picked themselves up.

"These graduates are all *first* ladies. First ladies to themselves and their families and the children with whom they are now reunited. They are ready for the inevitable challenges of living a clean and sober life. They know they're not alone. If they get scared or confused, they've got a friend in the alumni circle of the family treatment court and in their caseworkers. These ladies are now shaping a life they may have once thought they didn't deserve. I call that a happy ending.

"These ladies have taught me how to be a judge, and how to keep the bar of my expectations high while at the same time keeping my heart open. The most underrated and yet important characteristic of the law is mercy. My fellow judges and I, we are gratified that they have fulfilled the requirements of the family treatment court. I congratulate you, my ladies."

After the ceremony, Diane posed for pictures with

several graduates as they held their certificates. She met fathers and mothers, beaming and grateful at the sight of their daughters' resurrection. Rahema Elliot, chubby with eyes as bright and happy as those of the eight-year-old daughter whose hand she held, told Diane, "I'm gonna be honest with you, Judge Tate, Judge Bigelow told me if I didn't get my act together she was gonna send me to your court. When she told me that, I stopped playing around and got serious."

"You leave my judge alone," Jenee Kelly, said, bustling into the group surrounding Diane. "That was some tough love, Judge, but you always made me feel like I could make it."

*This, I will miss,* Diane thought, leaving the conference room and heading back to her office. *This, I will miss.*

Diane returned to her office and began attempting to bring order to the chaos on her desk. Overwhelmed and bristling with fatigue, she stacked files and assessed the significance of various forms and letters, deciding what to trash and what to keep. Another full day, a day of emotion, the frustration of community court, the joy of watching the women graduate. She twirled her desk chair around to face the wide picture window from which she could see not only Judiciary Square but the sky. How many times, she wondered, had she sat in this office simply gazing at clouds and finding in that act solace and hope? The five o'clock October sky was still studded with a few highlights of the day but showed signs of the impending evening.

Since Gregory had been formally diagnosed with Alzheimer's, Lauren picked him up in the morning and drove him to Caldwell & Tate. Having taken his medication, he could sit in his office much of the day, filing through the company's archives and records for a project Lauren had initiated. Caldwell & Tate's papers, some of its blueprints and digital files were to be donated to the D.C. Historical Society. A man who was losing his memory was in charge of compiling the history of the company.

Lauren had told Diane that most days Gregory managed well, and the younger designers still sought him out for advice. Either she or Mercer would take him to a nearby café for lunch or order something and eat with him in his office. She told Diane, "Mom, he remembers everything about the company, things even Mercer had forgotten."

He remembered all that, Diane thought but did not say, because the past was where he was headed. The past was his destination. The past was where he would end up. The past, an island offering no escape. Sometimes, she thought, maybe that was best. Who would want to have to face, sip from the cup of the present he endured and the future that lay in wait? Gregory had a dreadful disease, but all this—going into the office, giving him his own "job"—spared his pride, gave his life meaning, for as long as that was possible.

Diane turned from the window, stood up, and stretched, literally shaking off the hold of these thoughts. Tonight Bruce would come to the house after Lauren dropped Gregory off at home. Diane had finally said yes to Paula's invitation for an evening out.

"Can you believe the old geezer wanted to *get with this,* as the young folks say?" Paula smirked. "And on the first date!"

Diane was sitting with Paula in the basement of Westminster Church having a plate of fried fish, coleslaw, and greens. Diane savored the sound of her own laughter since it had become so rare and nearly unfamiliar. Paula was driving her to tears as she recounted her latest date with a retired engineer she had met online.

Paula reached across the table and handed her a napkin, which Diane used to wipe the moisture brimming in her eyes. "Hell, I didn't even do that during the heyday of the sexual revolution. And that picture he sent me online had to have been thirty years old."

"Stop, just stop!" Diane chided her as she put her hand on her chest to still the effervescent beating of her happy heart.

The Friday night jazz program at the church had been an easy and cheap date for Diane and Gregory for years. For five dollars, they'd heard jazz played by some of the city's best musicians and bought soul food dinners. Mixed in with a crowd of retirees and seniors and the occasional college students or tourist, they'd hear a jazz standard by Ellington or Miles Davis, or a local singer belt out her version of a classic by Sarah Vaughan or Billie Holliday. The church was the citadel of old-school, straight-ahead jazz, and Gregory had enjoyed the music and the mingling. He and Diane never failed to find friends or associates also in attendance.

Diane hadn't been to a concert at the church in several years but she found that nothing had changed. Paula had been coaxing her for weeks to join her for a night out—"A movie, dinner . . . something!"

Paula waved to a woman at a nearby table and bounded over to talk with her. Diane watched and thought about how far Paula had come, how far they had come together. Paula had stood beside her when she and Gregory got married and was godmother to Lauren and Sean. During Gregory's battle with cancer, Paula had given Diane a key to her house and told her she could use her guest room as a refuge any time she needed to, night or day.

Initially Diane had thought the idea generous but unnecessary, but the gift had quickly unlocked her need for solitude, silence, and self-care when she had grown weary of questions from friends and family about Gregory. The key opened the door to a room of olive green and a bed that cradled Diane as she'd closed her eyes for what she thought would be a quick nap only to find herself waking hours later. Sometimes Paula would sit on a recliner in the corner and watch her sleep. In the guest room, Diane's loneliness and unexpressed anger could live and breathe, uncensored and unjudged.

When Paula returned from talking with her friend, she said, "If you hadn't agreed to come tonight, I was gonna drag you out of that house."

"Thank you," Diane murmured, still warm from the onslaught of laughter.

She buttered a slice of cornbread and looked around the basement at the nearby tables. Men and women, not past their prime but seemingly entrenched in it, some heads bobbing, some fingers snapping to the beat of "The A Train" performed by a quartet upstairs in the sanctuary. A large screen on the wall showed the group playing.

"I feel like a widow. I don't mean to compare my experience in any way to what you went through after George passed," Diane said.

"You mean after George *died*. My husband died five years ago. He didn't pass, he didn't make his transition, he died. I get so tired of hearing all these useless euphemisms for a perfectly natural part of life, and you know I don't expect such imprecision from *you*," she said. "Rant finished, but I know what you mean. You have to face it though. You're experiencing a lot of what I went through. It's just that I'm a widow and you aren't. I go on. But I still miss him."

175

Diane pushed her plate aside and reached for the slice of sweet potato pie in the center of the table. She grazed at the pie with the tines of the plastic fork, carving Gregory's name into the creamy texture.

She thought of the diary she had found yesterday when bringing order to Gregory's sock drawer. The leather journal about the size of a paperback book was a heartbreaking testimony to what he had borne, what he feared, what he had found no words to say to her. The first entry was dated three years ago. The last was in May of this year, his script jagged and nearly unreadable. It had taken her several minutes to make out the last words he'd written: *Of all the things I will miss most . . .*

Slumping onto the bed, Diane had sat stunned, reading the rough outline of her husband's journey into a place that he feared promised the end of everything. The loss of everyone he loved. Her feelings were tumultuous. She felt cheated, angry that he had kept so much from her. She'd read the pages awestruck that Gregory had found a place to tend the ever enlarging wound that his life had become. She wished he had confessed his fears but the more she read, Diane knew that he had withheld these thoughts because he loved her. He wasn't able to spare her the sight of his decline. He could, he must have felt, at least protect her from being torn asunder as he was, haunted by what he could not evict from his life or even explain.

176

Diane slowly, meditatively, finished the pie, took a sip of water, and then said, "You know, at night in bed, I lay beside Gregory and take all of him in. It seems to be claiming him so fast. On my really bad nights, when I kiss him good night, it feels like an internment."

"What about the support group?"

"I went a couple of times, but with my caseload there's often a conflict. Somehow, I figure I can always find my own way. Besides, Lauren, she's always there, and even Sean sometimes helps out. Bruce is with Gregory now. And your calls keep me sane."

"Take it one day at a time. After all this time, it's still the way George died that gets me. One minute he's standing at the foot of the bed putting on his pajamas and the next he's slumped on the floor, dying of a stroke. One minute I had a husband and the next I didn't. I was buried, too. Sometimes it still feels like I am. I'm digging myself out a bit more each day. But you sound like you're digging your way in."

"Of course. I can't help but remember his bout with cancer. Comforting Lauren and Sean, assuring them that no, Gregory was not going to die, and that his prognosis was good. The absence of intimacy between us for nine long months. But Paula, *this* is different. We're going to lose this fight. I've begun to think that we're called *boomers* because just as we hit our stride, just as life begins to make sense, it all blows up in our face. It all goes *boom*."

"That's just too much to think about on a girls' night out like this. Can we pass on that right now?"

Upstairs in the sanctuary, the quartet had been joined by a buxom, honey-colored singer. The space pulsed with the sound of hands slapping thighs, murmured voices singing along, and snapping fingers offering up a lazy, syncopated undertow.

During the intermission, when the audience stood and stretched, walked over to greet friends, or went back down to the basement for more food or drink, Diane noticed a man staring intently at her. He was then walking through the crowd over to her. He was tall with a gleaming shaved head, a neat moustache, and a palpable solidity. He was substantial, yet fit, and he wore his size lightly.

"I think we've met before," he said leaning on one of the folding chairs in the aisle.

"Really, where?" Diane responded.

"Your last name is Tate?"

"Yes."

"Is your husband an architect?"

After a pause that drew attention to itself, she finally said, "Yes, yes he is." She hoped this man did not hear the falsity in her voice and she tried to defeat it by looking him straight in the eyes. "He's the co-founder of Caldwell & Tate Architects."

"Yes, yes, that's him. A couple of years ago his company built a brand new high school over in Brentwood. I was the principal there before I retired. They did a great job. The only school with solar panels in the city, very green, environmentally friendly. Full of light and color. The kids and staff loved it. You came to the ribbon cutting. After the speeches and pictures, your husband was being interviewed and you told me you were a judge in the family court. You asked me about the number of students at the school in the adoption or foster care system. If I recall, we talked about that for a while before Mr. Tate came over. I got another chance to thank him and then he whisked you away." He extended his hand and said, "My name is Alan Rich."

"I do remember now," Diane said, hoping that they would hear at any moment the announcement of the beginning of the second half of the evening that would preempt any inquiries about Gregory.

"How is Mr. Tate?"

His bated and genuine interest in her forthcoming answer forced Diane to blurt out, "He's fine, just fine. Please excuse me, I've got to go to the ladies' room."

She made her way through the milling crowd, breathlessly pushed open the door to the ladies' restroom, and scrambled into a stall. She could handle the odd friend who didn't know or hadn't heard, but on this night, a night designed as an escape, a new quandary arose: How to inform those who knew Gregory only from his work? Of course, his fellow architects had heard that

Gregory had retired or knew the truth, but what did she owe someone like Alan Rich? The thought of giving voice to either the truth or a lie struck her as punishment that she, Gregory, and even Alan Rich did not deserve.

When Diane entered the house a few hours later, she found Bruce sitting on the sofa in the family room beside Gregory. Bruce had volunteered a week ago to stay with Gregory sometimes if she wanted to go out.

He stood up the moment she entered, tossing his head back and his eyes to the ceiling. "How do you do it? Handle him, I mean? He kept talking about some meeting that he and Mercer had with the mayor years ago and keeps telling the same story over and over."

Diane checked her desire to tell her brother-in-law to stop talking about Gregory as though he wasn't present or as if he were deaf. "What've you two been doing?"

"Watching the History Channel," Bruce said reaching for his jacket and striding quickly toward the front door. Clutching the doorknob and avoiding Diane's gaze, he stammered, "We ate something, and he got to walking all over the house. I had to follow him to make sure he was okay. He took a nap and woke up as soon as I settled down for a rest of my own. He wanted a glass of water and then knocked it on the floor. In desperation, I hoped the television would calm him down. Diane, I had no idea."

"The symptoms seem to worsen in the evening and at night."

"My offer still stands, but I need time to kind of recover, you know."

Then, in a move that was both awkward and unexpected, Bruce leaned forward and kissed Diane on the cheek before hurrying through the door.

Diane locked the door, kicked off her shoes, and walked into the living room where she found Gregory staring at the television screen, watching the erection of the Brooklyn Bridge unfold. As she got closer she could hear him mumbling, his fingers drumming the arm of the sofa.

"When I finally got down to the district building Mercer was fuming," Gregory said. "Pacing up and down. Back and forth on the sidewalk in front of the building. I was late because I'd spent the night before tossing and turning and didn't get to sleep until five o'clock in the morning, and our meeting was at ten o'clock. Well, he starts to light into me and then I tell him to save it, and we rush up the stairs back into the building."

Gregory laughed loud, a hearty bellow, and clapped his hands. Suddenly aware of Diane's presence he turned to face her and, buoyed by her presence, he continued, "We cool our heels for another half hour, all the while going over the presentation. This is make or break for us. The chance to design the first office building in the U Street corridor since the riots. Our chance to make something rise from the ashes. When we get called into his office, he walks over to us like he's honored that we came. I'll never forget what he said: 'Come on in, brothers. Come on in.' Like me and Mercer grew up with him down there in Itta Bena, Mississippi, picking cotton. And he's got his staff, most of them black, all around him at the conference table. Waiting for us. Ready to do business. And he leans back in his mayor's chair and says, 'Sit on down. Y'all got a reputation that precedes you. A good one. Now tell me why y'all should get this contract. And make it easy for me to say yes.' And you know we did."

Diane had heard the story hundreds of times by now and she sat down beside Gregory and held his cheeks in her palms, looked into those still-magical gray-blue eyes and said, "Gregory, that's a wonderful story."

And when Gregory began again, saying, "When I finally got down to the district building . . ." Diane gently placed her head on his shoulder and said, "Yes dear, I know, that was one of the best days of your life."

# *Chapter Twelve*

## August 2013

This morning his wife hands him off like a package to Cecelia, who stays with him during the day. Diane cares for him but he cannot any longer care for her. And caring for her is the thing he wants never to forget. His wife kisses him good-bye and then it is Cecelia and him. She has brought the morning paper in and hands it to him.

"Here's your paper, Mr. Tate," she says, removing her jacket.

She goes into the kitchen and prepares a cup of coffee and they sit together at the kitchen table. Cecelia is a tiny thing: slender and small-boned, large eyed. He remembers that she told him she is twenty-one. He looks at the newspaper, reports from a world he is no longer a part of.

After they have finished their coffee, Cecelia sets a jar of coins on the table and pours out the pennies, dimes, quarters, and nickels. This is his favorite game. Gregory's fingers slide toward the coins, and he sorts them into piles. Across from him Cecelia methodically stacks her coins as he quickly builds towers of quarters. He is playing with money but he remembers the thrill of winning and the feeling of being first.

"You're too fast for me, Mr Tate. Just too fast."

"You're too slow. I think you let me win. Don't let me win. I want to beat you fair and square." Gregory pouts.

"All right, but be careful what you ask for." Cecelia laughs. "How many of these to make a dollar?" she asks, placing a quarter in her palm and holding it up for Gregory to see.

"I think it's three."

"Almost, Mr. Tate, it's four. Four quarters to make a dollar."

"I was good at math. I needed it in my work. I don't know what happened," he says staring at Cecelia quizzically.

At lunch, Cecelia stands over Gregory and begins to cut his chicken into small pieces. The knife, the fork, held in her hands instead of his, the concentrated look on her face as she cuts the meat into small pieces, disturbs him. Anything sharp—knives, scissors—are hidden from him. These are the things he still knows. His hand moves quickly and abruptly pushes Cecelia's hands away. The sudden sound of the knife and fork dropping and clattering onto the kitchen floor cuts through the anguish.

"Don't," he demands. "Stop, I can do that." The words are meant to hurt her and salvage his pride but they accomplish nothing. Cecelia reaches onto the floor and retrieves the fork and knife.

"Mr. Tate, now why you wanna be mean like that when I'm here to help you?"

He watches her go to the sink and wash the fork, dry it with a paper towel and place it beside his plate. Head bowed, Gregory grabs the fork and stuffs his mouth with the rice and peas and chicken.

"I'm sorry," he mumbles as Cecelia sits down across the table from him.

"Mr. Tate, you don't have to apologize. I know you didn't mean it."

"But I did."

After lunch, Cecelia tells Gregory that Diane has asked her to pick up some things at the drugstore. Gregory looks outside and sees the sun shining, closes his eyes, and presses his face close to the living room's picture window, his cheeks bathed in the sun's rays.

"Mr. Tate, get your jacket now, and we'll be ready to go."

He opens the closet and pulls out a thick winter parka, gloves from the top shelf, and a wool scarf. When Cecelia comes into the living room and finds him dressed this way, ready to go, she smiles and says, "I don't think you need so much, you'll burn up."

Gregory stands his ground. "I'm ready to go." And when she approaches him to remove his coat, he sits down on the sofa stubbornly crossing his arms.

"All right, Mr. Tate, we can't go out until you're

dressed properly. And look at you, you still wearing your house slippers." The sight of his feet melts his resistance, and he removes the heavy coat and scarf, removes his slippers and slides his feet into his shoes. He stands up and Cecelia stops him. "One more thing." She ties the laces.

Rising from her knees, Cecelia is suddenly gay and begins dancing around the room. She has earbuds in her ear and holds her iPod. She slips a bud into Gregory's ear and he hears "Don't Worry Bout a Thing" by Bob Marley. The song transports him to a room of red and blue lights, bathed in the smell of liquor and warm bodies. Fingers balled near his ears, he moves in time, in rhythm. Cecelia places the other bud in his ear and for how long he does not know, for how long he does not care . . . the party, the blue and red lights go on and on. He sees women held too tightly, hears men's gruff, easy laughter. He feels a slap on his back. He is unmired. His tears are for joy.

The song ends and Gregory tumbles back on to the couch and asks, "Where are you from, Cecelia?"

"You know I'm from Jamaica. You told me you've been there. I came here to join my mother. To study to be a nurse's aide. I came to America to take care of you."

"Yes, Jamaica, I've been there." Gregory removes the buds from his ears and hands them to Cecelia. "The water is so blue," Gregory says wistfully.

He looks further off and says, haltingly, "Marley, Manley, and Garvey."

"Oh, you know your Jamaican history, Mr. Tate. I tell them all the time you know more than you let on."

At the drugstore, Gregory walks beside Cecelia as she takes products from the shelves. They walk to the pharmacy in the rear of the store and she stands in the line. It is there that Gregory sees Randall Cullen: the short, muscular body, the jet-black hair Gregory always wondered if Randall dyed. They are friends. He still knows what it means to be a friend. They spot each other at the same time, and Gregory calls, "Hey Randall," just to hear himself say what he is sure is the man's name.

Randall unfurls a smile that is the most beautiful thing Gregory has seen in months, a beacon that reminds him of good things.

"Hi, Greg. Hi, man, how are you?" Randall asks as he approaches Gregory standing in line beside Cecelia. He peers at Gregory through those thick glasses as though searching vainly for signs of life.

Gregory marshals a confident smile and throws his arm around Randall's shoulder and pulls him aside, a few feet from Cecelia. Suddenly he does not want Randall to know that he is with her.

"You don't call me," Gregory says, waylaying the words, piercing his friend with an accusatory stare, moving in so close to him that he can hear Randall's breathing, see the pores on his face, smell the sweetish tinge of tobacco on his breath. "We can talk about the Middle East, those damned Republicans, the city council, like we used to."

Randall shakes his head. "Greg, we talked a month ago. When I got back from those six weeks in Athens. And then Diane invited me over for dinner. We had a good time."

"We did?"

"I brought you and Diane a vase and a small rug."

The hopeful lilt in his friend's voice stings Gregory as he realizes he must have again let someone else down, someone besides himself.

"I've checked on you and Diane regularly, but it's time for us to go to dinner again, okay?"

Gregory rallies with a smile and says, "Call me. Don't be afraid."

"Sure, sure. I will," Randall tells him. But Gregory hears the disappointment in his friend's voice and hates himself, hates that he cannot remember any of what Randall has told him, hates that this man who he still knows as a friend, is not a friend, but a liar.

"Who was that, Mr. Tate? A friend of yours?" Cecelia asks as she comes to Gregory's side holding a bag of prescriptions and they watch Randall walk away.

"I don't know."

As Cecelia prepared to leave that night, she told Diane that Gregory had seen an old friend in the CVS. "I think I heard him say his name was Randall."

"Oh, Randall Cullen. Did he remember him?"

"Yes he seemed to. They talked for a while."

"How was he today?"

"Oh you know, Mrs. Tate, it was a good day and a bad day. He performed pretty well on the games we played. But when I told him to get ready to go to the store, he dressed for winter. He couldn't remember how to tie his shoes. But he told me that Marcus Garvey and Bob Marley and Michael Manley are all from Jamaica. And when I asked him if that man in the store was a friend, he didn't know."

They heard Gregory's steps hurrying toward them from the living room, heard him furiously shouting, "Why, I can tie my shoes. Do you think I'm a baby? Of course I tied my shoes. I dressed for winter because it is winter, just look outside." He strode over to the kitchen window and pointed to the still light summer sky. "She's lying, why is she lying? Why is she lying about me?"

Diane gave Cecelia an envelope with her pay and signaled for her to leave them alone. She stood in the middle of the kitchen holding her husband, flooded with remorse, withered by fatigue, craving his once strong arms to comfort her.

"Why did she lie? Make her tell the truth."

The weekend stretched out before Diane. Before, when she came home from work, she would change into comfortable clothing, sprawl on the bed or sofa and vegetate before deciding if she would cook or they would order in. Now there was a part two to all her days, a studious girding for the unexpected.

She had grown increasingly vulnerable, unsure, felt sometimes unsafe alone with Gregory. It has not happened yet, but she could snap, surrender to the growing urge that quietly summoned her to ignore Gregory's needs and tend, without guilt, without shame, to her needs, her desires.

In the kitchen, Diane retrieved a package of lasagna from the freezer and slid it into the oven. Gregory sat at the marble island behind her, and she risked leaving him alone to go upstairs and change clothes.

When Diane returned to the kitchen, she said, "Cecelia told me you saw Randall today."

"I did?" Gregory asked, clearly surprised, his face a map of bewilderment.

"That's what she said."

"Mercer and I have that meeting with the mayor in the morning, so wake me up early. I have to go to bed early tonight."

"I'll make sure I do. Bruce and your mother are going to lunch with us tomorrow."

"All right, but not until after that meeting."

# *Chapter Thirteen*

## August 2014

As the months passed, Diane discovered new forms of agitation, as new types of bewildering, nonsensical actions committed by Gregory crept into their lives.

One night, one of her dress pumps went missing. An empty hanger bore no trace of a sheer, silk white blouse. Sean's graduation photo was gone from its conspicuous space on the mantel above the fireplace. Her favorite umbrella. An autographed copy of *Song of Solomon* that she stood in line for half an hour for Toni Morrison to sign, all missing. For only a fleeting moment did she suspect Cecelia. Looking in the most unlikely places, she found her blouse stuffed behind the dryer; the photograph of them with Sean beneath the sofa cushion; *Song of Solomon* protruding from a plastic bag of trash, grease stained and half the pages torn out.

Now, she couldn't find the topaz and silver necklace and matching earrings she'd bought in New Mexico. All weekend she had searched the house, her fury rising.

"Gregory, I don't have much anymore. So little. Why can't you leave me at least some things that I cherish?"

Feverish with paranoia, she was convinced the actions were not random. Gregory's mind, she was sure, was brimming with malevolence. Stealing like this took cunning, planning, forethought. Diane stood before her husband, herself a kind of wreckage. She had not washed in two days, brushed her teeth, or changed clothes all weekend. All she wanted was to find the jewelry. All she wanted, in the midst of this, was to hold on to one little thing. Even if it was material, tied to vanity and pride. It was *her* little thing, and he had stolen it.

"Just tell me where you put them. I won't be angry. Gregory, this isn't a game. The necklace and earrings, where are they?"

Gregory stood, like a shabby edifice, unmoved in a winter sweater and corduroy pants he had somehow found although it was August and the house was sweltering because the air conditioning was faulty. His answer was to lope away from her nonchalantly, another thing she'd come to hate, casting one last look at her that promised he would never reveal what she wanted so desperately to know.

Talking to Gregory like this set her on edge, made her hypersensitive. *There is no past. No future. Only now, this eternal moment. Now* lived in the extreme, a neon present tense. Each word, whether from him or from her, a possible precipice.

She knew not to touch him from behind because if she did, the inability to see her, to prepare a response often set Gregory howling and running from her. But she grabbed his arm anyway, shouting, "What did you do with them?"

Pulling out of her grasp, Gregory clamped his hands over his ears and stomped in circles around the dining room table.

"I didn't do it. I didn't do it," he said, head bowed forward, hands squeezing his ears.

"You did and you know it."

"No. No."

Trailing him around the table, Diane heard her voice, careening, mad: "You did, you know you did."

The doorbell startled them, and she thought it must be the air conditioning repairman. But when she opened the door and saw Lauren instead, Diane covered her mouth with her hands and reached for her, holding her so tightly, Lauren nearly clawed her way out of her mother's arms. They stood in the portal while Gregory raged in the living room:

"No. No. It wasn't me."

Freed from her mother's afflicted embrace, Lauren led Diane back into the house.

"He took my topaz and silver necklace. He hid them and won't tell me where they are. He's taken everything. Everything I had. I can't even have one thing of my own," her mother announced, her voice bruised with complaint and outrage.

Lauren took a deep breath, quickly deciding to care for her mother first.

"Come on, you need to lay down, Mom," she said, leading her up the stairs.

"Will you make him tell you what he did with them? You know the topaz necklace and earring set I mean; you borrowed it last year."

"Yes, Mom, I know, I know," Lauren assured her, gently guiding her mother to her bed. A bed that was unmade, stacked with clothes and a tray holding what looked like the remains of last night's dinner. Lauren removed the clothing and set the tray on the nightstand and sat on the side of the bed, rubbing her mother's shoulders. Weariness was a pall draining her mother's face.

"I can't believe it. Before you arrived I was chasing him around the living room, shouting at him, screaming in fact." Her mother stared at the ceiling, her eyes widened by disbelief.

"Mom, just rest now. Just rest for a while."

"How can I?" She grabbed Lauren's hand and said, "Go. Please check on your father. Make sure he's all right."

Lauren had packed an overnight bag and left it in the trunk of her car in case this turned into a long night's journey where she could not imagine leaving her mother alone with her father. Increasingly, she'd become referee between her parents as they sparred—one coherent, overwhelmed, and growing more and more bitter, the other locked in a netherworld.

"She's mean to me. Why won't she let me go? I

have places to be," her father shouted as Lauren walked toward him downstairs.

"Did you hide Mom's jewelry, Dad?"

"No. No," he shouted and folded his arms across his chest as he furiously circled the sofa.

At that moment, Lauren heard a knock at the door.

"Hi. I just stopped by to see how everyone was," Sean said when she opened the door. He stood staring at Lauren with a sheepish grin, wiping his forehead with a handkerchief. "I was in the neighborhood."

"Well, halle-fuckin'-lujah!" Lauren fumed, suddenly near tears. She wanted to slam the door in Sean's face but instead turned away and walked back to her father.

"What's going on?" Sean asked innocently, entering the house with careful, measured footsteps. The sight of his father, arms folded, mumbling angrily and circling the sofa stopped him in the hallway.

"Come on in. He's your father. He won't hurt you."

"Is he always like this?"

"If you were around more, you'd know the answer to that question."

The innocent confusion on her brother's face, the perplexity she heard in his voice enraged her. As their father had fallen deeper into the grasp of the disease, she had watched Sean's unease in their father's presence blossom. He always had an excuse for why he couldn't visit or stop by to give her or Diane a break. And when he did come by, the sight of their father shocked him so that he seemed to be saying good-bye before he had finished saying hello.

She was shocked, too. There was no getting used to it. But for her, there was no other choice. This was her task to perform, one that was onerous and yet, she had come to think, sacred as well. She wanted to ask Sean if he loved their father at all. As angry as she was, she could never go that low.

"I came by to help. You're always saying I never pitch in, but what can I possibly do here?"

"Talk to him. Take him for a walk."

"Talk to him how?"

Closing the distance between them, Lauren said, "Brother, I have to figure that out every day."

"You always had a special bond with him. Your own language, your own code. You're cut out for this."

"He's *our* father," she screamed. "Our. Father. Mom's upstairs trying to rest. I'm going to leave now and let you figure out how to do your share."

She grabbed her bag and stormed out of the house. Not until Lauren was three blocks away, having ordered a pizza from a corner take-out restaurant, did it dawn on her what she had done. Nonetheless, she forced herself to sit at one of the plastic tables outside and slowly eat, willing herself to believe that when she returned to the house, Sean would have found a way.

They all thought he avoided his father because he was irresponsible. He had been absent, but his father was not forgotten. Only Sean knew how it felt to look at his father now and see him as a mirror. Without language to bind them, without coherent thoughts, what was there to say? The disease had stripped Sean of the ease and comfort they had begun to rebuild after his father had visited him that day, which now seemed so long ago, when he first knew something was wrong.

"Come on. Let's watch TV," Sean said and slumped onto the sofa.

He heard his father padding toward him and sit down at the other end of the sofa. Sean picked up the remote control and saw that his mother had taped a list of the channels and corresponding numbers in large black letters on the back. Clearly this was meant to help his father, but he'd lost his memory and no matter how large the letters and numbers were, just as the shapes had once meant nothing to Sean because of his dyslexia, they probably meant little to his father now.

"Let's watch the Nationals, Dad. There's a game on, I think. You know the Nationals are your favorite team."

Gregory shook his head adamantly. "My team is the Orioles."

"But, the Nats are our hometown team."

Making a fist with his right hand and punching his left palm, like a boxer, Gregory insisted, "Orioles, always the Orioles for me."

"Okay, okay."

Sean flipped between channels as Gregory watched him quizzically and said, "The Orioles will beat the Redskins next time."

"You know, I think you're probably right."

Sean watched his father at the other end of the sofa, staring raptly at the screen. What, he wondered, did he see through those still alert eyes? Within minutes, his father nodded into a deep slumber. Sean went upstairs to see Diane and found her asleep as well. Coming back down, he saw Lauren enter the house.

"I'll do better. I will," he told her.

"Sean, you have to. That's our father. I need your help. Mom needs your help."

"I'll be here. I'll do more." He had said the words before. This time he meant them.

# *Chapter Fourteen*

## OCTOBER 2014

The bookstore was packed for a reading from the memoir of a prominent veteran of the civil rights movement, Eunice Benjamin. Benjamin, who had gone on to a career as a journalist and photographer, regaled the crowd with her reading and anecdotes about well-known political and cultural figures who had been major players in the black activism of the late sixties and early seventies.

Gregory sat in the third row of the audience with Diane clutching his hand and Mercer's arm thrown protectively around the shoulders of his friend. Gregory's attention span had been growing shorter and shorter and Diane counted it a minor miracle that he had sat for nearly twenty minutes listening or appearing to listen to the speaker. She was determined not to exile Gregory from life, from other people. Maybe during tonight's reading he would hear a word, a phrase, a question, that would give him a moment of joy, spark a brain cell into resilience. Life. She didn't want to go into hiding. She wasn't ashamed of her husband or his disease.

The audience sat hushed and rapt as Eunice Benjamin read a passage describing her days canvassing the backwoods of Mississippi for blacks willing to attempt to register to vote. She had just read a riveting account of a midnight ride down a darkened Alabama road with a carful of SNCC workers being followed by the police when Gregory released Diane's hand and moved to stand up. Mercer quickly pulled him back into his seat and Gregory said loudly, breaking the spell Eunice Benjamin had cast over them, "Bathroom, I have to go." Heads turned and Diane answered the quizzical looks with a humble, forbearing half-smile. Mercer guided Gregory out of the row.

She watched Mercer lead Gregory through the maze of tables stacked with books, past the shelves marked by category and genre, over Oriental throw rugs, and to the downstairs restroom. She turned back to face Eunice Benjamin, rearranging her body, sitting staunch and straight-backed in the folding chair, trying, with her show of resolve and indifference, to erase Gregory's outburst.

When the question and answer period ended, Mercer and Diane stood watching Eunice sign books as the staff collected the folding chairs. Friends who had entered after they'd arrived, or who had not greeted them earlier warily assessed Gregory, as though he were an unruly toddler whose behavior they had heard rumors of.

"How are you, Gregory?" Sadika Grey asked. She leaned in to hug Gregory and clutched his hand. "Gregory, it's Sadika. Diane will have to bring you to my shop one day. You'd like that, wouldn't you?"

Sadika was a sculptor and jewelry designer. Gregory had often visited her gallery and boutique in Adams Morgan for a unique birthday or Mother's Day gift for Diane. Diane had never seen her in any attire that was not African in origin. Tonight, she was dressed in a dramatic Senegalese-inspired flowing dress called a *bouba* and a starched *galae* of matching cloth reigned on her head.

"How is he?" she asked Diane as her smile collapsed.

"As well as can be expected."

"I mean it, Diane. Bring him to the gallery one day. It would cheer him up."

Diane wanted to ask, *How do you know?* But wouldn't she be just as verbally incompetent and unsure if the roles were reversed and it was she clumsily trying to talk to a longtime friend who had this disease?

Otis Shepherd, a loan officer at the city's only African American–owned bank, spotted them. He first shook hands with Mercer and then easily launched into a conversation with Gregory.

"Man, we haven't done anything since that Wizards' game a couple of years ago. You know, the one where they actually beat the Cavaliers when LeBron was on the team?" Otis smiled broadly. In response, Gregory lifted his hand and pointed his index finger at Otis. Otis told Gregory jovially about his grandchildren and his recent retirement. The ease with which he spoke to Gregory, the way he held Gregory's furtive shaky glance and would not let it go, burst Diane's heart with gratitude.

When Otis stood up to go back to his seat, Diane hugged him and he patted her on the back whispering, "Call me and Miriam anytime, for anything you need."

At home, Gregory turned to Mercer and said, "In the morning. The office," and shuffled into his study.

Diane prepared two cups of tea.

"Whoever thought I'd be drinking goddamn herbal tea," Mercer said. "Remember back in the day when you could just eat any damn thing you wanted to, when eating wasn't something you needed a doctor's prescription to do, when food wasn't something you took pictures of in a restaurant and sent to friends on their phones?"

Diane laughed as they heard Gregory rustling through papers in the next room.

"Is he gonna be okay by himself?"

"For a while anyway."

"I still can't get used to it."

"There is no getting used to it."

"Scares me to death, Diane. I'll be retiring from the firm in a year or two. I want to hang around long enough to mentor Lauren and the new leadership team. But all this has me thinking about my legacy, about having had three wives and no children.

Who'll care for me like you and Lauren care for Gregory?"

"Some days, Mercer, when I'm really brave, I ask myself what he's feeling. What he's thinking?"

"What can life be like for him now?"

"I can't convince myself that the life he's living, that he's trapped in, means nothing. That it's only emptiness and torture. Please, Mercer, I have to believe there's more than we can see. More than we can know. Maybe more than we need to know."

"Is he all gone?"

"I still see flashes of who he used to be sometimes. But I feel caught in a permanent state of grieving. I've suffered a loss. It's like a hurricane every day. I've lost my husband, and I still don't know what that will mean for me going forward. It can't go on much longer like this. It's too much. I came in from an evening meeting last week and found Lauren sitting in the dark right here where I'm sitting. In the dark crying. Gregory had trashed the study, and she had finally gotten him to sleep. She told me 'Mom, I can't do this. I love him, but I want my life back. I want the life you both prepared me to have. This isn't it.' What could I say? I want my life back, too? I've started investigating alternatives."

"You mean like one of those places . . ."

"Yes."

A heavy, solemn calm mushroomed between them. Sipping their tea, only the sound of Gregory in the room with his papers crackled the silence.

Then Diane said, "Mercer, I love that man. With everything the last couple of years have demanded of me and of him, I love him. I feel no relief thinking about putting him in an assisted living facility. I feel guilt. I feel remorse. I feel like I have failed. Gregory forced me to reconcile with a father I never wanted to forgive. He never believed I would remain as small and as afraid as, for a long time, I was comfortable being. I owe him too much. Especially for that."

## 1994

"Are you ready to make the call?"

The question was generous and long-suffering, asked regularly. It spoke to Diane of an unfulfilled promise Gregory assumed, perhaps imposed, but that she had never made. Asked quietly, without a hint of judgment, the inquiry was founded on his unshakable belief that one day Diane would reach out to her father. Gregory believed what she could not. He believed *for* her. His belief became an element in their marriage that she resented yet relied on to alter the DNA of her thinking. Each time he asked, she was consumed by shame and the fear that he would conclude that the mother of his children, the woman he had married, the woman he loved, was a coward. What else could he think when she reflexively reached out to him with an embrace, a hug, a kiss, as she whispered, "No, not yet." Gregory had his beliefs and she had hers. She was cynical, bitter, and terrified, subscribing to a relentless faith in the power of lies and secrets. She had found herself several times edging toward the brink of calling her father, but the thought of the length of the potential drop, or a bloodied fall, always propelled her back from the edge.

Margaret's heart attack, suffered when she was seventy-three, changed everything. Back then, Margaret was active in her sorority, was a member of the Mayor's Advisory Board for Senior Issues, and held fund-raisers to raise money for Dorothy Height's initiative to allow the National Council of Negro Women to purchase the building they were headquartered in on Pennsylvania Avenue. She served on the "Free D.C." committee to gain statehood for the city, and in previous years she had taken Lauren and Sean to Paris for two weeks. Three months before the heart attack, she had journeyed to South Africa on a trip organized by her church.

Diane had come to admire Margaret, was inspired by the way that she had created a life for herself in these later years of widowhood, a life that included an ongoing relationship with a gentleman she referred to as "my old, new boyfriend," whom she had dated before she met Ramsey and who was also then a widower.

The heart attack, which Margaret felt the first signs of while sitting in the pew at Metropolitan

AME one Sunday morning, was significant, but not fatal. During the weeks of recuperation, when Margaret stayed with them, Diane thought more and more about mortality and aging and wondered about her father. The distance and brittle stance of indifference that Diane had perfected cracked.

One evening as they cleaned up the kitchen after dinner, Gregory said to Diane, "Thank God I've said everything I needed to say."

"What do you mean?" Diane asked, pausing as she placed cutlery and plates in the dishwasher.

"She dodged a bullet. She's always possessed an air of invincibility, but my mother, like everyone else, is a mere mortal."

"Of course," Diane said.

Gregory stopped wiping the stove and said, "Diane, if you make me, I will ask the question every day for as long as we are together, for as long as we have. When are you going to make the call?"

Before she picked up the phone to call her father, before she ventured across the country to see him, she had to give her children what she had denied them, a grandfather and the truth. All these years, Diane had told her children what she had been told: "He walked away. He didn't love us anymore. I don't know why."

The truth would be more layered, tender, and raw than the hard-edged artifact she had been offered. Lauren and Sean were teenagers. And this would be the first time she had spoken to them at length about their maternal grandfather. Sitting beside Gregory on the sofa, enduring the quizzical, skeptical gaze of her adolescent children, who more and more seemed refugees from her love, who took every chance to brusquely struggle literally and figuratively out of her grasp, Diane, after days of imagining this moment, found herself speechless. It was Gregory who fueled the revelation, who found words she could not as he sat clutching Diane's hand, looking squarely and fearlessly into the faces of their children. "Your mother has something to tell you."

"Are you sick?" Sean asked, suddenly attentive and alarmed.

She wanted to say, *Yes, I have been sick. Sick with grief most of my life and now I want to get well.* There was nothing to say but everything, and so she used all the words she had sought to protect them from—rape, burglary, abandonment, and what she knew must be her father's shame, what she admitted was her own desire to punish.

"Why are you telling us this now?" Lauren asked, thrusting it all back at Diane.

"You have a grandfather that you need to know. I have a father I need to forgive. It's time."

Sean rose and Diane prepared herself to watch him leave the room, but he sat down on the sofa beside her and buried his head in her shoulder. "When can we meet him, Mom?"

The children were in bed and Gregory sat in a chair near the bed watching her make the call.

Now she was walking in the shoes of all the parents and children whose lives she mandated and adjudicated from the bench. Reconciliation, empathy, forgiveness—she routinely prescribed them for others. Now she felt their weight, how they loomed so large and unapproachable, how humbling and confusing it was to feel the sheer burden of words that demanded so much.

She dialed the Las Vegas number and he answered. *So this is all it took,* she thought, *all these years.* The sound of her father's voice, surprisingly soft and thin, halted her breath.

"Hello, can I speak to Samuel Garrison?"

"This is Samuel Garrison. Who is this?"

"This is Diane. Your daughter."

Whimpers, cast up from a place beyond imagining racked her father's throat. A convulsion he did not try to halt. Diane steeled herself against the sound of her father's shattered voice as he said, "I was ashamed. I never forgave myself. For what I did to your mother, you, and Ronald. It just got easier to stay away."

"Marcia gave me your number. Years ago. I could never use it till now."

"She's told me all about you. How successful you are. Your family."

"You never reached out; you never looked for us."

When planning the call, almost as an act of theater, she'd imagined hurling the charge at a climactic moment, but the accusation tunneled out swiftly, would not be delayed or denied.

Then before he could answer, both to wound him and to acknowledge the depth of her own sin, Diane said, "I should have called years ago. I could've."

"All things in time," he said.

*Not all things,* Diane thought but did not say. "We needed you. All of us. I was five years old when you walked away."

"I've had years to think of nothing else."

In the calls that followed, she developed a friendship with this man, a stranger who reactivated a primal, unquenchable desire in her to be loved. Samuel told her that after he left Washington, he moved around for a couple of years, avoiding everyone he had left back in D.C. He'd finally settled in Las Vegas, played the casinos and got lucky. Won enough money to open a dry-cleaning business. After Ella's death, he had remarried.

"I didn't attend Ella's funeral because I felt like it was me who had in some way killed her. If I had come, I felt like I'd have to turn myself in for punishment. When I heard about Ronald, I didn't leave my house for a week."

Diane sent him pictures of Gregory, Sean, and Lauren, and he sent her photos of his wife. Gregory talked to him on the phone. The children had stilted conversations with the man who was their grandfather.

"Can I tell you something?" Samuel asked Diane during one call.

"Anything. Everything."

"I had nightmares for years after what he did to us. He had a gun and held it on me while he forced Ella to tie me up. Then he raped her. Your mother. My wife. I never got over it. She changed, too. I couldn't touch her, comfort her after that. I could see it in her eyes . . . she hated me for not saving her."

"Did you ever talk to anyone professionally about it? A counselor? A therapist?"

"No. I didn't even know how to do that. When I met Inez, she made me feel as whole as I figured I'd ever be."

Diane thought of the two years she'd spent in therapy, another suggestion Gregory had made, and how their marriage might not have survived without it.

Diane and Gregory made plans to visit her father when the children were out of school, but Samuel Garrison died six months after her first call.

Marcia delivered the news and her father's wife, Inez, called Diane a few hours later and told her that she had discovered Samuel's body in his house.

"We talked a couple of times a week and when I didn't hear from him and when he didn't answer the phone, I knew something was wrong. He'd been in the house two days before I discovered him," she said. She told Diane all the arrangements were being made; all she had to do was come to Las Vegas.

Numbness returned, but this was different, not the numbness of before: a shellac around her heart, a glaze of resistance. This was a membrane separating Diane from the world, riddled with cracks and slivers. She had not cried where tears could be seen, but inside, she was sodden.

Inez met her at the airport. She was a woman of medium height, olive complexion. Her hair was a long sheath of solid gray that reached her shoulders. She was dressed in white capri pants and a striped top. She stepped forward from the crowd and hugged Diane. Tensing in the woman's embrace, Diane realized that Inez was her stepmother.

They walked silently to the parking lot and Diane loaded her suitcase into the trunk of Inez's car. As they prepared to pull out of the garage, Diane asked, "So he died alone and you found him?"

"Unfortunately, yes. Do you want to go to your hotel?"

"If you don't mind, I'd like to go see my father's body."

On the way to the funeral home, Inez told Diane, "This is West Vegas. When we were married, your dad and I lived in North Vegas, but in a sense, this is where he always lived."

Diane looked around at the streets. There were small businesses, boarded-up buildings, a pall of neglect and decay.

"He used to own a dry cleaners over there on that corner. This was before we met. But he got robbed so many times he closed it. But he always came back here. Even after we moved to the suburbs. He got people involved in clean-up campaigns and helped pressure the city to build a recreation center. He'd be in the library during election season registering people to vote. This was where his heart was. He didn't have a lot of friends, but everybody knew and respected him."

In the funeral home, Inez introduced Diane to the owner, Blair Harris, a small wisp of a man in a three-piece suit, his hair slicked back from a protruding hairline.

"This is Sammy's daughter, Diane. She just flew in from Washington."

"The state or . . ."

"The capital city."

"Welcome to Vegas, and I'm sorry you had to come under these circumstances. The memorial service is later this evening," Mr. Harris told Diane as he began walking toward the room where she was sure her father's body lay in repose.

The solemn, austere feel of the funeral home brooded around Diane as she slowly walked toward the front of the room and saw the casket. This is what she had come to do. To see her father.

Samuel Garrison was a large man, his head shaved and gleaming. His fleshy face was studded by a moustache. The powder and embalming fluid cast a gray shadow over his face. This was the face of her father, dead. It was not, therefore, the face she had longed to see all her life. The face she had first seen in a picture just a few months ago. Her father was dead, and because she had not really known him in life, looking at him now, she did not know what to feel or what to think. She did not know what she saw on his face. They said that in the casket you saw the face that the person had earned, but you could only see that face if you knew the person. Then you could judge. She did not know her father. Not really. He was dressed in a blue suit and gray tie, his large hands folded atop his groin. Despite the sins of omission, her father's face was a mask of calm. This was the posed theatrical face of the dead: cared for, designed to quiet the qualms of those who would have to look upon the face one last time. Diane searched the face for the story of her father's love for her mother or what it meant to watch your wife's rape. Her father's eyes were sealed shut, so she could not look into them to see whatever had, in the end, remained in his heart.

Inez sat in the front row of folded chairs that would fill later in the evening.

Diane turned around and said, "I'm ready to go."

"Would you like to get something to eat?"

Diane thought of the hotel room and wanted to

delay her arrival there as long as possible. "Sure. I would like that."

Inez drove out of West Vegas and stopped at a mall where they found an Italian restaurant.

"I thought I'd feel more," Diane said.

"Trust me, you will."

"Could you tell me something about him, anything? How long were you married?"

"We were still married."

"I mean . . ."

"I met Sammy at a bingo game. I'm a midwife and still practicing. I was always delivering babies, making families happy, and I wanted a family of my own. I had given up. I was almost forty when I met Sammy. I never thought I would find love. I don't know if that's what I found with Sammy, but it was enough. There isn't much of an Argentinian community out here; most of my friends are black. I had heard about him, this guy who a couple of years back won big at the casinos and owned a dry cleaners. I knew he had lost something that mattered to him and I knew that I would have to wait before he told me what it was. He seemed like a good man, though. We were both lonely and thought before it was all over, before giving up, we'd give love, give marriage a try. It was that simple. We were serious, at least I was. He said he was an old man but he wanted to start over. I wanted to try to have a child. But he told me he had a family once and something bad happened and he didn't want to risk having a family again. I said if we couldn't have a child maybe we could adopt. He didn't want to.

"I was happy for a while. We were like a normal couple. He liked showing off our life. He said I was enough. He had run all his life and he wanted to stop running. I didn't know what he meant until he told me everything. Everything about your mother, your brother, you. The terrible thing that happened. How he'd run away from all that, from you. I felt closer than ever to him because I finally knew what he'd been hiding. I felt so much love for him then. But the next day he felt ashamed for telling me. It's like he grew further and further away the more I knew him and the more I understood. I told him that one day he might see you again.

"After a while he stopped coming home at night, wouldn't tell me where he was, and so I left him. He had treated me bad, but after I left, he tried to make up. For a long time, I didn't speak to him or see him, then he called me one day and said he was tired and afraid of dying alone. Said if I couldn't be his wife, could I be his friend?"

"You said he didn't have many friends."

"People thought they knew Sammy, but they never did. People thought they were his friends but they weren't. But when you called, he was happier than I had ever seen him. He went to a lawyer and revised his will. Made the lawyer the executor of his estate, told him on his death, to sell the dry cleaners and divide whatever he got between me and you."

• • •

The next day at the funeral, Diane sat beside Inez and listened to the young men her father had hired to work in his dry cleaners tell stories of his mentorship, the young men he'd coached on the basketball team at the rec center, who'd called him "Pop." One man who had promised Samuel Garrison when he got out of jail that he would never go back, didn't, he said, because Samuel let him work in his cleaners.

At the repast in Inez's neat bungalow, the old men and women came over to Diane and gave her hugs.

"Sammy never told me he had a daughter. He shouldn't've kept you a secret."

As the repast wound down, Diane sat alone in a gazebo in Inez's backyard and that is where she finally cried.

She stayed an extra day in Las Vegas, remained in the place her father had called home. She lay in bed in her room the morning after the funeral meditating on the hypotheses, the lies, the secrets, the conjecture, and the final truth her father had told her. Samuel Garrison fled to Las Vegas, away from the scene of the crime committed against him and his wife, two thousand miles from all of it, left behind like scattered debris. Miles and miles, and he never looked back. Or so she'd thought, but he'd been looking back every day. Looking back when he hid it all from Inez, from the people in West Vegas who thought they knew him. And after he had revealed it, he'd had to hide it all once again—hide it or die. All those people he helped, were they stand-ins for her mother, for Ronald, for her? In the end, he didn't want to be alone but died alone in his bed and in his house anyway.

Before she left, Diane walked the Strip, garish, overwhelming, a Disneyland for adults. She went into the casinos, saw the machines where her father had hit it big enough to be written about in the newspapers, the sprawling rooms where he came weekly, up until the day before he died, still looking for luck. He must've thought luck was a form of forgiveness. When he won, he must have been able, for a moment, to put it all to rest. Before leaving for the airport she called Gregory.

"So, who was he? Who was Samuel Garrison?" he asked.

"He was my father."

Mercer smiled in appreciation when she finished. "I thought I knew everything there was to know about y'all."

Mercer had sat listening to the story Diane told, his eyes never leaving her face. Gregory had walked quietly into the room and sat on a hassock, oblivious to the fact that Diane was honoring him with piety and tenderness. "Even friends keep some secrets."

Mercer reached for Gregory's hand and shook it.

217

"You did good, buddy, you did real good by this woman here. Do you know that?"

Gregory smiled broadly, his eyes aglow looking at Mercer. He shook Mercer's hand vigorously up and down, until Mercer had to place his palm on their hands to quell the movements.

"And that's the man that I'm now planning to put away somewhere, Mercer," Diane said. "He did that for me."

# *Chapter Fifteen*

## MARCH 2015

The moment Diane opened the door to her study, Gregory pushed her aside, his face a mask of unreasoning fury. Her frightened gasp was swallowed up by the barrage of his hands grabbing her, his fists thudding and leaden, random yet precise.

*Help me,* thundered in her mind yet lay yoked, denied an exit by her throat.

*If I hurt you . . . If I hurt you . . .* Diane remembered as she sank to the floor, feeling her cheeks begin to swell.

Gregory, now spent, breathless and leaning against her desk, shouted, "My memories? Where are they? I want them back."

"Help, help me," Diane called, hoping Lauren was still downstairs. She burst in the room a moment later.

"Daddy, Daddy, stop, please stop," Lauren said, hugging Gregory, before carefully, almost gently, leading him from the room.

Diane rose from the floor, crawled to her office chair, and hauled her body upright.

"I made him lie down in the bedroom," Lauren said, entering the room again and firmly closing the door. "Are you all right? Did he hurt you?"

"Yes." That was the only word she could say.

*"My memories, where are they?"* he had asked, demanded.

It had been weeks since Gregory had spoken a full, declarative sentence. More and more, he broke through the simmering silence with a grab, push, or pull to express physically what he could not verbally. He would stand behind her and pinch her arm or bump into her on purpose. This, his doctor told Diane, was an expression of frustration and a language all its own. Yet periodically, coherence returned full blast.

"Are you okay?" Lauren asked again.

"No, Lauren, I'm not."

The bathroom mirror reflected the tender blush of a bruise beginning to form under her right eye, and Diane wondered how she would explain it at work.

Nightfall invited Gregory to rise from bed and roam the house, pacing from room to room. Their house, normally placid, slumbering at night, was now restless and alive. It was during these weeks that Diane allowed herself to wonder how long she, how long *they,* could live like this. Gregory had hit her. Given her a black eye. The lock and chain she'd installed on the bedroom door offered a fragile illusion of safety. They were both incarcerated in different prisons. He no longer knew her as his wife. She refused to accept that this man was not her husband, for if he was not her husband now, he never had been.

Days passed before Diane allowed herself to think and then speak the words. As caretaker, she was the closest and easiest target. The thought that they would not go on like this, that there would inevitably be an alternative, a separation, was never voiced. Speaking it to Lauren, to Sean, would turn her into stone.

"If I ever hurt you . . ." he had said. *Put me away.*

But back then, that was conjecture, hypothesis. Now, the *if* was real, and it rubbed her raw.

When Gregory gazed dismissively at the bowl of soup and pushed it onto the floor, Diane cracked as rudely, as instantly, as the ceramic. "Clean it up right now, you bastard. All that I've done and this is what I get."

Her pulse splashed bitterness into her bloodstream. Tears blazed down her cheeks. The sound of the profane words filled her with an edgy pride.

"Look at me," she screamed, marching around the table to face Gregory. Then it was as though her arm was not her arm, but she felt it rising, felt the full force of the slap trickling up, then the feel of Gregory's stubble against her fingers, the ripple of the slap in her fingertips. The slap that turned his face away. The slap that brought him to tears.

The tears no longer moved her, and she didn't care if he struck back. Maybe it would be better if they fought it out, she thought, fought it out . . . till the end . . . whenever that might be.

The slap transported her into an unfamiliar, virgin zone of new misery and guilt. She had slapped her demented, mentally confused husband. Yet the slap was the most intimate act between them in years because of the passion it unleashed in them both.

With an orgasmic radiance, the slap tingled in her fingers, pulsed throughout her body. She sank into the chair and watched as more tears filled Gregory's eyes, his stunned, bright, and knowing eyes. He knew that he had been slapped, hurt, and abused. There were more tears trickling down his cheeks than she had seen him shed since this all began. She sat stony, hardened, and too brittle to cry. Too ashamed to cry. Too stubborn in this moment even to lean forward and kiss the red and tender spot where her anguish left damning evidence. Gregory, wobbly and quietly weeping, pushed himself up with his hand on the edge of the kitchen table and walked away.

He could walk away from her. Find a hiding place where he would be safe from his crazed wife. But she could not walk away from him.

Could not grab her purse and keys. Could not go. She could not, she could never leave him alone.

Diane cleaned up the broken bowl and wiped up the soup from the floor, then stood at the counter and finally released her furtive tears. Through that veil, she looked at her hand, her fingers, and began furiously washing them. Drying them, she stifled a final sob and went to find her husband wherever he was in the house.

There was only one person who she could tell what she had done. Later that evening, when Gregory had sunk into a deep and abiding sleep, she called Paula.

"How do I find grace in this?"

"You're both walled off against each other. The only thing I can suggest, Diane, is that you climb over that wall. You're the only one who can. Maybe grace is on the other side."

Diane was now a family court judge who had been both a victim and a perpetrator of domestic violence. An officer of the court who could be arrested. Gregory's blows, her act of violence, each had pushed them across lines never before crossed. Made the unthinkable easy, even necessary. If Gregory could punch her, she could slap him. Husband and wife teetered on and then plunged over tipping points both dangerous and seductive. Seductive, because on the other side of the slippery demarcation lay the promise of relief, unreasoning, but entirely deserved.

Despite what Diane thought she had decided, the prospect of placing Gregory in a memory care unit in an assisted living facility remained so toxic she thought of it as a kind of radiation that she could only approach timidly and with care. Weeks passed during which Diane shared her decision only with Paula, whom she asked to help her find suitable facilities to visit and assess. Octavia Sanders, the social worker who facilitated the support group she irregularly attended, guided Diane through the maze of the new world she was entering. She gave Diane a stack of booklets and brochures that Diane and Paula spent an afternoon looking through while Bruce and his son Aaron took Gregory out for a ride and to a steakhouse.

Diane and Paula sat at Paula's dining room table, passing the colorful booklets between them.

"Listen to the names," Paula said, "Lighthouse. Morningside House. Golden Pond. Heartlands. They sound like synonyms for heaven."

"I had no idea that a whole industry had sprung up to care for every aspect of growing old. Caregivers relief, life management, someone to come to your house and pay your bills when you can't do it anymore."

"There but for the grace of God, my sister."

Week after week, she and Paula toured the upscale, attractive, and inviting facilities. Facilities that were beautifully decorated, colorful, serene, where everything about the décor and the atmosphere, and the competence of the directors they talked to, promised calm in the midst of a family's storm. Home away from home.

Paula had a friend whose mother was a resident of Somersby and who recommended it, so they toured Somersby's memory care unit, guided by a certified nursing assistant. What they saw were mostly black men and women who had been middle-class professionals—airline pilots, lawyers, social workers. They looked healthy and prosperous, like life had been good to them—until now. When they looked closer, they saw the tall pecan-colored woman pacing the halls and hovering around the exit, her eyes as large as saucers, distant and suspicious; the man leaving his room in a business suit, newspaper folded under his arm, umbrella in hand, carrying a briefcase; and the woman sitting in a rocking chair, holding a doll in her arms in an ironclad embrace.

The decision, in the end, was Diane's alone to make. There would be no family meeting. She would just tell them—Sean, Lauren, Mercer, and Bruce—what she had decided and she would do it on the phone to avoid a scene. But Diane knew that she had to tell Margaret in person.

In Margaret's apartment Diane watched her water a four-foot-tall philodendron she had named Oprah. Through the window, Diane could see the spires of the National Cathedral. Margaret valued her independence and had refused to move in with Bruce or into a senior citizens' retirement community. A half-finished crossword puzzle from the day's paper lay folded on the table beside Margaret's laptop computer. A CD of classical standards played in the background.

Margaret placed the plastic watering container in the sink and then joined Diane in the living room. In gray velour pants and a black sweater, Margaret possessed the air of a dowager: her gray hair in a style that was braided, complicated, and regal; massive hoop earrings dangling from her ears; various rings on her fingers; and her reddened lips full and plump.

"I know why you've come to see me, Diane. Lauren called and told me."

"I wanted to tell you in person."

"You have to think about yourself," Margaret said, reaching for a crystal bowl of nuts on the table beside her. "Believe me, my dear, no one else will." Margaret gently scooped a handful of the nuts, offered some to Diane, who politely declined. "I was fifty-five when Ramsey died. Fifty-five," she said as though she did not believe it. "We were supposed to be entering our golden years."

"How did you cope, Margaret?"

"You were there for the last of it. You saw what I went through."

"Yes, but I look back and remember now that I never asked you how you were doing, how you were holding up."

"If you had asked me, I'm not sure I would have known what to say or how to say it. But there was someone." Margaret took a tissue from the box on the coffee table and wiped her hands.

"Someone?"

"Yes, a friend. A former colleague from Howard."

"Was it meaningful?" Diane asked, choosing the word specifically for the multitude of definitions it possessed.

"Very much so." Margaret smiled proudly. "He was a wonderful man. I needed someone who wasn't family. Someone who wouldn't ask me anything but would listen to what I said or even what I didn't say. My husband was wasting away before my eyes. That man and I spent precious time together. No matter what kind of day it was, he helped me carry it, he helped me bear it."

"So you were . . . friends?"

"And after a while we were much more. He made it possible for me to have the strength to love Ramsey the way he needed and not be angry because there was so little he could give me. You look surprised."

"It's not every day that a woman hears her mother-in-law say she had an affair."

"I don't think of it as an affair now and I didn't then. My son is gone. The husband you once had isn't there anymore. He's not coming back to us. If you feel it's time to place him in one of those homes, do it. I trust you, and I know you'll find the very best one you can."

"Back when all this first started, the day we got the formal diagnosis, he told me that as we went through this together, to do what I felt was best, and especially if he ever hurt me. But back then, that's the kind of thing I would expect him to say."

"Diane, he meant it. I know he did. He loved you too much not to."

# *Chapter Sixteen*

## SEPTEMBER 15, 2015

The broad-limbed, sheltering trees were cloaked in early autumn dusk. Small mountains of leaves coated the sidewalks and lawns. The streetlights felt more eerie than illuminating as Diane sat in her car, hesitating to enter her house.

Across the street, she watched Tim and Sandy Neilson heading toward her, arm in arm, walking their golden retriever, Sonny. Tim and Sandy were among the first on the street willing to talk to Diane about the changes they noticed in Gregory, and Sandy, a justice department lawyer, had told Diane that her own mother suffered from dementia.

Wind rattled and blustered, swirling the piles of leaves, and she knew she had to go inside. When she opened the front door, she stepped into a pile of mail that had been slipped through the door drop and stooped to retrieve it from the floor. She tossed her briefcase and cashmere coat onto the sofa and turned on all the lights. Then she went upstairs to the bedroom and changed into a pair of fleece pants and a turtleneck.

In the good times, dinners had often been casual, just the two of them: Gregory entering the house laden with bags from the Ethiopian place on

Colorado Avenue. The bags of food on the counter. The smells humid, hot, fragrant, irresistible. That first look, that quick yet all-consuming gaze between them that affirmed he had come home. That look, so small and so much in it; *Hello,* his look said. *Welcome home,* she would beam at him. He often came home exhausted but wired, all of that at once.

Upstairs he would go, the heavy-yet-light footsteps. She would open the Styrofoam plates of food, a startling slash of more vivid color than she had seen all day: the split peas, a muted tender green; the lentils yellow as the sun; the tomatoes, tiny seeded hearts; peppers so hot their heat sprang forth. Above her, Gregory's feet padded across the bedroom floor as he removed the day's uniform, neatly, carefully hanging up the slacks, the jacket, tossing the shirt in the hamper.

Downstairs he would come, the steps lighter in slippered feet. The kitchen table now laden with food, the lamb and vegetables no longer in white Styrofoam cartons but on plates. Was this a night for paper plates, or had she lovingly spooned the meal onto fine china because they rarely used those dishes and they could make Tuesday night a celebration? There would be his beer, Sam Adams, and her glass of wine, chardonnay. They rarely said grace—*they were grace.* Eight, ten hours after walking out of the house, they had returned to it and to each other.

*How was your day?* The question might as well have been *Once upon a time,* for all that it inspired. The stories of that day would be told seeking sustenance, agreement, support—for it really was them against that stupid, bigoted, idiotic world.

But in the first week after Gregory's move to Somersby, Diane had slowly wriggled into the skin of an unalterably new life. She had given notice that in the spring she would retire from the family court, a decision a long time coming but that felt finally right. Howard University's law school had offered her a professorship that would begin in a year. A position that she had accepted. Howard University, where Ramsey Tate had attended medical school before heading the department of surgery at Freedman's Hospital, where Margaret had also attended before teaching social work for many years, and where Gregory had attended the school of architecture.

There was so much to look forward to, but the present she feared would never be past. There had been a call from Somersby about Gregory hitting one of the nursing assistants and his refusal to eat. These were common patterns of adjustment she was told, but she worried nonetheless about the decision she had made with so much guilt, anguish, and care. That call made it clear: her husband was institutionalized—no matter the charming name of the place or the lovely décor. She had left him in the care of strangers who she trusted would do for him only what was best.

On this night, after eating a quick, improvised meal of leftovers, Diane looked at the mail, mostly junk, bills, and an update about Medicare. She washed her plate and cutlery, and then went upstairs to her bedroom.

The day after Gregory had beaten her, she'd bought a chain lock and installed it on her bedroom door. It was a symbolic, second tier of defense in case Gregory dislodged the lock built into the doorknob. Diane stood in the doorway to her bedroom, quaking with memories of the fear she'd felt. If Gregory could hit her once, would he do it again? If he hit her again, what would she do to defend herself? The chain lock was modest and possibly inadequate, but both locks had withstood Gregory's occasional attempts to enter the bedroom at night.

Dismantling the lock was even easier and faster than installing it. As her hands rubbed the rugged spot bearing the imprint of the lock that had defaced the door and her union with Gregory, Diane opened the door wide, its creaking a kind of song.

"Can I get you anything while you're waiting?" the server asked, breaking into Sean's thoughts.

"No, no, I'll wait. My sister's always late." He smiled then reached for his glass of water and took a sip.

He looked across the street and saw the city's main library branch. The ceiling-high windows of the restaurant showcased his father's signature building. Because of its electric exterior design and the exuberant play of light and weather on the five levels of glass windows that formed the basic structure, Sean had always thought of the building as a book cathedral. The way the building arched toward the sky lifted anyone observing it and elevated everything that took place within its walls. Inside, the colorful, carpeted floors and soothing, sky-blue walls were totally surprising, as were the plush, comfortable chairs, and wide, solemn, burnished wood tables that made the building flush with a composure that honored what libraries were for, foremost, the work of the mind. Whenever he drove or walked past the library, he was honored to be his father's son.

He had finally attended one of the support group sessions his mother had told him about. While Diane chose not to attend, she had nonetheless urged that he and Lauren go. Near the end, he had raised his hand and asked the social worker, Ms. Sanders, "How can I make my father remember me?"

"He hasn't forgotten you," she said. "But he doesn't know you as an adult. He doesn't recognize you, but I'll bet he knows your voice. Talk with him about the childhood you've left behind. When you visit him, bring a photo of yourself when you were much younger. Talk about yourself in the third person, point to the photo and tell him about the person in the picture using your name."

Now that he was making good on his promise to Lauren and spending more time with his father, they often pored over family photo albums. They sat together, his father relying on a shrinking vocabulary and a battered ability for recall. They had lost so much, Sean would think, watching his father's fingers trace the faces in the photos. But the communion created from the silences and puzzles and empty space the disease imposed managed to fill him with a sense of the life lived between them, and something very much like love planted its flag.

Sean looked away from the sight of the library and saw Lauren walking toward him.

"So sorry I'm late," she announced as she sauntered to the table.

Lauren looked both ready for business and feminine in a burgundy-colored suit and sheer black blouse. Her light brown dreadlocks were chin length and framed a face that Sean thought was quite lovely. This was the sister who had confessed to him one night in high school that she had always felt like an ugly duckling, as they sat parked in his car outside the house and shared a joint.

Lauren tossed a small, black leather handbag onto the chair between them, settled into her seat, and grabbed a menu, saying, "Let's order. I'm starved."

"Not starved enough to be on time."

"Truce, please?"

Sean signaled for their waitress, as thin and lacquered as a runway model, and they ordered. Lauren grabbed a slice of pita bread from the basket on the table.

"You look good," Sean said. "So carrying the weight of Caldwell & Tate hasn't brought you down?"

"Is that what you're waiting for?"

"Come on, you made your choice, and I made mine."

"You're talking to one of the three managing partners. They made me a partner not just because my last name is Tate, but because in the short time I've been with the firm, I earned that spot. Mercer lobbied for me and that helped, too."

"Mom told me. Congratulations."

"And you?"

"I've got my crew renovating a couple of houses across the river. Anacostia is the new frontier. I just wish Dad could see all this, what I'm doing. And understand it."

"You ought to take him to one of your projects one day. I keep telling you, Sean, it doesn't look like it, but he's still there."

His father *was* still there. One evening, Sean had asked his mother why he felt closer to his father now than he ever had. He confided that more than once he had looked into Gregory's distant, always disconcerting stare and whispered, "I love you,

Dad." Why, he had asked his mother, did he feel able, emboldened to say that to a man who he was sure could not understand what he said, the words people spent their lives longing to hear.

"I don't know, Sean," she'd said. "Maybe it's because he is literally stripped to his core. There's nothing like pride or vanity or bitterness left for him. He's terribly, horribly free. And maybe, just maybe that opens up a region in our souls, too."

Their orders arrived, a dozen small plates of Greek, Lebanese, and Mediterranean food: hummus, eggplant, falafel, ground lamb, and more. Finding space on the table for all the plates was a feat that their waitress managed with skill and good humor.

They tackled the small plates before them as though their hunger was more than physical, as though it resided in a dangerous place they had both inadvertently touched. The restaurant, all hardwood floors, open windows, and chrome, the size of a warehouse, was loud as an echo chamber.

"I told Mom I could move in for a while if she wanted me to until she gets used to being in the house alone. There've been a couple of burglaries on her street," Sean said. "I talked it over with Valerie and she'd understand."

"What did Mom say?"

"What do you think? 'I can handle it.' "

"I'm not surprised," Lauren said. Her cell phone

rang and looking at the screen, Lauren said, "I'll call them later." She then looked at Sean.

"This has nothing to do with Mom, but I've always wanted to ask you, Sean. There's a test you can take to see if you might develop Alzheimer's. Would you take it?"

"I'd be afraid to know."

"Uncle Bruce says he counsels against it. Says the test isn't entirely reliable and there's no more you can do to fight it the day after you know you have the gene than the day before. And that it could affect your insurance, employment. What would I do with the information if it was bad? How would it affect the rest of my life?" Lauren asked, slumping back against her chair, fingering the rim of her water glass. "I mean, tell me, how do you even prepare for something like this?"

This was the third test. Each time, the plus sign in the window of the plastic stick informed Lauren that she was pregnant. Plus sign. Positive. So why was she flooded with a foreboding that increased with each test? She and Gerald were good, they were happy together. Why was she so certain that this child, real and tangible in her imagination long before peeing on a plastic strip in her toilet, would change everything?

Lauren looked at the results again and then tossed the test into the trash can. She wiped herself, pulled up her panties, washed her hands, and went into her bedroom. Lying on her bed, she hugged herself, willed herself not to cry, and thought of her friends Whitney and Marla who had taken her to the club where she and Gerald met. Both had had abortions.

"The relief was a godsend," Marla had told Lauren. "I got a second chance to have the life I wanted."

Whitney had said, "I felt a lot of things—relief, but also regret that I had not anticipated, and guilt. But the relief, that never went away. The other emotions in time, they did."

Why was she thinking about abortions when, for her, that was not an option? No matter what Gerald said, she would have this baby. Their child.

Everything in her life until now had felt ordained by her genes, her talent, her father. Having this child was *her* first adult decision. She would mother her child with bold intentions. But how would that child be fathered? Her father had told her to have a life. Now life had her by the throat, and she inhaled its tingling and raw effervescence. She was afraid but she could breathe.

Lauren looked at the clock. It was Saturday night and she was meeting Gerald and some friends downtown in a new Spanish restaurant near Union Station. As she dressed, to calm herself, she thought about her and Gerald, about the things that made them a couple that Marla and Whitney both teasingly and convincingly said they envied.

The Sunday afternoon Redskins parties that she

attended in the basement of his family's rambler in New Carrollton were raucous affairs where football became a blood sport among the seven Stone siblings and their girlfriends, wives, and children. Gerald's father, who worked for Pepco, was a Dallas Cowboys fan. His mother wanted the Redskins to change their name but said she'd support them win, lose, or draw.

Lauren didn't even like football, but on those Sundays, squeezed onto the leather sofa between Gerald and his mother, Nadine, she felt like she had another family. A family where no one was sick with a disease whose name she could not bear to speak.

Then there was the day Gerald had spent an afternoon with her as she drove to several Caldwell & Tate projects in the city, explaining, "I want to see what you do."

At a bar the previous week, they'd sat drinking and munching on exotic, artsy appetizers, all before going to see a review of comedians D. L. Hughley and George Lopez at the Warner Theater. His friend Lucian had leaned across the small table and asked, "So when are you two making it official?"

"Make what official?" Gerald had asked.

"What you got going on," he said, a broad conspiratorial grin beaming at Lauren and Gerald. "Y'all look like an ad for one of those dating services."

"We're doing just fine. Just fine." Gerald laughed,

throwing a possessive arm around Lauren. "Don't give her any ideas."

Lauren had laughed nervously and wanted in that moment to remove Gerald's arm.

"We're *born* with those ideas," Lucian's girlfriend, Caitlin, had said.

"*We're* not." Gerald laughed again, too loudly, Lauren thought, as he leaned across the table and theatrically slapped palms with Lucian. Then to Lauren, he said, "We've arrived where we were headed. Smack dab in the middle of a comfort zone and it feels real good, right babe?"

Lauren had looked at Gerald and chose silence as an act of mild defiance. Her mother had told her once that silence and inaction were two of the most unrecognized power moves.

"Anyway," Gerald had said, looking slightly annoyed but clearly driven to shut down Lucian's jocular inquiry. "Okay, I'll speak for us both. We're just fine. In our comfort zone. With no surprises."

Now dressed, Lauren put on her silver earrings and looked in the mirror one last time. She liked what she saw.

Five hours later, after they had returned to her apartment, after she had tasted the pungent remnants of rum and Coke on his tongue as they kissed, after they laughed about the evening they had just shared, she told him.

He was silent. But the silence was not silent at all; instead it was a crackling electric heat groaning in the space between them. He was sitting, his legs spread, arms resting on his thighs. At the sound of her words, her declaration, what Lauren thought of as *their* truth, Gerald hung his head. She wasn't sure if he was avoiding her gaze in anger or defeat.

*I'll touch him,* Lauren thought. Her first thought now was to comfort Gerald. Comfort him as though he had been wounded. Hurt by what she had revealed.

"Aren't you on the pill?" He raised his head so she could see the disbelief, the mistrust, in his eyes. That question answered everything she had wondered. Closed every door she thought stood open between them.

"Yes, but nothing's foolproof. Even with the pill there's a five percent chance of pregnancy."

Gerald stood up, able, it seemed, only to place distance between them as he paced. She watched him pacing, the noisy silence threatening to engulf them again. She thought to apologize, to say "I'm sorry," but then wondered why she would lie.

"What do you want to do?" He had stopped pacing and stood still, asking her. The fact that she could not read the emotions on his face terrified her.

"I want to have it."

The admission forced him to sit down in a chair across from her. "I'm not ready to be a father."

"I'm ready to be a mother."

"So I guess that's all that matters?"

"This is a shock, Gerald, I know that, but we did this together."

"I guess we did."

He could not say he loved her. How was that possible, she wondered, when she felt *her* love like a contagion? When she walked through her life giddy but balanced, convinced that if need be, she could fly.

"I wish you could say you loved me. But loving our baby, I'll take that. Not as a consolation prize, but as the way it has to be."

"I just need some time."

"Time for what?" she shouted. "To fall in love with me by default? Because I'm carrying your child? What do I have to do?"

"Lauren, calm down. We've got a good thing. A great thing. We've got our whole lives."

"I don't feel that way, Gerald. I've got today. I've got now. Right now, *this* is my whole life."

"I'll be there for you and the baby. Don't make me a bad guy. I said I'd step up. I won't let you down." The words were an unconvincing whisper.

Lauren thought, but did not say, *But I want you to hold me up.*

"I don't know, I don't know," he stammered. "I feel trapped by this, all of a sudden. Out of nowhere."

"Nowhere? What have the last six months meant to you? So that's where we've been, nowhere? So then all this has meant nothing."

"Did I say that?"

"Yes, in a way you did. Yes, that's how I heard it."

"I care about you, Lauren, you know that."

"But you don't love me."

Gerald hid his face in his hands.

There was nothing left. No other way to stand up for her child. And so that's what Lauren did. She stood up slowly, unfurling her body with a methodical grace and calm. Standing before Gerald she offered him her hand.

"I love you, Gerald. I love our baby. Tonight, love me. Love us."

Their coupling was a storm, for Lauren an act of greed and hunger, for Gerald both surrender and retreat. Lauren cradled him beneath her heart, clinging to him. When she woke in the morning, groggy, unfulfilled, he was gone.

Lauren couldn't tell her mother that the house was falling apart. Not now, with everything she was dealing with. The leaking faucets in the bathroom, the chipping paint, the worn hardwood. This house no longer felt like her childhood home. They had both changed.

Sitting on the carpeted floor flipping through channels as her mother thumbed through a textbook she was considering using for her classes at Howard next year, Lauren asked, "What if I'm having the baby because we're losing Dad?"

"There are worse reasons for having a child," Diane said, closing the book.

"Mom, I haven't heard from Gerald in two weeks, not since the night I told him. He's not answering my texts or calls."

"Give him some time."

"I won't beg him to do the right thing."

"Lauren, you told me he said he'd do exactly that. It's just that your definitions of 'the right thing' are probably different at this point."

"I won't ask him for anything he doesn't want to give. I don't need him. I can do this alone if I have to." Rising from the floor, Lauren reached for her mother, burrowed into the shelter offered by her arms. "Am I wrong? To want this baby? Was I unfair to him?"

"Of course not. He's not wrong for needing some time to take all this in."

"Mom, are you lonely?"

"That's a word that has a lot of different meanings."

Lauren gently pulled out of her mother's embrace and asked, "What do you miss most about Dad? Since all this started I don't think I ever asked you that."

"Him seeing me. Knowing me. Understanding me. When I come home now, that's when it hits me. How much I've lost. I'd give anything, Lauren, to get that back. I miss your father. I miss our life. Very much."

# *Chapter Seventeen*

## SEPTEMBER 2015

He cannot sleep on nights like this one, so he slips out of the room they gave him and walks the long hallway. Walks until one of the women who wear the white pants and the blue tops and the white shoes, appears and takes his arm, her palm at his back, and steers him back to bed. This night, he has decided to trick them. Before, he would leave the room fully dressed, his shoes sliding against the floor's surface. That was how they found him.

But tonight, naked and noiseless, he creeps along the long hallway of rooms where the others must be sleeping, the darkness broken by night-lights plugged into the walls in the meeting room, the den, the TV room. His clothes lay in a forlorn pile at the foot of his bed, for he tore off the shirt, ripping the tiny buttons, hearing them pop into the air and then land with a soft thud on the floor. Stepping out of his pants and underwear, he left them stationed, waiting for the return of his legs to give them life.

He moves through this place naked, unhampered. Up the stairs, although there is no need to, he tiptoes, holding the bannister, relieved of the confusion within confusion that haunts him during the day, looking into the faces of the others. He grabs the steel knob and slowly opens the door. The lower floor is miles behind him. So he walks, his shoulders and head high. It is enough to softly trek these long, narrow hallways, so many more than in the house of the woman who brought him here. He turns a sharp left, a sharp right, and another hall awaits him. His destination is surely close. Nocturnal smells singe the air—sleep, tossing, turning, an odd moan, a cry like an infant from behind the doors he passes. These things possess an aroma unique to and brought forth by the day's end. His naked body even smells different at night, perfumed by the day just past, humming in his muscles, etched on his skin.

Down these corridors he moves, further with each step away from the women who are like nurses. As he runs down the halls naked, Wallis Peebles, who was the first of the other residents to speak to him and tell him her name the day he was brought here, opens her door, clutches the collar of her robe at her throat, and calls out, "Where are you going? Can I go with you?" Wallis rushes out of her room with a sheet to cover his body and helps the nurse blanket him, swaddle him in the sheet, then stands in the middle of the hallway waving good-bye, calling behind him, "Bon voyage," as the nurse leads him away.

In this place, where loneliness festers and desire is a haunting, unforgotten sign of life, Wallis Peebles knows that Gregory has been sent as an answer to her prayers. He bears himself as though in the other life, before this place, he had mastered his world.

If she had not tried, one too many times, to leave on her own, without her family knowing where she was headed, she would still be in her apartment in the senior citizens' complex. She knew where she wanted to go, told the taxi drivers to take her to Woodward and Lothrop, downtown on Eleventh and G Street. But they all said what her nephew Kevin told her, that Woodward and Lothrop, where she worked as a milliner for twenty years, was torn down years ago. All she wants to do is go to Woodies and see one of her hats in the window.

All her life she has loved hats. A woman became a lady, a queen, in a hat. Her success at Woodies inspired her to open her own shop with money borrowed from her sister and brother, a tiny place squeezed in between a tailor shop and a Chinese carry-out on T Street, not far from the Howard Theater. There she flourished for a while, but then when women started wearing short skirts, pants, and stopped wearing hats, only the Sunday church ladies came to her shop. So she had to go back to Woodies. But it was there that she became the lead designer and made hats for the rich white ladies who gave society parties in Georgetown and on Capitol Hill, the wives of congressmen and senators.

She retired, was living on Social Security and her savings. Then she began to yearn for who she used to be. She'd get up in the morning, and after her coffee, her bowl of oatmeal, orange juice, and her pills, she would spend an hour or more picking out just the right dress, shoes, and hat. Satisfied with the ensemble, she'd spray her neck and arms with a mist of Jean Naté and, giddy with a sense of purpose, lock the door behind her and go out looking for her life.

But the city had been turned upside down. Made her feel like she was Alice in Wonderland. Nothing was where it used to be. She never forgot her address. She always knew where she lived. She just had no idea where she was going. She'd ride the bus she thought was headed to Georgetown and ring the bell to disembark, and stand on a street in Brookland. Sometimes she left her apartment without her wallet. Twice, a stranger, finding her sobbing on a street corner, flagged down a police car. When the police officers escorted her into the lobby of her building she felt famous.

Her nephew Kevin took over her finances and her life and brought her here, he said, so she would be safe. So he would always know where she was.

Now, opening her eyes in her small room every morning, she sees the beautiful hats lining the shelves. Hats she had made. Hats born of her hands. Hats that were her assignment from God. More and more she cannot remember who she made the hats for. Every hat always had a story but the stories are beginning to fade.

She loves the Bible study with the cheerful blonde lady who always remembers everyone's name and asks them to fill in the missing word when she reads phrases from the Bible. Wallis can still recite the Lord's Prayer and the Ten Commandments. She has prayed all her life and her prayers became more fervent after no one wanted to buy her hats, and there seemed nothing left in this life or this world to do, except to wander. She still knows how to pray. And she knows God has answered her prayers because of this man who roams the halls naked at night, as though dropped from heaven.

"I didn't eat when I came here at first either," Wallis says quietly to Gregory in the dining room. "But the food isn't bad." She gently pushes his plate closer to him. There is something in this movement that sparks a feeling in his stomach beyond hunger.

His plate is closer to him now. Although the people around him look healthy, he cannot be sure what the food will do to him. *I want to eat,* he thinks, looking into the sturdy face of the woman. He lifts a forkful of green beans into his mouth. The food does indeed taste good.

Gregory feels suddenly and deeply the hunger he has denied satisfying during the time he has been here, and before he knows it, his plate is empty. Wallis beams at him.

Fortified by the meal and this woman's smile, he announces "I can fix this place" and takes her hand. They rise from the table, and Wallis grips his arm, entwining her fingers through his. They walk down the hall to the library, the one place he has found peace. He opens the French doors and they walk to the bookcase where Gregory pulls a tube of paper from a space between the bookcase and the wall. He removes a rubber band from the papers and then slowly spreads them out on the long mahogany table in the center of the room.

Gregory feels Wallis lean closer, surveying the papers, her hands, her fingertips outlining the lines he knows that he had made. Lines that signify something bold and wondrous that he had once done. He hears Wallis whisper, "We both like beautiful things."

The receptionist was not at the front desk, so Diane took this solitary moment, which felt stolen and illicit, to breathe in deeply. Her closed lids nonetheless, sheltered the image of Gregory's face, the last time she'd seen it over her shoulder as she ran from his room. She inhaled deeply, courageously opened her eyes, and walked past the elevator and punched in the code that admitted her to the memory care unit.

Once there, one of the nursing assistants told her that Gregory was not yet available for a visit. He was taking part in a memory stimulation exercise, but she could sit and watch. She walked down the hallway and found the residents gathered in a large, open room adjacent to a kitchen area. The fifteen residents sat in a circle as Lynette quizzed them gently about their careers before coming to Somersby. One woman sat stylish and alert, dressed in a tailored red power suit as though waiting to convene a board meeting; a dark-skinned woman who sat assessing those around her as though she was in imminent danger wore blue jeans and a T-shirt; a man sat next to her in a gray running suit, his lips moving in a private, rumbling conversation that evoked in him ripples of laughter, which he abandoned in order to tell Lynette that he had been an accountant for D.C.'s office of management and budget.

"I kept the books. I kept the money safe," he said proudly.

Gregory sat placid and expressionless.

"I was a teacher," said a slight woman whose formerly blonde hair was now a dull white. She clutched a cane that she wiggled beside her chair. "I taught history."

"Do you still teach history?" Lynette asked.

"I have a class when this meeting is over. We're studying the American Revolution."

The woman sitting beside Gregory radiated a nearly crackling energy. Her hair was a curly mass of gray, white, and brown. In a riotously colorful blouse, floor-length black skirt, and large dangling hoop earrings, she looked like she was dressed for Halloween. The woman rocked back and forth in her chair, restless, shifting, impatiently awaiting the chance to talk.

"I was a milliner. I made and designed hats for Woodward and Lothrop," she announced, then pointed to a woman across the room. "Ask Bonnie. I made her a hat last week. Didn't I, Bonnie?"

"I don't know," the woman replied irritably, waving the words away with a dismissive sweep of her hand.

Nonplussed, the woman sat back in her chair, turned to look at Gregory next to her. She smiled and patted his hand then before throwing her arm across his back and hugging him.

*At least he has made a friend,* Diane thought.

Lynette announced the end of the session and the residents drifted off down the hallway to their rooms. Diane nervously stood up and prepared to walk over to Gregory, straining to gather the flailing loose ends of her emotions.

The woman who had been sitting next to Gregory was now standing, hovering protectively over him. As Diane neared them, she extended her hand saying, "I'm Diane, Gregory's wife."

"I'm Wallis. He's my friend," she said with childish glee.

"Yes, I see. Hello, Gregory," Diane offered tentatively, flushed with discomfort.

"Hello."

Lynette approached them and led Wallis away. Diane could hear the woman muttering her resistance as she continually gazed back at Gregory over her shoulder. Diane sank into the chair that Wallis had occupied moments before and, now that she was closer, drank in the sight of her husband. Despite that now permanently indifferent, jittery gaze, there seemed to be more of him.

They walked down the hall to Gregory's room, Gregory loping quickly ahead of her, out of reach. Diane longed to touch him, to hold his hand.

In his small room the request was simple: "Want to go home . . ."

"I can't, Gregory. This is the best place for you now. For a while anyway, until you get better."

Stalemated, they sat on the bed. Diane inquired about the food, the other residents, how he felt, all questions he left unanswered. Gone was the courage she had mustered. She was deflated, minuscule in the presence of this man, her husband to whom she was a mere visitor, someone making a foray into his world from a distant galaxy, a planet beyond his comprehension.

Gregory bounded from the bed and rifled through the papers on his desk. He returned to sit beside Diane and showed her a series of crude drawings of Somersby, the interior and the exterior. As he shuffled through the drawings he pointed to each one and told her, "I have to fix this place."

"You'll do a fine job. I know you will."

"I was an architect."

"Yes, you were. You were one of the best."

Gregory walked to the window and looked out at the courtyard, at a toddler playing in a thick carpet of leaves. The history teacher from his group, now bundled in a jacket, watched the child as a younger woman stood beside her.

Diane approached Gregory, stood beside him as he watched the scene.

He turned to look at her and said calmly, "You're Diane. Diane. That's your name."

Never had her name sounded so sacred. Months had passed since he had last spoken the word. *Diane.* Her name. Cradling his face in her hands, Diane kissed Gregory on the lips.

"Thank you," she said, whispering this, beating back the crushing rush of her heart. Stymying the rise of the one thing so hard to hold on to, hope. That he might say her name again. That he would remember her name. That he would never forget it.

"I was . . . I was . . ." he began.

"You were a father. You were my husband."

A good visit was one in which Gregory talked, though usually the words were a mantra: "Go home . . . want to go home." Diane was the conversationalist, telling Gregory about her last months on the bench, Sean, Lauren, and gossip about friends Gregory no longer remembered. On weekends, Margaret, Bruce, Lauren, Sean, Valerie, and Cameron often joined Diane and Gregory at a restaurant or for walks. During a walk along the Mall, the weather chilly, brisk, Diane walked with Lauren behind Margaret and Gregory, Margaret's arm entwined in Gregory's, both of them walking slowly, as Margaret whispered stories in his ear of childhood exploits, stories of his father.

At Somersby, Wallis Peebles was Gregory's shadow, scurrying away from him when Diane neared or sometimes refusing to leave them alone, forcing Diane, in exasperation, to find one of the nursing assistants to lead her away. Diane would arrive to find Wallis and Gregory making crafts, hiking the hallways for exercise, or sitting together eating popcorn in the theater. Increasingly, upon Diane's arrival, Wallis's hostility grew. Wallis was a blast of rolled eyes and pursed lips. Once, she was certain that as Wallis stalked past her, she heard her whisper, "You, bitch."

Regardless, Diane befriended the certified nursing assistants. There was Angela from Jamaica who had left a son and a daughter behind in Kingston, in the care of her mother, until she could get a visa to bring them to the US. Angela's Jamaican lilt soothed Diane, especially when she called her sometimes "my lovely," the nickname growing familiar as they grew closer. It was Angela who told Diane that Gregory wasn't drinking enough water and risked dehydration and a urinary tract infection, who revealed that in the first weeks of his residency at Somersby, Gregory had roamed the halls at night, attempting to punch codes into the security system. And it was Angela who said of Gregory and Wallis, "They're right good friends. It's good, you know, that they have friends."

# *Chapter Eighteen*

## NOVEMBER 2015

Diane stood in a virtual sea of food. The number of choices in the Whole Foods café was sumptuous and intimidating. A stand that held a dozen trays of different types of olives, another laden with cheeses from around the world. A fifteen-tray stand with familiar and exotic vegetables, fruits, toppings, and condiments for salad. She stood at the hot tray stand, trying to decide between deep-fried Brussels sprouts; stir-fried quinoa with shrimp; meat loaf; braised, locally grown beef floating in a bed of carrots, onions, and potatoes; herb-roasted chicken; and other dishes whose aromas tugged at her, making this one of the most difficult decisions in a day filled with hard choices. She had finally decided on the meat loaf and deep-fried Brussels sprouts when she felt someone's eyes, someone staring at her, as though she had been physically touched.

When she looked up, on the other side of the food stand stood Alan Rich.

"Hello, Mrs. Tate."

"Mr. Rich, I had no idea . . ."

"I've been staring at you for a while now. It was interesting to see a judge who couldn't make up her mind." His smile roused a tiny dimple she had not noticed when they'd met at Westminster Church. Had it been a year and a half or two years ago? However long it had been, Diane was flushed with unexpected pleasure at seeing him.

"Well, as you can see, I finally made my choice," she said, tipping her brown carton toward him.

"Me, I'm a quinoa man, myself," he said.

A tall, red-haired woman in a stylish hoodie and yoga pants reached over Alan to fill her carton with herb-roasted chicken, nudging him aside with a smooth yet definite shove.

"Okay, lady, the food's not going anywhere," he snapped. "This isn't Somalia."

"And this isn't your kitchen counter," she muttered.

Diane laughed and exchanged an amused glance with Alan, who moved away from the woman and came to the other side where Diane was standing.

"I was going to go home and eat," he said, "but would you like to join me upstairs? If you have the time, that is."

A torrential, freezing rain battered the streets outside. Between the rain and the wearying day she'd had on the bench, Diane had convinced herself not to go by Somersby on her way home. She'd pick up something to eat, shower, microwave her store-bought dinner, and eat in bed. That was the evening she'd had planned.

"Certainly."

"Great. Give me your carton and I'll pay for us both. I'll meet you upstairs in the dining area."

Diane saw Alan's dark, olive green trench coat stained by rain flow behind him as he hurried away toward the cashier. Giddiness flooded her at the thought of sharing a meal with a man she did not know, but wanted to.

Alan found her wiping a table near a window that showcased the bleak sky outside. She had placed napkins and plastic cutlery for two facing one another. As Diane sat down, he said, "Hold on," and strode over to the watercooler and came back with two cups of filtered water.

As they opened their cartons and took the first bites of food, Alan asked, "How've you been? I haven't seen you, your friend, or your husband at the church. Naser Abadey turned it out last week. I sometimes go on Monday nights when it's blues night."

Diane took another deep breath, again summoning guidance from a faithful, clearly inexhaustible supply of courage. "Alan, my husband Gregory has Alzheimer's, and he's living in an assisted living facility's memory care unit. He's been there for about two months."

"Oh, I'm . . ."

"Please, Alan, please don't say 'I'm sorry.' I know you are. I assume you are. It can't be helped. That night at Westminster, I was still learning how to own it and not melt down, like saying it was an admission of guilt or a failure."

"My mother died of complications from Alzheimer's. Caring for her tore our family apart. I know you're tired of hearing it, but I'd still like to say, I'm sorry, and I want you to know that's neither a platitude nor pity."

Diane hoped that her smile expressed all the gratitude she felt for his words.

"So, you've been shopping," she said pointing to a bag from a chain bookstore.

"Yes, for my nephew's son. He asked for a couple of those *Diary of a Wimpy Kid* books but I also got him an atlas and a dictionary."

"Do you have children?" Diane asked.

"No, and I'm divorced. Do you have grand-children?"

"Not yet. My daughter is pregnant, though."

"Congratulations."

"It's complicated."

"Isn't everything? Hard day?"

"Yes and yes and no. Did you read or hear about that case last week where a woman high on PCP killed her boyfriend?"

Alan nodded.

"A real tragedy. She was a senior at the University of the District of Columbia. Had never used any drugs before, got in with a drug-using crowd, and the very first time she uses PCP, goes on a violent rampage and kills her boyfriend in front of her three-year-old son. Stabs him to death."

She paused and moved the Brussels sprouts around the carton, took a tiny bite of the meat loaf and a sip of water. Then she looked again into Alan's horrified gaze.

"She had worked hard to pull herself out of and away from a very dysfunctional family but now she's in jail facing murder charges and her son is under my watch in protective custody. He was placed with a foster family that we've had problems with in the past, so the child's lawyer and I were going back and forth today trying to find a more suitable home."

"The child has a lawyer?"

"A guardian ad litem—to protect his interests as he goes through the system."

"So mother and child both have lawyers?"

"Uh-huh. And she's probably lost that child for good. So it was a real hard day."

This was how it used to be with Gregory, she thought—sifting through the remains of the day over a meal, the dinner table a confessional. Simply eating, an act that bound them always one to another. Her heart throbbed with regret. Then she stifled the onslaught of these overly familiar emotions and decided to look at Alan Rich. She wanted to be here, not back there where she could never be again. She silently commanded her thoughts to attention. *Look at this man. Really look at him. What do you see?* What she saw was the ease with which he occupied his body. The slightly chapped lips, the clipped moustache flecked with gray.

"Since I retired, I've been working with a nonprofit that mentors ex-offenders returning to the city after they've served their sentences. We work with them on everything: getting a degree, dress, tutoring, interviewing, and getting a job."

"So we're both in the trenches."

"Well, yours is a lot deeper than mine. You know, I play at Westminster sometimes. The piano. I've got a quartet I perform with now and then."

"That's wonderful. So you're a musician."

"Yeah, when I was younger I played in a local band. At one point, Motown was interested."

"Oh." Diane shivered with delight. "Why didn't you make a go of it?"

"I wasn't made for that life. The clubs were filled with inattentive, half-drunk audiences and rooms full of smoke. The other musicians were talented but too often just plain trifling. They'd miss rehearsals, let women problems interfere with gigs, and we never got paid what we were worth."

Having finished their meals, Diane and Alan lingered in the austere, nondescript dining room. A group of Ethiopian men sat huddled over their meals nearby, speaking their native tongue, their comradeship loud and jocular. As she watched

Alan stack their cartons and cutlery and take them to the trash container, she felt anointed.

Finally, Alan slid his business card across the table. "I enjoyed this, Diane. I don't know about you, but I can always use a friend. Will you call me?"

Diane searched her pocketbook for her own card and then handed it to Alan. "I'd be glad to do that."

When Alan took the card, he captured Diane's hand in his and held it encased in his palms. "That's good to know, very good to know."

At home, preparing for bed, Diane reached in her drawer for her gown, a faded pink-and-white cotton nightdress she'd worn for the last four or five winters. Rummaging in the rear of the drawer, her hands found the cool, slippery material of a silk negligee she had not worn in years. The ivory-colored gown lay in her palms and she inhaled its musky scent then rubbed the sheer fabric against her cheeks.

First, it was memory; then touch was the next to go. The good-morning, good-bye, good-night kiss—over time, Gregory could only tolerate them impatiently before slipping from her grasp, turning from the aching and abandoned lips Diane offered. They lived bound by a chastity strictly enforced by the stranger residing in her husband's body. They had always loved with passion and imagination, but now she was consigned to a kind of sexual exile. When she pleasured herself at night, in the dark, lying beside Gregory as he snored sweetly as a child, or in the last year, while he trekked the hallways of the house outside the locked bedroom door, Diane had called forth the sight of Gregory's face, staring at her intently and exhausted as he hunched over her, their bodies bound by the slick thread of their joint release.

In the bathroom, after a shower, gazing at herself in the steam shrouded mirror, Diane said, "I'm a mess."

She opened the towel and let it drop to the bathroom floor. Her hair was uneven, unruly. It was time for a trim. Finally, in the last month, she had begun sleeping through the night again, but the circles under her eyes were evidence of the long parade of fitful nocturnal struggles. She had to get back to the gym. What had Alan Rich seen, looking at her?

Maybe she was a mess, but Diane allowed herself to recall the incendiary thoughts and feelings Alan had inspired. She had sat across from him one part the respectable, middle-aged judge, and one part a woman drawn physically to a man and striving mightily to hide it. She felt her thighs stained by a moist trickle of desire. Beneath her touch, the skin of her breasts was soft as a newborn's. She had buried, forgotten, and been stripped of so much. She whispered as her hand retrieved the towel, "Please, God, not this, too."

• • •

The coffee shop was chapel-quiet. Watching the people at other tables staring at phones and computer screens with the intensity of scientists in a lab breaking a genetic code, Diane thought how the coffeehouse had become a kind of church, and coffee itself, a sacrament.

A profusion of small wooden tables and matching chairs. A windowsill that was home to philodendrons desperate for watering. Exposed brick walls. Posters of an eternally young Bob Marley, his broad, toothy, ecstatic smile an invitation, and a debonair, white-haired Tony Bennett. Three bookshelves of poetry, self-help, and biographies of radical political activists beside the counter and cash register and makeshift kitchen—that was the décor.

This neighborhood off of the busy, traffic-clogged Rhode Island Avenue had been christened Bloomingdale. Communities that, in Diane's childhood, were known by a major street or thoroughfare now were designated by sprightly names conjuring up feelings and images of contentment.

Diane smiled when she saw Alan walk through the door and hold it for a young blonde entering behind him. She had called him three days after their dinner at Whole Foods and made a date to meet today, a week later. What, she wondered, was the etiquette for this? His buoyant, seductive energy inspired a surge of starkly sexual desire. Alan removed his sheepskin-lined hat as he walked toward her table and there was his bald shiny pate. He loosened the buttons on his sheepskin jacket, seeming eager to present himself, his full self to her. He sat down, easing into the small chair gracefully.

"It's good to see you again." He smiled jovially as he stuffed his leather gloves into his coat pocket. "You beat me to the punch. I wanted to call, but for all my forthrightness that evening, I was unsure of the etiquette, you know what I mean."

"I'm still unsure myself. We'll figure it out," Diane said with more confidence than she felt.

"What were you thinking about when I walked in?"

"I was thinking about the personality of the city now, how cookie-cutter it's become with the same mix of coffee shops, yoga studios, overpriced gourmet restaurants, and bakeries. Apparently, funkiness in the way we used to know it has been banned. When was the last time you saw a hog maw or a chitlin? Or a store that sold pickles or pickled pigs' feet in one of those big jars?"

"Don't tell me you eat that stuff. Nostalgia has its limits, you know. It's probably just as well, as my mama used to say, that back in the day we had no idea how toxic that stuff was."

"It kept generations of our people alive." Diane laughed.

"I know a hole-in-the-wall place off Columbia Road that's got the city's best sweet potato pie, the required amount of dirt and grime, a sister behind the counter wearing a hairnet, potatoes fried in two-week-old bacon grease, and in the summertime, they got no air conditioning. Wanna head over there now?"

"Oh, come on," Diane chided Alan.

"So in other words, you were sitting here waiting for me thinkin' *really* deep thoughts?"

Alan asked her what she wanted to drink and went to the counter and ordered two coffees.

Settling back at the table, Alan pried the plastic top off of his coffee. Diane reached for several packets of sugar and three plastic pods of creamer from the pile he had placed between them.

"So you like your coffee sweet? Or should I say, you like coffee with your cream?"

"Guilty on both counts. And you like yours black?"

"And strong."

In the midst of this back and forth, Diane realized that she was flirting. She was sporting a new haircut. Putting together a pink cashmere turtleneck sweater and black shawl draped over her shoulder with black earrings and matching necklace had consumed nearly an hour, as she searched not just for the right clothes to wear, but for a new persona to present to this man who she hoped would not be a stranger much longer.

"You know," Alan began, "Alzheimer's makes family of us all. When my mother had it, I was the only man in my support group, but I couldn't have cared for my mother without it."

"The assisted living option hasn't been a panacea, but it's given me back more of my life, and that's the main thing."

"With me, Alzheimer's affected my relationships with my sisters, who didn't inherit the compassion gene and who pushed off the major responsibility for our mother onto me. They say men aren't intuitive; that's a lie. My intuition was working overtime. But you know what got me through all the ugliness of the divorce? My mother. Visiting her in the home where everything had become so simple. I'd go to the home sometimes fuming because of an argument with Beverly and sit there with my mother answering her questions about friends of hers who had died years ago or listening to her telling me again about something she'd done before I was born. It was like therapy. My wife didn't love me anymore, and having to care about my mother kept me from becoming bitter."

"What drew you to work with ex-offenders?"

"Seeing so many of the young men who had either been in classes I taught or who attended schools where I was a principal end up behind bars. I wasn't able to stop the pipeline at its source so I figured maybe I could help at the end."

"I saw the same thing working as a public

defender. That's why I turned to family law. Do you miss anything about the school system?"

"The kids mostly. There are still so many good, decent kids in the schools you never hear about. They get swallowed up by all the labels: inner-city, at-risk. Bush promised not to leave any student behind while Obama's got administrators racing to the top like crabs in a barrel."

"Are you hungry?" he asked when she was done with her coffee.

"Actually, yes."

They drove in separate cars to Chinatown and ate a leisurely dinner. When they parted, standing in front of Diane's car, Alan leaned in and enfolded Diane in an embrace pulsing with unspoken promises. Diane surrendered to Alan's touch, grateful for the possessiveness it contained. Closing her eyes, it was his face and his only that she saw rising to fill the shadowy vacant space.

# Chapter Nineteen

Sean's first visit to Somersby had confirmed all his fears. His father, a man who had helped shape the landscape of a city, was now confined to this place. It was as "nice" as his mother and Lauren had told him, but the quiet to Sean sounded like what waited for him in his grave. The residents all looked fine until you looked closely.

So, most days, he took his father out, anywhere: for a walk in a nearby park, for a slice of pie and cup of coffee at a diner in College Park. He'd joked with Valerie that although he didn't have to employ cunning, violence, or threats, each time he walked through the doors of Somersby with his father out into the world, he felt he was involved in a prison break.

Sean reached his father through stories. Stories, wasn't that all that conversation was? The stories he told his father were narratives peopled by his clients and his crew. Gregory had come to nod his head in what seemed, and felt to Sean, like understanding.

He had arrived early today to take his father to Ruth's Chris Steak House for dinner to celebrate his birthday. Valerie, Cameron, his mother, sister, and Mercer would meet them there. He tied his father's tie around his neck, a singularly confounding task that he recalled his father teaching him to do when he was twelve.

"We've got a few minutes, Dad," Sean said, sitting down. His dad's room made him feel claustrophobic, but here at least they had some privacy. "I finally did it. I let Archie go."

"Archie."

"You know, the guy I've been telling you about who I've depended on for so long but who's got a drinking problem?"

The blank stare no longer pained him, for he knew it did not necessarily signal incomprehension.

"It was the best thing to do but it was still hard, y'know. I don't know how you and Mercer did it. People look at the finished product and have no idea how much it cost in human terms to erect or renovate a building. Maybe they shouldn't know."

"I have to pay the staff," his father announced. Then he looked at Sean, his eyes narrowing in assessment and said, "I want to give you a raise."

"Dad, I told you, I don't need a raise and I'll take care of the payroll. You don't have to worry about that." Here he was in the present and also back in the terrifying roller-coaster past with his father. Pretending. Make-believe. Creating a now from the soil of a past his father hungered for and was deeply rooted in. More and more often when Sean visited, Gregory imagined that he was an employee of Caldwell & Tate. Sean had learned how to glide through his father's alternate reality, with only an occasional stumble.

"Riggs Bank," Gregory said, a bank that had closed its doors in the city years ago.

"Yes, I went there yesterday and made a deposit. Just like you told me to," Sean spoke the words of deceit calmly.

"Did you bring the receipt?" Gregory demanded skeptically.

"I sure did." Sean reached in his pocket and handed his father a deposit slip he had filled out earlier in the day, for this visit. This transaction had become a ritual between them. It did not matter that the deposit slip bore the name of his bank, Wells Fargo. His father imagined himself still at the helm of Caldwell & Tate, managing accounts, overseeing staff.

Gregory walked over to his desk drawer and placed the slip of paper in a small wooden box he had shown Sean the first day he visited him. "My money, in case I die. You know. My money," he had said placing his hand on Sean's shoulder. Sean had looked into the box and seen only a pile of tiny scraps of paper.

"Go ahead and blow them out, Daddy. Go on."

Diane watched as Gregory warily assessed the two candles in the shape of a six and a nine lodged atop a coconut birthday cake. Overcoming his skepticism, Gregory leaned forward and expelled a half-hearted exhalation, then slumped back heavily against his chair.

The candles extinguished, Lauren began slicing the cake. Diane, Sean, Valerie, Cameron, and Mercer sat around the table in the private dining room at Somersby where they had come after an early dinner at the steak house, to celebrate Gregory's birthday.

Through the French doors that separated them from the larger dining area, Diane saw some of the other residents watching the unfolding of this occasion. Fredrick Connor, a burly ex-fireman; the history teacher, Emma Bradley; and Trent Simpson, a small, wiry man who wore a patch over one eye as the result of a childhood accident, all waved at Diane through the doors. She waved back. Residents were informed of birthdays and Lynette had told Diane that earlier in the day, lunch had concluded with residents singing "Happy Birthday" to Gregory and eating slices of cake.

And there was Wallis, at a table with three other women, who sat in what seemed to Diane from this distance to be nervous, twittering awe of her. Wallis held forth with a monarch's confidence, her face an elastic, expressive mask.

"I brought you a gift," Lauren said, handing Gregory a box wrapped in glistening silver paper. Gregory simply placed the box on the table beside his untouched slice of cake, so Mercer said, "I'll open it for you."

"It's an electric shaver, Gregory," he said. "Old man, you're beginning to look like a caveman with that beard."

"When you want to shave, Daddy, that's what it's for."

Gregory nodded at the sight of a thick cardigan sweater that Sean lifted out of his gift box. There was a wool scarf from Mercer.

With more ceremony and seriousness than was required, Diane left her seat beside Mercer and sat down beside Gregory and slowly brought out of a large shopping bag a plush, tan leather briefcase.

Setting it on the table before Gregory, she said, "For a new set of dreams."

"Mom. That's beautiful." Lauren sighed, leaning in closer to admire the gift.

"You can use it for anything, Dad," Sean said.

"Don't leave it anywhere near me, man, or it's gone," Mercer joked heartily.

"Go on, open it," Diane urged him.

Gregory opened the snaps and reached inside. He retrieved several framed photographs. Diane moved closer to Gregory and the others stood behind them as she told the story of each picture: Gregory and Diane smiling into the camera from a table on a cruise to Bermuda. Diane and Gregory dwarfed by the pyramids of Giza on the trip he had longed for all his life. There was a photo of Lauren in hair rollers, wolfing down a slice of pizza at a birthday party sleepover when she turned sixteen. Sean shooting hoops in the backyard after his barbecue birthday party when he turned eighteen. Diane, chic and beaming, in a formal gown and Gregory in a tuxedo on the dance floor of the Grand Hyatt at the party Gregory had thrown for her fiftieth birthday. Gregory stared at the photo of Lauren, then pointed to Lauren, saying, "That's her."

"Yes, Daddy, that's me." Lauren giggled in delight.

"I saw a picture of the pyramids in school," Cameron said as he held the photo of the trip to Egypt in his hands before Valerie lead him back to his seat.

A gentle knock on the French doors interrupted them, and Diane looked up to see Wallis standing outside the door. She was dressed in a thick caftan as bold as a box of crayons and she was carrying a gift.

Lauren looked at her mother quizzically.

"Open the door, Lauren." Diane sighed.

But before Lauren could move, Wallis burst into the room.

"Hello," Wallis said cheerily, as though they had all been expecting her.

Wallis barreled toward Gregory, thrusting a gift into his hand. Gregory's eyes brightened and he smiled for the second time that evening and took the small box clumsily wrapped in silver paper. Blushing, he sat up in his chair, clearly revived.

Then Wallis hugged Gregory, her breasts stationed in his face, her hands and blazing red nails squeezing his head. Gregory lay against her sublime and relaxed. Releasing him, Wallis spotted an empty chair and dragged it beside Gregory, trying to squeeze between Diane and Gregory.

"Move, move," she ordered Diane, pushing her so hard she nearly fell onto the floor.

Cameron asked Valerie, "Who is that lady, Mommy?"

"That's enough, that's enough," Sean said, standing up. He shared a gaze with Mercer and both men approached Wallis, who, as they neared her jerked wildly in fright and turned around, her fists pummeling Sean's chest. The altercation and the noise brought Lynette running toward the room.

"Stop. Stop. Help," Wallis screamed.

Lynette expertly moved Sean and Mercer away from Wallis and led her out the door, soothing and comforting her. "Now Wallis, come on. It will be all right."

Diane was trembling. Enraged, confused, she felt assaulted, like the victim of a theft. Rare were the moments when they could replicate what it felt like to be a family again, when celebration was easy and heartfelt.

All evening, through dinner at the steak house and on the drive back to Somersby, she had been watchful, waiting, expecting disaster to derail her intricately planned evening. Would Gregory become suddenly disoriented in the restaurant and demand to leave? Would he stare in stoic, blank indifference at Cameron and reduce the boy to tears when he refused to or could not respond to the boy's frightened inquiries?

Neither had happened. And she had foolishly congratulated herself too soon, beaming when Gregory opened the briefcase, certain that her concerns this time were unjustified. This evening would be the special and love-filled gathering she had planned. Who was this woman, Wallis, to Gregory, she wondered. She didn't know but Gregory did, she was now certain of that. That woman, as lost as Gregory, had ripped out her heart. She had no idea how she would rise from her chair.

Sean now sat beside Gregory, his hand on his shoulder, whispering into his ear.

Mercer shook his head and said, "I wonder what *she* was like back in the day."

Summoning a composure from the scattered threads of her emotional tailspin, Diane turned to Lauren. "It's been a long night. I'm sure your father's tired."

Lauren and Sean gathered the paper plates and sodas. Mercer leaned over and kissed Diane on her cheek good-bye.

Diane helped Gregory stand up and they headed to his room, Diane carrying all the birthday gifts except the gift from Wallis, which Gregory clutched tightly under his arm. When they entered Gregory's room, Diane calmed herself by concentrating on placing the photographs in the briefcase carefully and strategically like sentries on Gregory's desk and bookshelf.

She had tried to ignore the woman, had convinced herself that she was a mere annoyance. Foolish. Vain. That's what she'd been. Seething with anger at herself, at Gregory, and at a woman she could not believe was a threat to her relationship with her husband, Diane crossed her arms against her chest to calm her rampaging nerves. "Gregory, why did Wallis give you a birthday gift? Is she your friend? Your special friend?"

"Wallis is my wife," he said adamantly, pushing her away for emphasis.

As nausea roiled in her stomach, Diane watched Gregory place the boxes on his desk and sit so still on the bed that he seemed to be meditating.

"It's your birthday, and you're sixty-nine years old today," she whispered, determined that at least one thing between them would be true before she left.

Outside, the snowflakes resembled falling stars. Diane longed to float upward into the billowing darkness overhead. Sean reached for her as a spasm forced her to lean over a few feet from the car and expel the evening's hearty meal.

"What happened back there?" he shouted, rubbing her back while Lauren opened the trunk and retrieved a wad of paper towels that she thrust in her mother's hands.

Inside Sean's car, Diane sat in the passenger seat wiping her face and taking small sips from a bottle of water Lauren had given her.

"What happened?" Sean insisted.

"I asked him why Wallis gave him a gift. I asked him if she was his friend. He told me she was his wife."

"Mom, he doesn't know what he's saying," Lauren said, comforting her.

Diane looked at her children beneath the ceiling light Sean had turned on. She saw their faces mapped in concern and disbelief. Looking from Sean to Lauren and back again she asked, "How did we lose him? How did we lose him so completely, so fast?"

Wallis steps into a hallway that is as quiet as she imagines the beginning of time must have been and pads to Gregory's room. His moan welcomes her as she unbuttons her nightgown and lets it fall to the floor in the room's patient, somber darkness. He cannot see her still tear-stained face. Wallis still seethes with the humiliation of being forced from the birthday party. She had never found a man worth her love. Now she has and they want to keep them apart. Sliding beneath the covers,

279

beside Gregory, Wallis eases into his waiting arms as her sobs erupt like a howl. Gregory whispers "shh, shh" and holds her close, Wallis's body a bulwark in the night.

# Chapter Twenty

## December 2015

Half a dozen prescriptions huddled around the lamp on the nightstand beside Alan's bed. He'd warned Diane away from his left knee, worn from years of running. She suffered from sporadic back pain only partially relieved by yoga and walking. Performing this dance, their bodies were aging, yet eager and sure-footed. Diane's kiss was fierce and anguished, all tongue, thrusting and impatient. Alan's longing was unvanquished and so the slick, moist, hide-and-seek of the first moments soon gave way to Diane mounting his solid fullness. The ecstatic shudder melted into a satisfaction sprung from the soil of tenderness, gratitude, and desire.

After, Diane lay swathed in the sheets resting on Alan's chest, washed up on the shore of him, stretching her arms around his girth. Gregory was all angles and length and muscle. Only the second man she'd had sex with in over thirty years, Alan was round and soft, his flesh sheer, grand invitation. Thirty years ago, she was sure he would not have moved her. Now he had consumed and resurrected her.

"Thank you," she whispered.

"You're more than welcome." Alan laughed, his chest rumbling in delight.

"I've wanted to do this for a long time," she told him.

"I've wanted to do this since that night at Westminster, but you were a married woman so I went home that evening and had a stiff drink and told myself such is life."

Their laughter mingled, glowing in the dark. Diane closed her eyes and listened to the sound of Alan's breathing and her own shallow, contented breaths. They both slipped into a sated slumber, shifting positions so that Diane lay on her side.

When they woke a half hour later, Alan turned on the halogen lamp on the nightstand. He kissed her earlobe, squeezed her, and told Diane, "You're still a married woman."

"Is this going to be too complicated for you?" she asked.

"It'll probably get complicated for us both. I kind of hope it does."

Alan released her and sat up, plumping the pillows behind him. Diane turned on her back, her head resting on his groin. She lay gazing at the bedroom walls where, like the walls in so many of the rooms of his house, Alan had hung moody, artistic black-and-white photographs of musicians. B. B. King sat in his dressing room cradling his guitar, Lucille, in his lap. Billy Strayhorn played a baby grand. Sarah Vaughn gripped a microphone in a close-up, her eyes closed, her face mapped with sweat as she sang on stage at the Apollo.

"Gregory told me that some woman at Somersby was his wife. In his mind and in the life that he's living, I've had to conclude that's the truth."

"What was he like before?"

"He wanted so much and felt he had a right to everything. He wanted all that and more for me and our children. He was brash, impatient, loyal."

"I like you. I more than like you," Alan said, "and I'd like to feel I knew where we were headed. Where we could go? I need to know that."

*Need,* such a small word that sprawled over everything they were or dreamed of. *Need,* the thing that defined them when they entered the world dependent on others for everything, and when they left the world hoping only to be let go with grace and acceptance. Didn't Gregory need someone, something he had found in Somersby with Wallis? Didn't she need what Alan was offering?

"One, we've been seeing each other for less than two months."

"You know that has nothing to do with what I'm talking about."

"And the kind of clarity you want evaporated for me four years ago."

"Wouldn't you like a new kind of clarity?"

"Alan, I can't just impose it. It has to rise from the muck and mire, from the chaos of everything. And it will. In time."

"Are we arguing or bickering?" he asked

"I guess we're being a couple."

"You still looking forward to stepping down from the bench, your honor?"

"Yes, and with less and less trepidation every day. In the early period of our battle with Alzheimer's I used to look forward to going to work, because there I was in charge, I set the rules. But as the disease progressed, I began to feel my work was a reflection of my other life, not an antidote to it."

"Whatever happened in that case a while back with the little boy whose mom was high on PCP and—"

"Her trial starts in a few weeks and we finally found him a stable foster home."

"Isn't that one for your team?"

"I just hope it's a win for that little boy."


The following night, plucking her earrings and watch from her jewelry box as she prepared to go to the Kennedy Center with Alan, for the first time Diane did not instinctively reach for her wedding band. Two gold bands melded together in a basket weave. She and Gregory had not wanted diamonds, supporting the growing international push to boycott diamonds from Apartheid South Africa, and they had wanted to use the money a diamond ring would cost for a down payment on a house. Gold bands had been enough.

When she finally removed it from its resting

place in the velour-lined top drawer of the jewelry box, the ring seemed so minuscule. The gleam of the gold was dulled and bore nicks and scratches. It was now a perfect symbol of all they had weathered. She wore the ring now out of habit and because, as Alan had reminded her, she was still a married woman. But now the ring felt false. In all the ways that being a married woman, a wife counted, she was not. The ring represented her and Gregory, but she was the only one with memories of what it meant.

Her children, her family, her friends all asked her what she felt for Alan, where were they headed. Alan had reintroduced her to joy, but she was careening, falling toward and into a new version of herself. She was beginning to love herself all over, love herself anew. This love was a country to which she was ready to pledge allegiance.

There had not been a Christmas tree in the house in years. But the upheaval of this year, moving Gregory into Somersby, the fact that she had actual plans for her future, the bitter sweetness of it all increased Diane's longing for a tree.

Alan drove her to a pop-up Christmas tree stand next to a gas station on Georgia Avenue. The evening air was moist, cold, the lot fragrant with the scent of pine. The trees had been picked over, manhandled, for Diane had waited until December 23 to act on her desire. They searched through the limp, leftover trees, bundled in cord, and the few standing upright on display, and managed to find a fresh, hardy-limbed tree. Alan tied it to the top of his car and they went to a nearby big-box hardware store and bought lights. The rest of the evening was spent putting up the tree and decorating it. When Diane tossed the last handful of silver icicles onto the tree's branches, she burst into girlish laughter and for no reason hugged Alan.

She made grilled cheese sandwiches and a salad and they sat together for the rest of the evening assessing the tree and sharing stories of their own Christmases past.

And now, on Christmas Day, her family was all here for Christmas dinner. Alan was one of the hosts for a holiday dinner for the formerly imprisoned men that he mentored, a celebration at a northeast recreation center.

Bruce and his son Aaron, Sean, Gregory, and Cameron sat in the living room watching the football game and Diane was in the kitchen. Margaret sat at the table slicing tomatoes and cutting lettuce for a salad. Lauren, two months pregnant but still not showing much, smoothing a bed of marshmallows over the top of sweet potatoes, said, "The more things change the more they stay the same. Just look who's in the kitchen."

"Thank God." Margaret laughed. "The men would just be in the way."

Standing next to Diane, who was placing kale

into a pot, Valerie brushed melted butter over a pan of rolls.

"You've been so good for Sean, Valerie. Please tell me he's been good for you."

"He has. Sean has grounded me. He's got his demons, but he's easy to love."

"For years, we thought we'd lost him."

"He feels terrible about that time. And he's mad at himself for those years. He's still trying to figure out how and why he let that happen."

"Maybe he'll never know, but asking at least proves my son has a conscience."

When Diane recalled this day, she would remember looking around the dinner table at Margaret beside Gregory, helping him eat; at Lauren, easy, comfortable with Cameron, her arm finding its way over his shoulder, again and again. Sean, proud and confident beside the woman he loved.

# Chapter Twenty-one

## MARCH 2016

Diane and Gregory had been together all day. Diane had picked Gregory up from Somersby to spend the day with her and all morning, she had enlisted his aid with small cleaning tasks around the house. She watched as he washed dishes, wiped the stove and counter. He helped her make the bed. Now, he stood at the kitchen counter stacking knives and forks.

After a lunch of tomato soup and chicken sandwiches, she helped Gregory into his jacket, slipped into hers, and they walked the length of their block. Back home, they napped. As Gregory slept, Diane watched a dribble of saliva stain his chin. There was no more desire. She no longer wore his ring. Another man was her lover. Alzheimer's had sacked and looted their relationship, stripped it to the bone, yet they were mated, soldered to one another beyond rings, ceremonies, and contracts.

Diane's mentor, William Larson, a respected judge, had died recently of a stroke. At Somersby last month, Trent Simpson had succumbed to a heart attack in his sleep. A friend of Alan's from high school died of diabetes-related complications.

The son of a fellow judge hung himself in his garage after years of battling with clinical depression, and Randall Cullen, Gregory's longtime friend, had just died of prostate cancer.

Diane found herself suddenly entrenched in a season of relentless death and dying.

But more terrible than anything she had ever seen or known this closely, this intimately, was Gregory's suffering. According to his doctors, what she read, everything she knew and saw, Gregory was in stage three, or stage six, of Alzheimer's, depending on how the horror of the disease was calculated. He could live, declining in increments, for two years, a decade, or more.

And there was more suffering to come. His immune system would gasp for breath, impossible to retrieve. That mind, devious and cruel, would disrupt his body's desire to move, his yearning to eat. Lethal blood clots and infections sown by the steady shutdown would ultimately stop the intricate and elegant biological system from working. This was not just Gregory's fate to bear but hers to bear with him. A fate that could be distant and encroaching, drawing nearer every day. Her husband was dying. But no matter what, she would not turn away from the awful sight.

Later, Bruce came by to take Gregory back to Somersby and Diane sat with Margaret and Lauren in the living room, drinking lemonade, and watching a movie on television.

As a commercial came on, Lauren said, "Daddy won't know he's a grandfather."

"Oh, stop it," Margaret said. "I don't care what those doctors say. All the studies and research. Gregory will know he's a grandfather."

"How?"

"That's between God and Gregory. When he holds that child the first time, believe me he'll know."

"How are you and Gerald?" Diane asked.

"We're not dating anymore. It felt too weird to me. We're waiting to become parents. That's all I can say."

"Sounds to me like you're together in the way that matters most now," Diane said.

"I thought your generation didn't believe in marriage anyway," Margaret said.

"Grandma, you have to stop reading the Internet. I'm not 'my generation.' I'm me. Look at Sean and Valerie. They're engaged."

"Life is long, Lauren, and you have no idea how much of it still awaits you," Margaret said.

"In one of our talks right after he got the official diagnosis, Dad was rushing to tell me things, things he hadn't said and was afraid he wouldn't get to. He told me to have a life beyond my work."

"Well, dear, you now have a life, a real one." Diane laughed.

"And you aren't alone in it," Margaret said. "You aren't alone."

Sean had begun to "steal" afternoons like this one, to drive to Somersby and tell Gregory, "Come with me, Dad. Let's go for a ride."

This was a day of excessive, inordinate spring charm. The sky, flecked by speckles of sun lighting the mosaic of frothy blue and white, hovered confidently over the city. The playful winds and the hint of humidity promised a perpetual reign of days like this.

Gregory sat beside Sean in the front seat, stylish in a thick, heavy cardigan, the curls of his white hair peeking up at the edges of a Washington Nationals cap. Sean allowed him to play with the radio dial. When the sound of rap music with its jittery belligerence blared through the speakers, Gregory nodded in satisfaction and Sean laughed. Sitting with his father at Somersby or going over on Sundays to join Gregory as he watched football or basketball, Sean thought of the inadequacy of words, how they mangled meanings and were just as often roadblocks as they were passageways. At Somersby, he watched his father sit with Wallis in the sunroom, in the library, in the den. The two of them now flagrantly joined. Her chatter, endless, easy, soothed his father as much as it boggled Sean's mind.

Today, Sean wanted his father to see the city's frenzy of construction. The skyline was now permanently bejeweled by cranes; the equipment mammoth in strength could be humbled by a strong wind. The staid, mannerly city of Sean's youth was now brash and cocksure. New buildings arched upright and edgy. Downtown now had its own version of Park Avenue, lined with glitzy glass emporiums and temples to glamour.

Sean scanned his father periodically, ensuring that he hadn't unlocked the passenger side door or wiggled out of his seat belt or wet himself. Long, tender silences settled between them as they drove around the city. But he couldn't trust the silence. He hoped the cerebral backlog of memory didn't set his father on edge, agitate him, or fill his eyes with tears.

On the corner of Ninth and H Street N.W., Gregory looks up at the twelve-story building that has greedily taken possession of the width and length of the entire block. The cold efficiency and pompous grandeur of the structure makes him dizzy as he stares up at it. Why is the building here? Where is Doggett's rugged gravel and earth parking lot? Where is Security Bank? The sensation of bewilderment and waste descends. Emotions and thoughts that never find a solid place to land strangle him. In the grip of this terrible sense of loss and bereavement, he cannot tell this one beside him, the one who acts like his son and calls him *Dad,* although Gregory knows they are, in fact, the same age. He can never tell any of them—not the woman who calls him *Daddy* or the woman who was something important to him, which he feels deep inside but can no longer recall. He has learned how to deceive them as they came to him, diplomats from a region beyond reason or dreams. He won't ask the young man what happened to the bank, the parking lot, the liquor store. He sits wondering as he does every day how he will find Mercer, how Mercer will ever find him.

As they drove past a construction site on Massachusetts Avenue, Sean told Gregory, "Dad, a man fell into a hole there last week and died."

His father had always told him that the men and women who actually did the work that transformed his drawings into buildings worked fourteen- to sixteen-hour days. Stamina, strength, and courage was required, he said, and yet most people saw them in their hard hats, their jeans, and looked quickly past their sweat-drenched faces and grimy hands. The pedestrians who passed the construction sites, unaware that craftsmen and artists were at work, could not imagine the intelligence, delicacy, and precision of thought required to mount and work a crane, to work sixteen stories high, to check the wiring in a building with three hundred units.

The din of construction on the site of the National Museum of African American History and Culture on Fifteenth and Constitution Avenue drove Gregory to place his hands over his ears to block out the sounds that once he had loved because, as he had told Sean, it meant a building was being born. Circling the area teeming with tourists, Sean found a parking space a block away and he and Gregory sat in the shadow of the museum. Each story of the structure, designed like an inverted crown, leaned outward, the burnished grill and iron squares, protruding like molded sunbeams. Sean still preferred his father's design, which had arched boldly skyward.

"Dad, that building is where our history will be told. One day, I came here and watched them lower a Jim Crow train car, the whole thing, onto the lower level."

Gregory folded his arms at his chest and pointed to the structure. "I made that," he said proudly, narrowing his eyes in studied assessment. So the hundreds of hours Caldwell & Tate had spent on their design, their bid for one of the world's most prestigious architectural projects had not been forgotten. His father had gotten it all wrong but, in a manner that made Sean smile in satisfaction, he had gotten it right.

On days like this, Sean gave his father all he had. And he took all that his father was, a fractured husk of a man. Valerie had dared him to "love what was left" of his father. That's what he was trying to do.

When Sean parked in front of his parents' house, Gregory peered out the window and said, "Home," a lilt of indecision in his voice. Gregory stood for several moments leaning on the car and looking at the house.

Camille Baker, their next door neighbor, hurried down her front stairs and exclaimed, "Why, Gregory, it's so good to see you. Diane told me where you are now. I'm so sorry I haven't had a chance to visit you. You look good, you look so well. I saw Diane leave a few hours ago. Sean, I'm so glad to see you are taking such good care of your father." This torrent of words drove Gregory to cling to Sean as though dodging an assault.

"Thanks, Camille. Let's go inside, Dad."

In his mother's bedroom, Sean placed a stack of his father's lightweight clothing in an overnight bag. Gregory inspected the bedroom with benign curiosity, then used the toilet. When Gregory came out of the bathroom, he wandered over to the bedroom door and stood, his hands rubbing the place that still bore evidence of the lock Diane had installed.

"I couldn't get in."

"She loved you, Dad. It wasn't you she was afraid of. It wasn't really you."

Today her husband would meet her lover.

Even as she so neatly thought of what was about to happen, Diane knew that this day was fraught with possibilities for closure and confusion. She never used the word *lover* when she talked about

Alan. Yet in her mind, she played with the word. *Lover.* A word that was so much more generous and complicated than the sexual overtones it evoked. She felt beloved, respected, and cared for. The damning emotional isolation had been replaced by a personal revival.

Alan was in her life and an integral part of it. They had met each other's friends; she had attended his high school reunion in Paterson, New Jersey. He and Sean had attended a hockey game, and Paula, Lauren, Sean, Valerie, and Cameron had joined them for a birthday celebration dinner for Diane that Alan hosted at a Cuban restaurant in Silver Spring. They talked every day, and she regularly spent weekends at his house. She had met his neighbors, who smiled knowingly as they walked down the stairs some evenings toward Alan's car.

That this day would come, had to come, was an unspoken expectation rooted inevitably between them. She relied on Alan for advice, yet had long sequestered what they had from whatever was left with Gregory. This zone they had created was a fortress, but one that camouflaged a fragility she did not want to test. His mother had died of Alzheimer's-related complications. He had been to the hell, so her reports from her own purgatory were unnecessary. She had given Gregory so much, and the prospect of giving more loomed large and dark on her horizon. To invite Gregory into what she and Alan had felt like a betrayal of them both. Still, if Alan wanted her in his life, her husband would have to come with her.

Alan stepped through the door into the hallway and hugged Diane, who rested in his customarily extravagant embrace. Each meeting between them had the feel of a reunion, and Diane longed for a simpler greeting, one that signaled more confidence that what they had would last.

"Come on back to the kitchen. I made iced tea and I have some empanadas, those small meat pies. We can have a quick bite before we go."

Alan removed his jacket and cap and tossed them on the living room sofa and then wandered into Gregory's study, its walls covered with plaques, trophies, and framed newspaper articles about the buildings Caldwell & Tate had helped design and build.

"He was a real trailblazer. I'm intimidated whenever I come in this room." He laughed uneasily. This confession unsettled Diane, and so she reached for Alan, slipping her arm through his and leading him back to the kitchen.

"What's all this?" he asked, pointing to a stack of textbooks.

"I'm choosing books for the courses I'll teach in the fall."

Alan stood thumbing through them. "You sound excited."

"I am."

"Thank you for inviting me along today. I've wanted to see Gregory again. Of course, not like this, but you know." He reached for the pitcher and filled a glass that Diane handed him.

Diane placed three empanadas each on small plates, one in front of her and one in front of Alan.

"Remember when I told you that Gregory thinks a woman at Somersby is his wife?"

"Yes, I do."

"A week ago I discovered that it isn't just something in his head. She, this woman, she's having sex with Gregory."

"Well, good for him."

"Yes, it is," she said weakly

"You don't sound convinced."

"I am. I am." The declaration rushed out.

The evening Diane had discovered Wallis and Gregory in bed together remained an offensive jolt in her memory. As she'd approached Gregory's door she heard the muffled moans, deep and throaty and began walking faster, fearing that Gregory was in distress. Reaching for the doorknob, the other voice, a gritty murmur, morphed into a high-pitched, ecstatic squeal. Gently opening the door, she'd seen a woman's bare, fleshy back and the outline of the woman's broad hips, straddling the figure beneath her. Gregory's hands, grasping in the shadowy darkness, slithered around the woman's waist. She knew the woman was Wallis. A tremor of quiet laughter filled her throat at the sight and the idea of these two wayward, lost souls engaged in intercourse. The laughter was overtaken by a literal spasm of anger that brutally cleared her head.

Bristling with an outrage she could not fathom but only feel, Diane searched the quiet halls for Lynette or any of the other certified nursing assistants, determined to report what she had see . But had she witnessed a crime? Calling Lynette, frantically searching the hallways, the den, and the TV room, she nearly knocked the woman down as she turned a corner.

"I heard your call, Mrs. Tate. What is it, did something happen? You look upset."

At the sight of Diane's face, Lynette placed a steadying hand on her shoulder and Diane heard herself stammer, "It's, it's nothing, Lynette, nothing at all." What could she say that was neither shameful nor demeaning to her sense of pride? Was she angry because she had found her husband having sex with another woman or was she angry because the man involved in that act was lost to her in all the ways that had once sealed their love?

"Are you sure?" Lynette had asked, clearly unconvinced.

"Yes, I'm sure."

In the parking lot, she had tried to catch her breath. How long had they been spending nights together? She told Paula, who had laughed and asked, "Aren't you relieved? In all the sadness of this thing, here at last, is something to be grateful for."

Now she told Alan: "I felt horrified, stunned, puzzled, a little bit of every imaginable emotion when I opened his door and found them making love."

"Come on, you call that making love? You make it sound like what we do. Remember, my mother had Alzheimer's. For them it's an act that's more biological than emotional."

Diane sat across from Alan chewing the empanada and suddenly had no appetite. "They're not animals."

"We're all animals."

"You know what I mean."

"Do I? Tell me about this woman."

While she had lost her appetite, Alan sat chewing on a meat pie, before reaching for another as he waited for her answer.

"Her name is Wallis. Wallis Peebles. She's seventy-eight years old but looks much younger. She used to be a milliner and she latched on to Gregory as soon as he arrived. She has more speech and abilities than Gregory. She cares for him."

"Gregory could be like a toy or a teddy bear to her. Do you think it registers with Gregory who he's having sex with? He no longer has any way of processing that."

"Stop. Stop." This clinical explanation that Alan clearly thought would comfort Diane instead reminded her of all that Gregory was not and all that he could no longer understand. "You don't need to remind me of all my husband's lost, of all he does and doesn't know."

"I'm just telling the truth. It's not the same as what we do, so don't say it is."

"Why are you being so hostile?" This was their first argument.

"I'm not hostile, I'm honest. What did you do when you saw them?"

"Ran. Ran because I didn't want to see it. But now I'm relieved. Alan, he may not know what love is anymore, or the multiple meanings of sexual experience, but I know it gives him something. Something he needs."

She had read that although Gregory forgot the visits from family and friends shortly after they occurred, if the visits had been positive, the good feeling they invoked could last and impact his immune system for hours. Each visit in some way extended his life. Was that a good thing? But what other choice was there? Did sex with Wallis Peebles bring Gregory satisfaction? Joy? Health?

"Are you jealous?" Alan asked.

"For a moment or two I was. It made no sense. I mean, of course there was the residual sense of— of . . ."

" 'He's my man,' and 'Bitch, what the hell are you doing?' " Alan laughed cynically.

301

"Sort of."

"Well, he's in a different world. His world. Their world." Alan reached across the island and held her hand. "You have to accept that."

"I have. Alan, what do you think the last couple of years has been about? I've earned a PhD in accepting things I can't control."

"Have you?" The question sounded like an interrogation.

"Yes."

"Well, I think we'd better get going."

Diane knocked gently on the door before entering, a new practice since the night she found Wallis and Gregory together. Gregory was not asleep but lay resting on top of the quilt on his bed, staring at the ceiling. He barely stirred when they entered.

"Gregory, hello, dear," Diane said, leaning over to squeeze his hands as they lay folded on his chest.

Alan pushed a rocking chair near Diane and she sank into it while he brought over the desk chair beside her and sat down.

She was suddenly aware of the severe limits and artificiality of Gregory's life. As they'd entered the memory care unit, she'd explained to Alan the number of rooms on each floor and told him about the activities for the residents. Yet showing it to Alan, she thought how hermetic, small, and encased it seemed. Alan kept murmuring, "This is nice, very nice," but suddenly it all seemed meager. This was what was left of life for Gregory, and seeing it with Alan at her side filled Diane with a flash of guilt and shame.

Looking at her husband, whose eyes revealed no glimmer of recognition, Diane could hardly breathe. The three of them filled the room to capacity. How would she introduce Alan, she wondered. What would she say?

Alan reached for Gregory's limp, elastic hand and shook it.

"You don't remember me now, Mr. Tate, but your firm built a school I was principal of back in 2002. It was the most beautiful school I ever taught in. The students, the staff, we loved that building and we all worked harder because it was the kind of building that required us to do more and be more to reflect its refinement. I had a lot of respect for you back then, how you asked me and the teachers and the students what we wanted in the new school before you started designing it, how you made the building about us. I know I wanted some things you said were impractical and we went toe-to-toe, head-to-head sometimes, but you usually won in the end. And when I looked at the building and started working in it, I'm glad you did."

Gregory's eyes were a void that gave neither of them anything. He listened with a faux patience and then turned on his side, giving them both his back, curled in on himself, and drifted off to sleep.

In the hallway, Diane told Lynette that she was worried. "I looked in his drawers and closets and it seems some of his socks and shirts are missing."

With a look of chagrin, Lynette said, "We've had a problem with some items being washed and returned to the wrong resident. They can't always inform us of the mistake."

"But I labeled all his clothes, everything."

"I know, I'm sorry, Mrs. Tate."

At that moment a resident walked toward them wearing one of Gregory's sweatshirts.

"That for example, belongs to my husband."

"I'll try to get it back."

"Try?"

"The residents, as you know, are sometimes volatile and—"

"So Gregory's clothes just disappear and become the property of anyone else just like that?"

Alan held her shoulders and said, "Thank you. Come on, let's go, Diane. It's not the end of the world."

In the car she fumed. "For all the money I'm paying, you'd think they could at least keep track of his clothes."

"What's really wrong?" Alan asked.

"I feel so empty. I hadn't told him about us, about you. I didn't know how. I had hoped this visit would be one way to start that conversation. But even if I say the words, tell him about our relationship, what would it even mean?"

"Is this what you want for the rest of your life? Don't you want more?"

"I haven't thought that far ahead."

"Not even since we've been together?"

"Alan, it's only been a couple of months."

"Why do you always say that like weeks and months have anything to do with feelings?

"You can go forward. You can always go forward."

"I'm here with you. I call this moving forward."

# Chapter Twenty-two

## June 2016

Forward, that was the only place to go, Diane often thought. Forward. There was no way to tell Gregory about Alan and so she no longer tried to. Whatever he shared with Wallis Peebles, that belonged to them. Apparently they were content in the universe they had created. In the months that had passed after Alan went with her to Somersby, she formally retired from the bench. She was moving on. There was no place else to go.

"Are you sure you're up for this?" Diane asked Lauren one day. "We can stay here if you want."

Lauren and Diane sat on the backyard deck. The garden Diane had tended and coaxed filled the yard, vivid and simmering with color and life. Lauren sat with her arms resting protectively on her abdomen. She'd cut her locks and now wore her hair in a close-cut, natural style that exposed a face Diane sometimes thought she had never seen before.

"I'm okay with the walking, Mom. Please, I wish everyone would stop treating me like an invalid. What did enslaved women do? No one can believe I still come into the office. What else am I supposed to do? I gotta support my baby." Lauren giggled at her own insouciance.

"So have you and Gerald chosen a name?"

"If it's a girl, I like Simone, and if it's a boy, I want Daniel. Gerald says he's fine with that."

"Daniel, that's Gregory's middle name."

"That's why I chose it."

"I'm proud of you, Lauren."

"Mom, you know this wasn't the plan."

"You could have made a different choice."

"Not now. I couldn't imagine a different choice."

"And Gerald, he'll be a good father. That's all that matters now. You two aren't broken, you didn't fail at anything. You're just making a family. The way families, quiet as it's kept, have always been made."

"I still love him a little."

"Good, then you'll be able to one day forgive him for not being ready to be everything you felt you had to have. Do you want to go to the Museum of African Art first or Macy's?"

When the phone rang, Diane rose from the plush deck chair, regretting that even for this moment she had to leave this late morning sun, a sun that had not just warmed her but blossomed a fullness within her that she held fast to as she hurried inside to answer the phone. Leaning against the wall in the kitchen, already slightly annoyed, fearing that she would hear the voice of a Saturday morning telemarketer, Diane heard instead the voice of

Leah Temple informing her that half an hour ago it was discovered that Gregory was missing. He had apparently left Somersby. The building had been thoroughly searched, and Gregory was gone.

*Gone.* The word landed, a rock from space, a sudden blow, a groin-tightening fright. There it was, despite her best efforts standing in her kitchen to erase it, slithering cold and wet.

Leah's voice was apologetic, straining to be clinical and composed as it narrated what could be an impending disaster. She summed up all the steps taken after it was discovered that Gregory was missing. All the rooms were checked. All the residents were taken from the building and the rooms checked again. Diane imagined a huddled mass of the elderly, some in wheelchairs, some on walkers in the parking lot, monitored and calmed by nursing assistants as everyone from Leah, to the receptionist and cooks, looked for Gregory again.

"Are you there, Mrs. Tate?"

"Where else would I be?"

"I know this is terribly upsetting for you. We've contacted the police, who've issued a Silver Alert."

Diane heard the echo of all the Silver Alerts she had seen on news reports about missing seniors. Grainy photographs of an elderly man or woman, the white hair, the face that looked like everyone's grandmother or grandfather.

And here she was now. In hell. She nearly gagged as her throat clogged and then constricted, her body urging her to release it all, what she had been told, what she knew, did not know, what she feared. To her amazement, she heard herself ask, "How could this happen?"

But she knew how it could happen, saw again herself in bathrobe and bare feet that early morning before the sun rose, chasing Gregory down their street, calling his name, willing him to stop, slow down, to hear her call. The human will can outwit even the most rigorous surveillance. But she had put Gregory in Somersby, convincing herself that this could never happen.

To forestall telling Lauren even for a few moments, driving to Somersby, thoughts of suing the facility, of Gregory never being found, of Gregory found, Diane asked again, "How could this happen?"

Diane couldn't drive fast enough and yet despised the idea of arriving. Maybe, she thought foolishly, crazily, grasping for a way out, a mistake had been made. By the time she and Lauren arrived, Gregory would have been found, somehow overlooked by the staff, not found in the two and possibly three checks of every room, every space in the building. All her training in the law codified for her the tangible, the real, the myriad of "realistic" possibilities, yet all her years in the law, her years as a judge, had taught her, too, that there was a higher law. The law of the unexpected, the miraculous. The law of the saving grace.

At every stoplight, she allowed herself to turn from the road ahead and scan the streets, crowded on this sumptuous summer morning with people. *Ordinary people,* she thought, not people like her who have, with one phone call, had their lives upended. People shopping, walking into and out of stores, waiting at bus stops, hailing taxis, clutching their children's hands as they steered them across the street. She was looking, too, scanning really for a sighting of Gregory. She caught sight of a gleam of white hair, a tall man in khaki pants, striding quickly, racing really, to catch an oncoming bus.

Diane nudged Lauren and shouted, "Is that him?"

"Mom, I saw that guy a minute ago. That's not Dad. He's not as tall as Dad, and he's darker. He was wearing sneakers. Dad never wears sneakers. He was wearing thick-rimmed glasses."

"He looked like him."

"Mom, trust me, it's not him."

Leah had told her that Gregory was dressed in khaki slacks and a light blue shirt and a baseball cap. So she was willing him, conjuring up the missing mate, seeing him in every tall, white-haired man. After the man who was not Gregory boarded the bus, after he rode away, out of reach, out of the possibility of questioning and further examination that might prove Lauren wrong, an ocean swelled between the two women, a stretch of emotional territory that separated them from the husband and the father neither would admit they already missed as if he had been declared gone for good.

*Disappeared. Missing Person.* Gregory had slowly descended into all those personas. Diane gratefully sank in to the silence that bound her to Lauren, finding in it a balm temporarily stilling the eruption of fear.

Before leaving the house, she had quickly briefed Lauren on all that was being done, the Silver Alert sent out to radio and TV stations. Soon Gregory's picture would be on the news. Reverse 911 calls would go out to residents living in communities near Somersby, letting them know that an elderly person with Alzheimer's was missing and might be wandering in their neighborhood. It was Lauren who, sitting beside her in the car, Googled *wandering seniors with Alzheimer's* and told Diane that if not found within twenty-four hours, up to half of them could suffer serious injury or death.

"Most likely, we'll find him. We're near downtown Silver Spring. There are police cars everywhere and those police officers have his picture." This was what Leah, harried and concerned, told them moments after Diane, Lauren, and Sean, who met them at Somersby, settled in her office.

Downtown Silver Spring, a phalanx of stores, restaurants, theaters, malls. Everyone hurrying by, everyone in their own world. Who would notice Gregory? What if he was mumbling? Got violent when a concerned person approached him? But wasn't that better than walking along the empty streets of the neighborhoods around downtown? Middle-aged homeowners inside, the few young children indoors playing video games? No one to see Gregory walking down their quiet streets.

"How could this happen? Where was the staff?" Diane asked, seething and so anguished she could barely remain seated.

"I wish I could say it isn't so, but no facility is fail-safe," Leah said with a shake of her head.

"What my mother wants to know," Sean said coldly, "is literally, how this could have happened."

"At this moment, I'm sorry to say we simply don't know. No one that we've talked to on the staff or among the residents saw him leave."

"I told you a few weeks after we brought Gregory here about finding one of the doors unlocked," Diane said.

"We took care of that, Mrs. Tate, and the person responsible had a poor security record and was fired."

"It seems some others need to be fired as well," Sean said.

"There will be a review and an investigation, I assure you of that."

"Why would he wander now? Did anything unusual happen?" Diane wondered aloud.

"I think it's because his friend Wallis was hospitalized for a lung infection yesterday. Since she was taken to the hospital, Gregory has been agitated."

"Does he know where she is?" Lauren asked hesitantly, "I mean *can* he know?"

"We explained that she had to go away, but that she was coming back."

"So he's looking for Wallis?"

"That's my best guess."

"We have to go look for him. We can't just sit here and wait. Your father is lost. He needs to be found."

Two hours earlier, Sean watched his mother and Lauren walk away from Somersby, each searching for Gregory in different sections of the nearby residential neighborhoods. They would all keep in touch by cell phone.

Sean drove to the commercial area along Colesville Road, parked his car, and walked along the nexus of glass office buildings, looking through the wide windows at security guards inside pacing the deserted marble and chrome lobbies. Praying for a sighting, a vision of his father.

After a while, all the lobbies began to look the same with the same black security guard, and he had even searched the Metro station, purchasing a card, and going through the turnstiles, walking the length of the platform in both directions. He had entered the restaurants and shops along Georgia Avenue that had resisted upscale gentrification—

the music store that sold R&B albums and CDs from the sixties, seventies, and eighties, the store that sold sheet music, the Korean nail salon, the comic book store. He even went into the fire station and told the men there to be on the lookout for his dad.

The heat, the frustration, the fear that this was all in vain—it wore him out. Now he sat at a Greek diner waiting for a gyro plate. He hadn't heard from his mother or Lauren and wondered where they were. He had texted them to update him, told them where he was and to meet him here. No news was supposed to be good news, but it wasn't in this case.

As the waiter brought his plate, his phone vibrated. It was Diane: *Any luck?* He hated to think that was what they were depending on. Luck. He thanked the waiter and texted back, *Not yet.*

Lauren walked along the residential streets, searching for her father. The houses were shuttered against her, residents huddled inside their air-conditioned rooms. She had opened the gates and walked past the picket fences of several houses, knocking on doors where no one answered.

She'd try one more door. The neat, solid, two-story brick house beckoned her. Was it the sight of a bicycle resting on its side? The balls and Hula-hoop scattered around? Maybe it was her thirst, the heat penetrating the broad straw sun hat she wore, her blouse matted to her skin, the hunger taking root in her stomach. She was suddenly desperate to hear another voice, even if it was one telling her they had not seen her father.

An elderly woman answered the door, her olive-toned face framed by a hijab. Lauren saw the woman's thick black brows and burning brown eyes fill with unease in her presence, for she was a stranger.

So quickly, before the door closed, the words tumbled out: "I'm sorry to disturb you, but my father is an elderly man suffering from Alzheimer's and he's left his assisted-living facility. I wanted to know if you have seen him."

Lauren held up her cell phone and showed the woman a picture of Gregory. Then two young children, a brooding little girl in shorts and a pink shirt and a boy with an open, curious face, came up behind the woman, whose arms found their shoulders and brought them close to her body. Then a younger man came to the door, tall, with the same skin and eyes. The woman spoke to him in Arabic.

"Papa, she's looking for her father. Her father, he's lost," the boy said.

"Come in, come in," the boy's father said. "Sit, please." The words both an invitation and requirement as he gazed at her stomach.

Lauren sat eyeing the Koran on the glass coffee table, a news anchor speaking in Arabic on the TV and felt safe in the room with all the dark rich colors, gold and green and red. "This is my father, he's elderly. He has Alzheimer's. He's lost, and my family is looking for him."

The man studied the photo on Lauren's cell phone and then handed it back to her. "I have not seen this man. You have of course told the police?"

"Yes."

"Would you like something to drink, to rest for a bit?"

"Thank you."

When the man left the room, Lauren's sobs spilled forth. All day she had felt that to give into the tears might portend all she feared. Now she sat in a stranger's house weeping with a shattering abandon, not caring who heard or saw her display. When she could cry no more, she sat both renewed and overwhelmed by a fatigue she felt embedded in her bones. She couldn't stop looking. They had to find him.

The man padded quietly into the room. He placed a glass of water and a small plate of meat pies on the table. "Eat. Replenish yourself," he told Lauren with an authority both compassionate and firm. "Then you will join me and my family in prayer for your father's safe return."

She always swallowed the big frog first. Working with families in crisis all these years and being the child of a family in crisis herself had taught Diane not to be afraid to enter the darkest space first and then circle back to the promise or even a flicker of light.

Fortified by the fact that the darkness had not yet swallowed her resolve, that in the darkness she still heard her heartbeat and the hum of her breathing, that in the darkness the world did not crumble beneath her feet, or if it did, she could pull herself out of the rubble, she had learned to make of the darkness a promise yet to unfold.

So, walking to the Greek café where Sean had texted her and Lauren to meet him, she moved with a stalwart heart that was already broken, a heart that she had repaired and mended because if the worst was yet to come, she would need a strong heart. She would be prepared for her heart to break over and over as it must.

She was too stunned for tears, for this was beyond all her fearful imaginings. In the novels she loved, the march of life was relentless, the shocks and surprises unfolded right up to the last page. If only her life were a text, one that she could let slip from her hands as she fell asleep reading in bed, the book shoved, harmless and inert beneath the sheets.

Their deepest fears for Gregory's safety had so far gone unspoken between the three of them. Now, she had been buffeted, tossed, her brain and senses and feelings scrambled.

The big frog was widowhood. She and Gregory had prided themselves on not being afraid to talk about death:

"If something happens . . ."

"If something happens to me before you . . ."

". . . this is what I want you to do . . ."

". . . this is where the important papers are stored . . ."

A therapist friend told her once that the process of grieving a spouse took an average of seven years. *Seven years,* Diane had wondered. Who had done the polling? What questions were asked? How could you tell when the grieving was done? She still grieved her mother, her brother, and the father she had not known. Had grieved them all her life.

Gregory had gone looking for the woman who had replaced her in his mind as his wife. But *she* was his wife, would be his wife beyond "till death do us part," for the parting was nothing more than a new beginning.

They had to find him. She had allowed herself the folly of thinking that there was some moving on because her husband was broken. There was no moving on, could be no moving on even as she lay in Alan's arms, laughed at his jokes, and beamed in the joy and comfort of his friends. She would be lodged in this space, the wide circumference of love that took in everything, all of them.

Gregory is engulfed by all the sounds in the world. Adrift in a roaring sea of dissonance.

Standing on the corner of Colesville Road a few feet from the entrance to a Ruby Tuesday, the crowd swoons around him. When he left Somersby, now two miles behind him, he strode the streets with a determined gait and one thing in mind—to find Wallis. Now, standing on this street, he feels only fear—agile, alert, freezing him in place.

He knows that there is only one person who can help him to find her. His best friend. His partner. Mercer. A headache nests at the base of his skull. Thankfully, it has not yet launched a full attack. But fear roils his stomach and several times it has taken all his strength to push back, push down against the terror that is a muscle poised to gush up and out from his insides.

So many people. Too many people. Immobilized in their midst, he has been bumped, cursed, and is near tears. But stubbornly, he decided that he would not drown. Not if he can find Wallis. Not if he can get to Mercer, who will help him find her. All these months, all this time, this is where he was headed anyway, to meet Mercer. Past and through the stop signs that have hijacked his mind. He just wants to get to 1213 U Street. Their office.

Out on the street, alone, hurrying away from Somersby before they realized he was gone, he was exultant, flush with courage. Courage he has longed to call forth. It was like taking baby steps: walking the first block away from Somersby, then the second block, and all the blocks that followed. Through the sea of cars, the sun, steady and hounding. He nearly tripped, for no reason that he could see, other than that suddenly, in these first moments of the freedom he had longed for, freedom overwhelmed him, freedom literally took his breath away. He stopped at each light, the memory of the place he was headed for blazing more brightly in his mind than even the flashing green and red lights telling him when to stop and when to go. He hurried across each street, for the cars were like animals he cannot trust. There was nothing around him that looks like what he knows, the one thing and the one place he remembers: 1213 U Street.

The voice of doubt huddles in his brain and he hears it throb with ridicule: *Where? Who?*

All that walking and here he is, forsaken, deserted on the corner of Colesville Road. How can he go farther? But he is a brash, eager young man who believes in himself, who has become an architect, designing buildings in the year of 1978, in the city of his birth, the nation's capital. He can do this. This remembrance, that he is more than the despair that now plagues his days and nights, activates his voice, and his first request for help.

The woman is walking fast toward him, her head slightly down, avoiding his gaze, clutching a shopping bag. He positions himself slightly in front of her and that movement makes her look up. She is startled.

*Is she afraid?* He marshals a steadiness in his voice that is pure make-believe. "Twelve thirteen U Street?"

He hears the sharp, quick intake of breath at the question. This close, she has to look at him. And he sees her full on. Asking her was not accidental. He assessed the quality and cut of her tan linen suit, the leather bag on her shoulder, and the colorful, designer shopping bags she carries. All that told him she would be the one to help him. He has chosen well, he thinks, for he has always been good with people, intuitive and knowing. Mercer signs the contracts, he seals the deal, ropes the client in. The woman is attractive, her skin flawless, her brown eyes curious and confident. If he was not looking for Wallis. If he didn't need to find Mercer . . . The train of thought, barreling down the tracks of his mind stops, as he understands the look on her face.

There is a pause as those wide eyes narrow skeptically and then she laughs. "That's a long way from here."

Her laughter relaxes him. But her look turns, despite the laugh, into a trap and she moves a few feet aside from the entrance to Ruby Tuesday and he follows her. Now they stand encased in their own bubble.

"Are you lost?" she asks, placing her hand on his arm. The question sounds sincere but does not calm him. He hopes she has not felt him flinch at her touch.

"Twelve thirteen U Street."

She is looking at him more closely now. Now he is being examined and he wishes for the return of the smile but knows he will probably not see it again.

"That's a long way from here," she tells him again. "That's in D.C. You could ride the Metro but you should probably take a taxi. Are you sure you're not lost?"

The concern on her face could prevent him from finding Wallis and Mercer.

"Wallis . . . Mercer will . . . I need to . . ." This explanation, so clear to him that it has taken all his remaining strength and belief in this adventure to say, seems only to confuse her. He spoke slowly, calmly, willing the upheaval inside to subside. But he sees the alarm on her face.

When the woman puts her shopping bags on the street beside her, reaches into her purse, takes out a square, pink object and puts it to her ear as she looks around, he knows it is over.

"Just a minute. I'll find a policemen who can help you." As she looks away from him, likely trying to spot a policeman right here and right now, he walks fast through the crowd, bumping into people, not pausing to say "Excuse me," when he sideswipes and nearly knocks down a woman eating an ice cream cone.

Walking fast, hearing the calls of the woman, breathless and terrified. The woman who wanted to call the police reminds him that he is not really free.

Whatever triumph he has felt in leaving Somersby

is temporary and he knows it cannot last. Even if he finds Wallis. Even if he finds Mercer. A block away from the woman with the phone, he slumps onto a cement bench in front of a row of restaurants. He is hungry. He is thirsty. But now he is afraid to speak to anyone. For now he fears that they will all see in him what that woman saw. His hands fumble in his empty pockets. Sweat congeals in his armpits, warms his back and neck and mats his shirt to his skin. He smells the sweat and the terror inside it.

He has no money but he can still get a taxi to take him to the office. Mercer will pay for the cab when he gets there. He cannot allow himself to sink back into pity and despair. He cannot, because Wallis is waiting for him. She would want him to find her. So he stands up and walks to the corner of Georgia Avenue, past the windows of restaurants where he sees people eating and drinking, happy and laughing. Through those windows he sees a world he wants to live in. With Wallis and with Mercer.

On the corner he hails a taxi and once inside, he tells the driver, "Twelve thirteen U Street," and settles back into the seat, safe for the first time that day. Refreshed and soothed by the air-conditioning, Gregory relaxes, closes his eyes. He remembers waking up that morning and looking for Wallis. They always met at breakfast. At night, she came to him, though sometimes, he went to her. When he walked into the dining room this morning and did not see her sitting at "their" table, he asked where she was. Lynette told him Wallis was sick.

"Remember? I told you yesterday she had to go to see the doctor but that she would be back soon."

In Wallis's room he found her bed empty, unmade, as though she threw off the covers, walked into the night, and disappeared. As though there had never been any Wallis at all. The nursing assistants found him lying beneath the sheets on Wallis's bed and escorted him back to his room.

He struggled in their steely grasp and demanded, "Where is Wallis? Where is Wallis?"

"She'll be back soon. She had to go to see the doctor," they told him, but he did not trust them. Wherever they had taken her, Wallis was waiting for him. Expecting him. Just like Mercer.

He has thought often of how he and Wallis could escape, and when he met Wallis and knew he would not have to be alone when he left, he began to routinely linger near the exit of the memory care unit and watched staff members and visitors punch the pad on the wall. Their fingers, like a magic wand, unsealed the door. Fingers placed inside certain squares made freedom possible. He watched as though he was not watching. In time, he knew where to place his fingers.

One afternoon, in the deserted hallway, he risked a trial run, his fingers quivering as they raced over the face of the pad. Then he heard the click of the lock.

This morning, after they told him Wallis was

hospitalized and made him leave her bed, he heard them say that she had been taken to Holy Cross Hospital. After he lay in his own bed, he dreamed of escape. Later, he entered the hallway and found it empty. Unseen, his fingers punched in the code and unlocked the door securing him in the memory care unit.

When the taxi stops, he does not know where he is and he tells the driver the address again. "Twelve thirteen U Street."

"Mister, this is the address."

Where, Gregory wonders, are the cranes looming over the dirt-filled, dug-up streets, nearly impossible to navigate as the city builds a subway system atop the decade-old ruinous decay left from the riots? The street is crowded with people. A CVS stands where his favorite bar is supposed to be. There are no empty, boarded-up storefronts but a profusion of shops large and small, new apartment buildings, people lined up in front of the box office of the Lincoln Theater, which is supposed to be shuttered.

"No, this isn't it."

"Look, mister, this is where you told me to bring you. I want my fare."

Ignoring the driver's belligerence, Gregory opens the door and stands before the place where his office should be, a building that is now a restaurant. The driver has gotten out of the taxi and is nearing him.

He enters the restaurant and knows he is lost. He

has never seen this many white people on U Street. A young girl with pink hair and dressed all in black asks him if she can help him.

"Mercer," Gregory shouts and then he is stunned by the brusque grip of the driver on his back attempting to turn him around. When they are face-to-face, he punches the driver, collecting in his fists all his bewilderment and rage.

There is a scream and chairs scraping the floor and before he can turn around to look again at those happy, laughing people, living the life he wants to live with Wallis and Mercer, two men whose faces he cannot see are grabbing him and he is pleading, "Wallis . . . Mercer . . ."

The squad car pulled up to the entrance of Somersby just as darkness was falling, and two female police officers helped Gregory out of the backseat. After the altercation at the restaurant, Gregory was taken into custody and traced back to the Silver Alert and then Leah Temple was called. Bedraggled and sweat-soaked, Gregory shuffled past Diane, Sean, and Lauren, who stood, relieved, in the lobby.

"I know you all want to be with him, but let us check him out first, make sure there are no injuries, that his temperature and heart rate are okay," Leah says.

Half an hour later, Leah rejoined them and said they could see Gregory. Lauren rushed into the room and hugged Gregory, Sean fell to his knees and held Gregory's hands tightly. Diane stood behind them, the impact of the day washing over her, blinking back tears at the sight of Gregory staring at them all with a distant, benevolent curiosity. Gregory wore clean clothes and his hair had been combed, yet Diane could see that his body was tense with the static of longing and dissatisfaction.

Sean tapped Diane on the shoulder and said, "It's been a long day, Mom. We'll leave you two alone."

Diane kissed Sean and Lauren good-bye then turned to Gregory. "You went to find Wallis, didn't you? And Mercer?"

Hearing those names, Gregory's eyes grew bright and he grabbed Diane's hand, pulling her onto the bed beside him. His adventure in the day's virulent sun had left his skin burnished with a sheen that countered the weathered, solemn gaze on his face.

The weight of the day, the force of the nine hours during which she had intermittently imagined and beaten back the worst possible outcomes, had chipped away at her strength. Even as her hands, like the fingers and palms of the blind, confirmed Gregory's face and body, his substantial, definite presence, Diane grieved. For the tight weave of the life they had once shared was now unalterably frayed and tattered. Never had she felt so close to Gregory as today, when scenes from their past constantly erupted, invading and skewing her thoughts. He had been brought back, returned, but not to her. Never again to her.

He had walked out of Somersby, strode through the front doors unaccompanied, back into the world looking for Wallis. All day, Diane had thought Gregory's absence had existed as an affront, a potential tragedy, a betrayal of her faith in the staff of Somersby, a wound. But this day had been about one simple desire: Gregory wanted to find Wallis. And this act, which Diane now considered more brave than foolhardy, confirmed that forward was her only destination. He had gone looking for Wallis. She had it in her power to reunite them.

As they drove to Holy Cross Hospital, Gregory sat mumbling, muttering to himself fragments of what sounded like the long remembered, recalled, savored, and hallowed conversation with the mayor on the day that Gregory and Mercer inked the deal for their first building for the city. At a desk in the lobby, the receptionist directed them to Wallis's room, and Gregory reached for Diane's hand as they walked down the hallway beneath the harsh fluorescent lights.

Wallis lay asleep in the room, whose medicinal, antiseptic smell was a presence all its own, as were the snores of the woman in the bed on the other side of the partition. At Somersby, Wallis reigned like an *enfant terrible*, but here, Diane saw her for what she was—a tiny, fragile, elderly woman. She was connected by tubes to machines purring as they provided oxygen, hydration, and life. Gregory leaned into Wallis, peering at her closely, his trembling hands smoothing the lightweight blanket beneath which she lay. There was nothing for Diane to say or do, save witness this, the fierceness of life.

A nurse bustled into the room and greeted them with a gracious smile. "Are you family?"

"Yes, yes we are. How is she doing?"

As the nurse checked the intravenous fluid drip, she said, "She's doing quite well. She should be able to go home soon."

Wallis opened her eyes, blinking groggily. When she turned from Gregory and saw Diane, they darkened with suspicion.

As the nurse pulled out a thermometer and softly asked Wallis how she felt, Diane, feeling more and more like an intruder said, "I have to go to the bathroom, I'll be right back." Instead, she stood outside the room leaning against the wall. Her cell phone rang and Lauren asked where she was.

"I'm with your father at Holy Cross Hospital. I brought him here to see Wallis."

"What?"

"I'll explain it to you tomorrow." She could not tell her daughter at this moment the strange, replenishing, liberating emotions she felt, so she said, "It's Wallis now that he needs, it's Wallis that he loves."

When she returned to the room, she found them both asleep—Gregory dozing as he clutched Wallis's hand. Waking Gregory gently, Diane told him that it was time to go, assuring him that if he wanted, she would bring him back to see Wallis tomorrow.

Back at Somersby, Diane helped Gregory undress and get into his pajamas and then she sat by his bed in the half-light and watched him fall asleep.

Walking toward the exit, Diane passed Wallis's room. She opened the door and turned on the light. Shelves of Styrofoam heads—white, dark brown—and frozen mannequin faces with bright red lips and thick black brows, exaggerated eyelashes, frightful in their blankness, gazed out into the limited horizon of the room.

Hats were everywhere, some on the heads of the mannequins, others on the shelves. There was a black silk, broad-brimmed hat with a veritable garden of white lilies and black feathers that arched several inches high; a red wool felt hat with a purple veil; a hat like the one made famous by Princess Diana, ivory straw with a large bow in the back; a hat bold and startling, made of two wide open funnels joined by a large black ribbon of bibbing.

Diane stood in the midst of forty years of the precise and artful work of Wallis's hands. For the first time, Diane wondered who Wallis had once been, how old was she when she made her first hat and knew that there was no going back. She stood in the small space, surrounded by all of Wallis's history and her yearnings, and was silent and shamed by the extravagant display of beauty she never would have imagined Wallis capable of.

Overcome, overwrought, flush with a fever-like fatigue, Diane remembered the day, months ago, when she and Wallis found themselves alone in the hallway outside Gregory's room:

"Leave him alone. He's my husband," Wallis had said. "I waited all these years for him and now he's come. Come *for me*. Come *to me*."

# Chapter Twenty-three

## July 2016

"So how is Master Daniel Burris Stone?" Alan asked as Diane lay next to him in bed.

"Still the world's best baby. Lauren says he sleeps through most nights."

"Congratulations, Grandma. How's the father taking it?"

"He comes over a couple of evenings a week after work to help out. He's in awe of his little boy and against all claims to the contrary, he was ready to be a father."

"All I know is, circumstances can *make* you ready. Have you decided about Somersby?"

"There's no sense moving Gregory anywhere else. The trauma of separating him from Wallis might induce a setback from which he'll never recover. I've formed a committee of resident relatives that Leah has agreed to meet with regularly about any concerns, from security to laundry."

A late-night talk show host was five minutes into his monologue on the plasma TV, and Diane yawned, stretched and sprawled, burrowing into Alan's side. There was the warmth of Alan's lips on her face and then the question.

"Where do you see us going, Diane? I want us

to be together. I want—I need you to be my wife. You're my solid ground."

Staring at the ceiling, she said nothing as the question ballooned in the room, swelling like a bruise.

"My heart's on my sleeve," Alan said. "It's been there since the beginning of this. You had to know how I felt, how I feel. I know it's been less than a year, but—"

"Alan, I care for you deeply. But I could never divorce Gregory. I just couldn't do that."

"Even for a new life?"

"I have a new life."

"One of your own choosing."

"I chose you."

"You've chosen part of me."

"What do you want that I haven't given you?"

Alan reached over and turned on the halogen lamp on the night stand. In the muted, shadowy flush of light, Diane was prickly with exposure and pulled the blanket up to cover her chest.

"A life that belongs to us. I want to be your husband."

The word *husband* severed her heart, and Diane touched Alan's broad, trusting, open face.

Removing her hand, she said, "I can't give you that."

"I know it wouldn't be easy."

"That's not even an option for me. I'll never divorce Gregory. You're being unreasonable.

Unreasonable and selfish. This is the life I have. I can't change it. I can't give you a do-over. I can't give you a happily ever after." The words charged into the still, small space between them. Words that were muscular, brutal, a bulwark that offered her shelter.

"I know of cases where spouses have divorced their mate who had Alzheimer's and . . ."

Sitting up on her elbow, she said, "Don't say it, Alan. Please don't tell me that lie. Maybe if I'd been miserable with Gregory or considering a divorce before the disease struck. And even then I'd feel I owed him some kind of guardianship. But I had a good marriage. I'm not living on memories. I'm not tied to the past. Even if Gregory dies before me, there will be no other husband for me. I know that now. I couldn't improve on what we had. I wouldn't even try. I can't be your wife."

"I want to give you a life, a real life."

"If this was any more real, I don't know what I'd do." Diane turned away from Alan and stared again at the ceiling. He slumped onto the bed and burrowed beneath the covers, turning his back to her.

Rising from the bed, she took refuge in the bathroom, locking the door behind her. If he'd known her at all, she thought, sitting on the rim of the bathtub, he would have known what he asked was impossible. Yet as she sat on the tub shivering with anger, Diane knew she was angry because she had considered a life without Gregory. A life free of Somersby, of Wallis, with memories of their marriage, memories of Alzheimer's just that, memories.

The affection she felt for Alan was deep, important. A kind of love, but not the kind he craved. Alan had resurrected her fluency in the art of affection and concern, it was acknowledged and received. That had been enough.

But now her anger was a blazing, blunt force. She, too, had imagined a life free of Alzheimer's. Only now did she allow herself to realize that she had not imagined a cure, a magic pill, a discovery to turn back the clock. She had only imagined and dreamed of an end. An end to Gregory's suffering and with it, the end of her suffering as well. She had been noble and brave and terrified and confused.

But she did not want to marry Alan. She would have to carve out some place that was her own, a place that nourished her even as she remained tied to Gregory but not tied down. She didn't want to marry Alan; she wanted to marry herself. His offer of love and devotion inspired her to fight even more, for this new, gestating self she had yet to meet. What *would* she do with the rest of her life?

Months ago, Diane had gone through all of Gregory's papers with Lauren and decided what to donate to Caldwell & Tate's archives and what they would keep. Looking through the stacks of photo albums had become a ritual of remembrance and gratitude. The photos captured a bountiful, blessed life, a life she had taken for granted. Her personal history was full to the brim—birthday parties, graduations, weddings, Thanksgiving dinners, awards ceremonies, Christmas mornings. And now a new album held photos of her grandson, Daniel Burris Stone, being breastfed while held by his mother, sleeping in his father's arms, sucking his tiny fingers in his mouth, held by Gregory, baptized at two months old.

One evening, Diane opened an album and on the first page saw the photos her father had mailed her a few weeks before his death. The photo of her parents on the day of their wedding: Her mother stunned, eyes bright. Her father solemn, wary, facing the camera but clutching Ella tightly around her waist. The photo of Diane sitting on her father's lap as all of them—her baby brother, her mother, and father—lay sprawled on a blanket in Meridian Hill Park.

She was the child of a family fractured by a crime and the loss and abandonment that consumed them in its wake, but the picture captured how her family had started, all the love and hope that had once formed the contours of their world. Her father had abandoned them. She had turned her back on her father.

But Gregory, she thought, turning to a page of photos of her, Gregory, Lauren, and Sean, watching fireworks, he had offered Diane another chance. Another way. He had stood firm, stood tall, always facing her and never looking away, his arms open wide.

The search for a new home was a pilgrimage. Diane ventured into the gleaming condominiums and apartment buildings, each walk-through a solo flight.

She claimed her new home moments after stepping across the portal. Two months into evenings spent researching on the Internet, talking with a Realtor friend of Paula's, and spending hours forgoing her car and walking the streets of the refurbished, remade city, Diane found the building. A twelve-story tower on New York Avenue. Sleek teak cabinets and quartz countertops in the kitchen. The stone shower, the small, elegant chandelier in the dining room were all touches that she was sure Gregory would have liked. The floor-to-ceiling windows ushered sunlight into all the rooms and lifted her as she stood in the model two-bedroom. She had been unaware of how stifled and choked she felt at home until she stood in the top-floor unit. Each day she would look out into a skyscape that reflected the design of the life she now planned: open, free-form as clouds. She chose the top floor to conquer her fear of heights. That would be one more thing she would have to get over. Give up.

She had expected to feel some remorse, even regret as she began deciding what to donate and what to take with her to her new home. She had done this for Gregory and now she was doing it for herself. What was home and where was it?

When she examined the house closely and saw how it had aged—the sagging gutters, the water-stained ceilings in the basement, the decades-old bathroom fixtures, the cracks in the drywall—Diane decided what to do. The mortgage had been paid years ago. She would let Sean and Valerie live in the house, make repairs, pay the property taxes. It would be their wedding gift. She was moving out and moving on but Diane wanted the house to remain in the family.

"You looked surprised to see me," Diane said. "Did you write us off? Fire me without notice?"

She hadn't called Alan in almost two months, afraid to risk summary rejection over the phone. Instead, she'd shown up uninvited, without warning. Waited, parked outside his house for twenty minutes before approaching the front door and ringing the bell. Now they sat in his living room.

"I wasn't expecting this, that's all," he said.

She thought of the dance of their bodies moments ago when he'd chosen not to sit beside her on the sofa but in an armchair across the room. Silence froze them in place. They sat not looking at one another, as though the gaze they had once hungered for was now taboo.

Finally, Alan asked, "How've you been?"

"I moved out of the house into an apartment. A condo on New York Avenue. I'm having a house-warming party in a few weeks and I'd like you to come."

"So now we're supposed to just be friends? I asked you to marry me. You said no."

"I said no to marriage. I didn't say no to you."

"You're talking like a lawyer, like a judge, playing word games."

"I'm asking you to think not just about what you want and need but what I can give. It's not just about you, Alan. It's about me, too."

"I didn't call you because I figured we had said everything there was to say. I was all out of words."

*That is exactly how I feel,* she wanted to say but did not. "I'm glad you didn't call. I needed time to think, to collect myself."

As Diane spoke, Alan stood up and neared the sofa, leaning on the baby grand piano.

"I wanted to put those pieces back together," he said.

"Only I can do that."

"What do you want, Diane? Why did you come?"

"I can't be your wife, but I'm yours if you will have me."

# *Chapter Twenty-four*

## SEPTEMBER 2016

Sean and Valerie married in the chapel of the Metropolitan African Methodist Episcopal Church, where the funeral of abolitionist Fredrick Douglass was held. Where First Lady Eleanor Roosevelt and poet Paul Laurence Dunbar spoke from the pulpit. The site of the memorial for Ramsey Tate.

This was the Tates' family church.

Uncle Ray had walked Diane down the same aisle. Paula was her bridesmaid; Mercer, Gregory's best man.

She had faced Gregory, holding his hands, imagining flight even as she held on to his fingers tighter with that thought. Her mother's face had unfurled in her mind, and she vowed to have all the happiness Ella had been denied, all the happiness that had been stolen from her, all the happiness she had not lived long enough to reclaim. Her mother, whom she had never forgiven for denying her knowledge of her father, for being small, afraid, selfish, and protective of her secrets and lies. On that day of frightful exhilaration, holding Gregory's hands, that tiny stone of anger had lifted.

So lost in thoughts of her mother was Diane that

she had to be asked twice, "Do you take this man to be your lawfully wedded husband?" Gregory's thumb wiping away her tears brought her back.

She'd whispered, "I do," and then shouted, "I do," as the congregation had broken into laughter.

Metropolitan AME was still not a large structure. But its red brick facade, white spires, steeples, and stained glass windows imbued it with the feel of a building both grand and welcoming. Its design was an architectural conversation that captured the aspirations both heavenly and earthly of the original founders of the denomination, and this, one of the city's oldest African American congregations.

When Diane and Gregory arrived, the pews were half-filled and people were filing in. Diane saw Valerie's mother and sisters. Valerie's uncle would walk her down the aisle. Cameron would be the ring bearer. Family and friends surrounded them; Gregory the nexus of hugs and kisses. He bore it and took it in. Margaret entered on Bruce's arm and her approach parted everyone. She reached for Gregory's hand and draped it over her arm as they entered the sanctuary. During the ceremony, Gregory was flanked by Margaret on one side and Diane on the other.

Sean and Lauren were baptized at the church. But the family's attendance had been sporadic and occasional. Despite the years of distance, whether it was due to Gregory's cancer, business troubles, or Alzheimer's, something occasionally brought Diane back—for the community, for the collective affirmation of faith in what she could not see and did not need proof of. The new, young pastor had visited them at home before Gregory went to Somersby and even now sometimes visited him there.

There had been so much she felt she could not bring here. Her anger. The day she slapped Gregory. Her wish for it all to end. Her longing for Alan. Everything she did at Somersby was sacred, an act of faith, but she loved this place. Her union had been sealed here. Once, she had feared Sean would never see a day like this, pledging to care for and love another. Diane smiled at the sight of Lauren rocking Daniel on her knees and rubbing his back. Beside her, Gregory snored lightly and she clutched his hand. Then Margaret nudged Diane in time for her to see Sean slipping the ring on Valerie's finger.

The office would have to do for now. The walls were bare and she would take her time decorating. The tapestry from Istanbul would probably fill the wall facing her desk.

Diane surveyed the wooden bookcase, most of the shelves bare. On the middle shelf, photos of Gregory were lined up: there was Gregory, beaming and triumphant, accepting an award from the Architectural Society of America for the Main

Library. Mercer stood beside him as he held the statuette aloft for them both. Then there was a photo of him at Somersby, sitting on his bed, the window and shades behind him; the photo captured the absence, the vacancy clouding his eyes. The last photo was of all of them, before the beginning of the end, before Alzheimer's. She and Lauren sat on either side of Gregory on the sofa, their heads resting on his shoulders. Sean sat at Gregory's feet. On this bookshelf in her campus office, she would find her family each time she looked. Next week she would bring in photos from her week-long trip to Aruba with Alan. The photos showed her dark and radiant on the sand, beneath the sun. The photos showed her laughing.

On the desk were copies of speeches and articles Diane had written over the years. As a family court judge, she had spoken at conferences, before civic and nonprofit groups, before foundations, before other judges and other lawyers. An invitation from the editor of a small press anthology of essays about new trends in family law had prompted Diane to go through her papers and speeches, to look back on her work, and to begin thinking on a topic to write about.

Her colleagues were a mix of legal scholars and practitioners who loved teaching the law as much as practicing it. A ruddy-faced professor of civil law had arranged a coffee date with Diane right after the first faculty meeting last week. The chair of the department had asked her to do an informal presentation at the monthly faculty brown bag lunch in November. A part-time adjunct, who was also a partner at one of the big K Street law firms, wanted Diane to contribute to his blog.

This was what she had begun to call the third half of her life. There had been the years with Gregory as they created a family, lived a life, then the arrival of Alzheimer's, massive, merciless leaving nothing untouched. And now there was this, all this, that she had taken on and all that she still looked forward to.

She sometimes wondered if the disease would afflict her. Paula had told her about an NIH trial study to test if the level of plaque in one's brain predisposed one to Alzheimer's. Paula had signed up, and Diane had signed up to be part of the study as well.

When she told Alan, he'd said, "You're braver than me. I'm old-school—I wouldn't want to know."

"Even though you saw what it did to your mother?"

"I can't think of any ways her life would have been different if she had known in advance. And some people might not be able to handle it. Think what they might do."

"Knowledge can be a powerful, liberating thing. I want to know. If the news is bad, yes, I might be so depressed there will be no way I can live each day I have left to the fullest or plan or prepare. But at least Alzheimer's wouldn't have the last word. I could say good-bye, still knowing what that word means. I could hear it from others and appreciate it more."

She would teach. She and Alan were going to Italy next summer. She would let herself love him. She would care for and love Gregory until he died. And she would love him after he was gone. Be a grandmother to Daniel and when Sean and Valerie started their family. Where was the fragility, the diminishment that was once the only promise for this phase of life? How could she have known it would be like this?

How did anyone ever know what they were capable of?

Looking at her watch, Diane gathered her briefcase and left her office. She took the elevator to the second floor and entered her classroom, a seminar with eighteen students. As she settled at the head of the conference table, she listened to the conversations now winding down and snippets of gossip. Diane smiled and handed out the reading for the next class meeting. After a discussion of the required reading for this week's class, she looked around the conference table at the faces of her students and said, "Tolstoy wrote that 'All happy families are alike. Each unhappy family is unhappy in its own way.' In my twenty-five years on the bench, seventeen of them in the family

345

court system, my goal was to make it possible for children and adults to sustain happy families. I was never able to actually order, to mandate happiness. But I tried to."

As Diane stood up and began writing on the whiteboard, she thought of her own happy-unhappy family. A family that included a woman more adept at loving her husband than she, a lover who regularly joined her when she visited her ailing husband. Her children, now adults, but who would always be her children. And there was this woman, older, more beautiful and loving than ever, who had stepped forth into the world. Stepped forth into the world in her name.

# *Acknowledgments*

This is a novel that I never imagined I would write. Like all my most satisfying writing projects, this is one that I was literally "called" to write. While unprepared for the summons, I reported for duty because there was no other choice. My goal was not to write "about" Alzheimer's but to use Alzheimer's disease as a way to explore the way we live our lives, how we love, create families, survive, and endure. Every novel I have written has been about families in crisis journeying to redemption and love. There are many people to thank, who opened their worlds to me. The world of families with loved ones with Alzheimer's, caregivers engaged in honoring the needs of these absent but still present members of our communities, the world of architecture, contracting, and family law.

The secret weapon that all writers rely on is good editors. I was lucky to work with two exceptional editors, Krishan Trotman and Chelsey Emmelhainz. Both were sharp readers and both in different ways taught me how to shape and envision this book. I thank Carol Mann, my agent and good friend for over three decades. My husband Joe offered, as always, love and support and belief in me beyond measure. I also want to thank my dear friend and mentor Sidney Offit who, year after year, makes me feel so lucky to be his friend. John Bess, always there to help. Judges S. Pamela Gray, Tara Fentress, and Anita M. Josey-Herring. Marshall Purnell, the late Barbara Laurie, Edward Johnson, and Andre Banks for giving me new eyes with which to look at my city. Aminata Ipyana, Rosemary Allender, and Bettye Wages for close reading, wise insights, and an investment in making sure I got this story right. Loretta Bowers and Denise Love for sharing with me the details of their journey of supporting loved ones stricken with the disease. Cissy Stoner, Renay Blackwell, and Iracy Wooten for inviting me to "sit, be still, and know" as I spent time in a memory care unit, and for inviting me to read and discuss writing before one of my best audiences, men and women living with Alzheimer's. Sam Taylor and Walter Woodyard, Julie Daigle, thanks for your input and suggestions.

# *About the Author*

Marita Golden is a veteran teacher of writing and an acclaimed, award-winning author of over a dozen works of fiction and nonfiction, many of which are taught in college and universities around the country. As a teacher of writing she has served as a member of the faculties of the MFA Graduate Creative Writing Programs at George Mason University, Virginia Commonwealth University, the Fairfield University low-residency MFA program, and as Distinguished Writer in Residence in the MA Creative Writing Program at Johns Hopkins University. She cofounded and serves as president emeritus of the Hurston/Wright Foundation.

Among her books are the novels *After* and *The Edge of Heaven* and the memoirs *Migrations of the Heart, Saving Our Sons*, and *Don't Play in the Sun: One Woman's Journey Through the Color Complex*. She compiled the collection of interviews *The Word: Black Writers Talk About the Transformative Power of Reading and Writing*. Her most recent book is *Living Out Loud: A Writer's Journey*. She is the recipient of many awards including the Writers for Writers Award presented by Barnes & Noble and Poets and Writers, and the Fiction Award for her novel *After*, awarded by the Black Caucus of the American Library Association.

Visit Marita at www.maritagolden.com.

For a free copy of Marita's e-book *I Want to Write*, a helpful and inspiring guide to creating a productive writer's life, visit maritagolden.com/book-bonus.

**Center Point Large Print**
600 Brooks Road / PO Box 1
Thorndike, ME 04986-0001 USA

(207) 568-3717

US & Canada:
1 800 929-9108
www.centerpointlargeprint.com

.

LARGE PRINT
Golden, Marita.
The wide circumference of
 love

MAY     2017